Suddenly Tempted

SUDDENLY Tempted

KATIE EVERGREEN

APEX Billionaire's Club Book 1

Revised edition 2025
Choc Lit, London
A Joffe Books company
www.choc-lit.com

First published as *My Extreme Billionaire* in 2019

This paperback edition was first published
in Great Britain in 2025

© Katie Evergreen, 2019, 2025

This book is a work of fiction. Names, characters, businesses, organisations, places and events are either the product of the author's imagination or are used fictitiously. Any resemblance to actual persons, living or dead, events or locales is entirely coincidental. The spelling used is British English except where fidelity to the author's rendering of accent or dialect supersedes this. The right of Katie Evergreen to be identified as author of this work has been asserted in accordance with the Copyright, Designs and Patents Act 1988.

No part of this book may be used or reproduced in any manner for the purpose of training artificial intelligence technologies or systems. In accordance with Article 4(3) of the Digital Single Market Directive 2019/790, Joffe Books expressly reserves this work from the text and data mining exception.

Cover art by Alexandra Allden
Cover images © Shutterstock (man's clothes)

ISBN: 978-1781898444

To my brother, Gordon, who gave me the confidence to call myself a writer. This book would not have been possible without you!

CHAPTER 1

DEVLIN

"Devlin! Devlin! Over here!"

Devlin Storm hadn't even left the building and the shouts had already begun. He stepped out into the crisp, cold winter air, nodding his thanks to the doorman. A crowd of reporters stood beside the path, bundled up in ski jackets and furry hats but still shivering. A line of red cord stopped them from approaching him, as well as a burly security guard, but they all thrust their microphones his way.

"Any word from the conference?" yelled one woman.

"Where will you be on the rich list this year?" said another.

"Any celebrity scandals?" shouted a man.

"Sure," he called back to the guy. "Me, like always."

He turned away from them, pulling up the collar of his Brioni suit against the bracing wind that cut through the Royal Alpine luxury resort. The mountains were all around him, a ring of giant peaks so covered in snow that they were almost invisible against the grey sky. Patches of dark forest stood out here and there, along with the lines of the cable cars and ski lifts that carried people up from the resort to the runs.

All in all, it looked pretty bleak — certainly not the kind of place you'd expect to pay £11,000 a night to stay in.

But this was one of the most exclusive resorts on the planet. Nestled in the foothills above one of Switzerland's picture-postcard towns, you could barely walk three paces here without bumping into British royalty, American billionaires, or European bankers. Especially this weekend, with the annual APEX Club Retreat taking over the whole resort. Half of the world's wealth had to be right here, shivering in the unseasonably cold February weather.

"Hey, Devlin," called a voice behind him. He ignored it, thinking that one of the journalists had broken free to chase him. He heard his name again and turned back, a dark look on his face. When he saw who it was, the scowl turned into a smile.

"Blake? I didn't think you were here this year?" he said, stopping and turning.

Blake Fielding, billionaire founder of social media site, Heartbook, jogged the last few feet, stopping beside Devlin and wrapping his arms around himself, bouncing up and down on his toes. Unlike most of the other billionaires in the resort, Blake wasn't dressed up — he wore a woolly sweater and jeans, with a quaint little bobble hat on his head — but that was his thing. Preppy and approachable.

"Yeah," Blake replied, his teeth chattering. "I wasn't going to be here, but my board practically forced me out of the building. Told me I needed a holiday and this retreat's the only place I can properly wind down. Can't argue with the board now, can we?"

Devlin laughed.

"They wield the real power," he said.

"That's the truth," Blake agreed. "How are you?"

Devlin shrugged. The last thing he wanted to do was start talking about how his life was going. Not now. Despite Blake being the type of friend who would listen without judging. No. Devlin always let the newspapers do the talking for him, and they tended to stick to the same old story: Devlin

Anderson Storm, twenty-nine, self-made billionaire, designer whose clothing line and retail empire stretched around the globe. Devlin Storm, the bad boy, who dated models and actresses and left a string of weeping women in his wake. Devlin Storm, the man that men wanted to be, that women wanted to be with, and whose arrogance was almost as legendary as his good looks.

"Oh, you know, same old, same old," he replied, grinning. "Rich, famous, and as handsome as ever."

"I'm glad to hear it," said Blake, slapping him on the shoulder. "Listen, a few of the gang are hitting the lodge. Nate, Jackson, Christian, all the old faces. You want to join us?"

The APEX Club was exclusive, and his close circle of friends even more so. The kind of close-knit community where Devlin could shuck off the skin that had thickened around him and be amongst friends who weren't scared to bring him down a peg or two. All the members knew what it was like to be able to buy whatever their hearts desired, because one of the prerequisites was to have a bank balance with at least nine zeros. They all knew what having that kind of money meant in real life too. The assumptions, the prejudice, the loneliness.

"Count me in," he nodded, stomach twisting at what else the weekend held in store for him. A drink or three first would do him good.

They hustled their way through the crowds and into the warmth of the lodge. Devlin felt his face tighten at the change in temperature and made a mental note to book an oxygen facial as soon as he landed back at home.

"That's a chiselled jawline I'd recognise even after too many Sapporo," a voice cut in from the other end of the rich mahogany bar. "Devlin Storm, as I live and breathe."

Devlin smiled at the man with tousled brown hair and an empire of sweet stores. "Jackson Brodie, you *look* like a man who's had too many Sapporo."

Jackson pulled Devlin in for a hug, hitting his back with the force of someone who'd drunk so many beers he'd forgotten how strong he was. Luckily, Devlin's back could take it.

"I'm getting in a round, what'll it be?" Jackson asked, forearms resting on the bar.

Devlin laughed. "You're getting in a round at a free bar? That's good of you."

"Well, Nate put in an order for a Remy Martin so it's a good job it's free or I'd be kicked out of APEX." Jackson crossed his arms and skulked, jokingly.

Nate Parker was in the social media business, like Blake, only his forte was dating apps. Nate could have bought himself a bottle of Remy Martin with loose change. They all could. But none of the men Devlin knew through his club were men who'd use that as a tool, none of them except Devlin himself. He sighed and waved at Nate who was standing at the other end of the lodge with a man Devlin hadn't seen in years.

"I'll have the same then. Thanks, mate." Devlin strode across the floor towards Nate and his friend, a grin growing on his face. "Christian Carroll, who dragged you into the twenty-first century?"

Christian Carroll rolled his eyes and tugged awkwardly at the Tom Ford shirt that he had buttoned right up to his chin. Devlin laughed and pulled him in for a hug.

"Last time I saw you, you were knee deep in wild grasses," Devlin said, letting the man go. "Now look at you, all dressed up."

"It's all against my will, Dev," Christian replied, his New York accent clipping his words. "And I've been forced out of my comfort zone and into a shirt because my old man is insanely annoying and badgering me to go home. So, obviously I came here instead. Couldn't resist the lure of some guy time before I face whatever he's got in store for me this time."

Christian's family were the Carrolls of New York department-store fame, but Christian had opted out of a life of wealth and had been building his own charitable business constructing schools abroad. Much to his father's chagrin.

"Drinks, gentlemen." Jackson appeared with a tray of Waterford crystal cognac glasses, a bottle of Remy Martin, and a wide grin.

Behind him, Blake hovered with the nervous energy of someone watching a bottle of the good stuff teeter precariously on the end of an arm of a man far too drunk to be careful. Devlin took the tray from Jackson with a single nod and placed it on the end of the bar.

"A toast," he said, pouring the warm, spicy drink into each of their glasses and handing them out to Jackson, Nate, Christian, and Blake. "To the men we once were and the better men we are today."

Nate snorted on his cognac. "Who forced you to swallow a motivational, self-help guide?" he jibed.

"Your mum," Devlin joked back, to a roar of laughter.

He sipped his drink, staring at the flames from the fire raging in the inglenook. Though the lodge was warm, Devlin could see the winds picking up outside. Snow was blasting against the windows and the fir trees swayed as though made from paper. Devlin had spent enough of his life in the mountains to know an approaching blizzard when he saw one.

His stomach dropped. He needed to get out of the resort before he was snowed in. "Guys, I might have to take a rain check. There's something I need to do."

"Everything okay, Devlin?" Blake tilted his head.

Devlin nodded, slapping Christian on the shoulder and giving the others a salute. He downed his drink in one great gulp and headed towards the door of the lodge, hoping he hadn't left it too late. An icy wind whipped snow around him as soon as he stepped out, and he shoved his hands in his pockets to stop his fingers turning blue. Devlin had only made it a few feet before Blake called after him.

"Hey, Dev, you okay? You seemed a bit, I don't know, distracted back there. It gets to us all sometimes, you know. All this... Sometimes we all need a bit of what money *can't* buy. Happiness. Love. Find love, and everything else makes sense."

A sad laugh escaped Devlin's lips, appearing as a cloud of breath in front of him before he could stop it.

"I'll bear that in mind, Blake," he remarked, pulling himself together and winking. "Next time I'm sitting in my twenty-million-pound mansion with a bottle of Dom and a woman whose name I'll have forgotten by the morning."

A flash lit up the path and Devlin turned to see a reporter there, a cameraman right next to her.

"Devlin, would you care to comment on what you just said?" asked the woman, who was grinning as if she couldn't believe her luck.

"Sure, I'll say it again," Devlin boomed. "I'm rich, I'm happy, and I couldn't care less about anyone else or anything else, especially love. Now go print *that*."

He turned his back on the reporters, walking around the corner and heading for his cabin. His own words haunted him, and he felt bad for saying them. He'd no doubt see it in the morning's papers, or even hear himself saying it over and over on social media if the reporter had been recording the conversation. He'd have to pretend once again that he didn't care about anything or anyone other than himself.

And it *would* be pretending.

Devlin sighed. He wasn't even sure how this reputation had started. He hadn't always been a rogue, a bad boy. Back when he'd first started his business, eleven years ago, he'd just wanted to create something beautiful and do something good. But he'd soon learned you needed a tough skin in this world, and his skin had toughened with every passing day until he'd convinced himself he couldn't feel anything anymore.

And as for the stories about supermodels and Hollywood starlets . . . They were just that . . . stories. All except for his ex, of course, Claudia Romano. She had been a supermodel and an actress, and even though they had parted company a year ago she had taught him the greatest lesson of all: not to trust too easily. He'd known things weren't working, had ended it cleanly, only for her to turn around and sell their story to the highest bidder. He hadn't trusted anyone with his life story since.

He didn't exactly mind the rumours about his dating life, they helped boost his reputation and sell his designs. But after all this time being showboated as a bad boy, how was a man with Devlin's reputation ever supposed to find someone who genuinely liked him as a person and not the lifestyle he brought with him?

He shook his head. He was way too busy for love, especially this weekend.

This weekend he had a job to do, one that required every ounce of his strength.

Ahead, a door opened in the main building and a group of revellers spilled out, two men and three women. Their laughter filled the evening air, followed by a series of excited squeals as they recognised Devlin. Two of the women ran up to him, shivering in their thin party dresses.

"Can we get a photo?" said one. "Nobody will believe we met you otherwise!"

Devlin didn't reply. He just stood there and let them take their selfies. He didn't even smile, just glowered at their cameras the way he always did. He started walking before they'd finished, ignoring their pleas.

He didn't want to be here anymore. He'd had enough of this place. The APEX Retreat hadn't been the chance for R&R he'd hoped it would. He'd only come because it was an exclusive event, and in the eyes of the world *exclusive* meant that's where they'd find Devlin Storm.

Well, there was another reason he was here, of course. One he hardly dared think about.

His cabin was dead ahead, and he ran the last few yards, grit and ice popping beneath his shoes. He knew he had to move fast, or risk being trapped in the resort for days until the snow cleared. Crossing the luxurious, open space of the cabin, Devlin picked up the phone and waited for it to automatically connect him to reception.

"Hello?" said a voice, one so sweet and lyrical that it almost softened his mood.

Almost.

"It's Devlin Storm," he replied. "I need you to ready my helicopter. I'm leaving tonight."

There was a pause at the other end, one that went on long enough for Devlin to guess what the sweet-voiced girl on the line was about to say.

"I'm sorry, sir, but all flights are already grounded. There's a storm approaching."

"No," he growled, standing up to his full six-three and gripping the phone hard. "There's a Storm *leaving*. This Storm. Tonight."

"It's too dangerous," the girl argued, with real concern in her voice. Her compassion was genuine., "Please, don't risk it."

"Tonight," he said. "*Now*. Make it happen."

He ended the call without waiting for a reply. This was bad. He had a job to do in the mountains, and he needed to do it now. Tossing the phone onto the sofa, he walked up the wooden stairs to his bedroom. It was packed full of the things he'd brought with him — way more than he'd ever need for one weekend — but he left it all and walked to the corner where a small, black suitcase sat. Checking that it contained everything he needed, he picked it up, grabbed his thermal jacket from the hook, and made his way to the front door.

He'd head straight to reception. He could demand access to his helicopter face to face, and of course it wouldn't hurt to see the owner of the voice he'd heard on the phone. Something about it wouldn't leave his head.

"Focus, Devlin," he said to himself.

The only thing that mattered was getting out of the resort right now.

CHAPTER 2

DARCY

"Hello? Hello?"

Darcy Wainwright pulled the phone from her ear, looking at it as if it had sprouted a mouth. It hadn't. It was just a phone, and the man on the other end had hung up on her.

"Oh!" she declared, turning to the girl sitting next to her. Penny Anderson glanced over, a knowing smile on her face.

"Let me guess," she said in her prim accent. "An APEX Club member, making ridiculous demands, in a tone of voice better suited to scolding a naughty child?"

Darcy nodded.

"You get used to it," said Penny. "Most of the people who stay here are nice, but there are some who really make you want to . . ."

She gripped the cord of her own phone and wrung it between her hands. Darcy laughed, covering it with a hand. The lobby was busy with all the wealthy on display. The suits and shoes and shiny watches. The minutiae of the rich that made them stand out from the everyday crowds, and all of them here, spilling out of the convention centre, heading for the banquet rooms. There were around a hundred of them, and Darcy scanned the crowd for familiar faces. It was like being at the Oscars, she thought, there were so many famous people here. It was one of the reasons she'd agreed to work at the Royal Alpine resort — the other reason being she had literally no idea what else to do with her life. It wasn't like there were a lot of jobs going for twenty-three-year-old American girls stranded in the middle of Europe.

"Who was it?" Penny asked, leaning in conspiratorially. Darcy smiled, lowering her voice to a whisper.

"Devlin Storm," she said, and Penny squealed.

"Oh my god, I am so in love with him. I've seen him around. I can't believe you spoke to him. What was he like?"

"Arrogant," replied Darcy.

"Well, duh," said Penny. "He's always arrogant. What did he ask for? More silk for his sheets? More gold in his bathroom? A delivery of gorgeous models?"

"He wants to fly out tonight. He was asking for his helicopter."

Penny glanced at the bank of giant windows that made up the south wall of reception. Through them was a perfect view of the Alps, their peaks dizzyingly high. The sky was darker now than ever, even though it was only mid-afternoon, and flecks of snow battered at the glass. It was dark enough that Darcy could see her own reflection there — her shoulder-length brown hair, her slim face, and the big, brown, doe-like eyes she'd inherited from her mother. She fiddled with the collar of her shirt, feeling overdressed and uncomfortable. It wasn't her style, but you couldn't exactly turn up to work in a place like this in jeans and a T-shirt.

"Well, even someone as rich as Devlin Storm can't control the weather," Penny said. "Management let us know an hour ago — no flights in or out. He's in for a long stay once this blizzard gets going. It's one of the biggest we've seen in years."

"So what do I tell him?" Darcy asked. Penny shrugged.

"You're new. You'll soon learn that people like Devlin Storm don't listen to anyone. If he wants his helicopter, he'll get it. But nobody will fly it for him. Incoming."

Darcy sat up straight as a young, dark-haired man walked up to the desk. He was incredibly dashing, with a beaming smile that was contagious. She grinned back.

"How may I help?" she asked.

"I was wondering if you could assist me," the man said in a gorgeous British accent that was even posher than Penny's. "I've been trying to call home, but the phone lines seem to be down. I need to speak to my father."

"I'm so sorry, sir," Darcy stuttered. "The storm has brought down all the phone lines. But I'll be sure to let you know as soon as they're back up and working again."

"Thank you so much," he replied. "My name is Edward Harrington. I'm just heading to the APEX drinks in the lodge, but I'll be at the banquet later if that's too soon."

He nodded politely, then walked away.

"Like I said," Penny whispered, "most of the guests here are perfectly nice, and perfectly gorgeous too. Case in point, that one is tenth in line to the British throne, or thereabouts. I hope his call isn't about an urgent treason plot because it doesn't look like the phones will be back anytime soon. The storm is closing in."

As if on cue, a blast of wind shook the building hard enough for Darcy to feel the floor tremble. The windows rattled in their frames, and the crowd *oohed* and aahed as they filtered through the door to the banquet hall. Darcy was so busy watching them go, and searching for celebrities, that she didn't see the figure approaching her desk until he'd slammed both hands onto it. She flinched, rocking back in her chair so hard she almost tumbled out of it.

"Oh," she said, flustered. She glanced at the man there and became more flustered still. Devlin Storm was even more gorgeous in real life than he was on the covers of the magazines. It was like he'd been carved from marble, every line of his jaw perfect even past the scattering of stubble. His short hair had been teased and tousled by the wind, and the first thing Darcy found herself thinking was how much she'd like to tease and tousle that hair with her fingers.

Darcy! she yelled silently at herself, her cheeks blazing. At this rate, she was going to have to throw herself out into the snow and wind. But how was she supposed to cool down when Devlin was fixing her with eyes the colour of an alpine lake — deep and green and sparkling with cold sunlight.

"Uh . . ." she muttered. "Hi?"

Devlin raised an eyebrow, looking at her with such an intense expression that she felt like pushing her chair back just to escape it.

"No," he said. "*Bye*. Are you the woman I was just speaking to?"

Darcy nodded, not sure if she could trust her mouth. Devlin may have been handsome enough to turn her insides to molten lava, but nobody got to speak to her like that.

"I don't think you understand," he growled. "I'm not accustomed to asking twice."

"I'm sorry, *sir*," Darcy said, fighting to keep her tone civil. "But as I said on the phone, there is a blizzard approaching. All flights have been grounded."

"That's not good enough," he growled, leaning over the desk. He smelled of pine trees and the cold, fresh air, and it took Darcy's breath away. "Nobody tells me I'm grounded."

"I'm sorry," Penny interjected. "Darcy is right, there—"

"Let me speak to the management straight away," Devlin demanded, completely ignoring Penny. "If they want to see me back here, if they ever want another dime out of me, they'd better get me my helicopter."

Darcy's mouth dropped open. He sounded like a petulant child.

"Am I speaking to an idiot?" Devlin said. "Now!"

Darcy had pushed herself out of her chair before she even knew she was doing it. She didn't retreat, she leaned over the desk until her face was just inches from his.

"You have no right to speak to me like that," she pointed out, anger making the words boil up from inside her. "How dare you!"

"Darcy!" hissed Penny in warning. "Enough!"

"Your helicopter is grounded, and there's nothing I or anybody else can do about it," said Darcy, folding her arms across her chest. "So, why don't you take your entitled attitude somewhere else and wait for the storm to pass like the rest of us?"

The silence in the lobby was deafening. Fortunately, the other guests had all passed through into the banquet hall, leaving Darcy and Penny alone with Devlin Storm. Darcy could hear her heart pulsing heavily in her ears, and her cheeks were burning more fiercely than ever.

Swallowing awkwardly, she took a couple of steps back, wondering how long it would be until she lost her job. She had no doubt in her mind that Devlin would report her to the management. He must be furious. But when she looked at him, his expression was unreadable. Darcy couldn't decipher the seriousness on his face. She also couldn't get over the sheer size of him even though she was standing too. Tall, broad, massive. He towered over her, studying her with his green eyes in a way that made her feel like she was melting. She bit into her lower lip and sat down heavily. The only trouble was that her chair had rolled away and what she sat down on was the floor.

"Oof!" she cried. Penny was there in a flash, helping her up. Darcy groaned, more from the embarrassment than the pain, rubbing her behind. Devlin shook his head as if he couldn't believe what he was seeing.

"You have five minutes to get a pilot to the hangar," he said. "Because in six minutes, I'm leaving."

He picked up his suitcase and strolled away.

"What do we do?" Darcy asked, her heart drumming against her ribs.

"You go after him," Penny said. "Try to stop him. I'll call Abigail."

"But—"

"Go!" Penny insisted, waving her hands to chase her out from behind the desk. Darcy did as she was told, trying to ignore the wave of panic that swelled inside her. Devlin had crossed the lobby and was heading out through a door marked 'Staff Only'.

"Mr. Storm!" she called after him. "Please, you can't go through there!"

She reached the door before it could close, running into the corridor beyond. Devlin was walking fast now, his long legs carrying him down the hallway in a few great strides. Darcy ran to catch up, calling his name to deaf ears. Devlin exited through the door at the far end, a fierce gust of wind blasting sleet and snow into Darcy's face as she followed. The cold air instantly cut through her shirt as she shivered behind him.

"P-please!" she called. How on earth had she ended up in this situation? She'd only been working at the resort for a week, and now here she was chasing an intolerable, arrogant, rich man through the snow. It was just her luck! Devlin was halfway to the low, squat building that held the guests' helicopters — a parking lot for the rich and wealthy. He hadn't looked back once to see if she was okay, or to even check that she was following him. She upped her speed, the snow crunching beneath her cheap shoes, the wind freezing every nook and cranny. She didn't think she'd ever been this cold before.

Devlin opened the hangar door and walked inside, letting it snap shut just as she was reaching for it. She cursed him as she pulled it open, grateful to be out of the cold. The building looked even bigger on the inside than it did on the outside, at least fifteen sleek, powerful choppers lined up side by side. A small desk sat beside the door and a balding man peered up at them through his glasses.

"The Bell 525 Relentless," Devlin said. "I need it ready to go, and I need a pilot."

The man shook his head as he stood up, brushing crumbs from his overalls.

"I'm sorry," he said. "Everything's grounded. I—"

"You'll do exactly what I ask," Devlin stated, pointing a finger at the man. "And you'll do it now."

"Mr. Storm," Darcy said. "That's enough. You simply cannot fly."

Devlin turned to her, a look of confusion sweeping his face. He opened his mouth to speak but was cut off when the door behind Darcy swung open. A middle-aged woman in a sharp suit and heels blustered in, shielding her head with a clipboard. Darcy recognised Abigail Lamb, the CEO of the resort, and took a deep breath of relief. Devlin could argue all he wanted with the receptionist, but he couldn't argue with the boss.

"Miss Lamb," said Devlin. "At last, someone with a bit of sense."

He glanced at Darcy with a dismissive look of contempt before turning around. A great, hulking mountain of muscular back filled her line of sight and told Darcy exactly how important she was to this man-child.

Abigail took a moment to compose herself, smoothing back her silvering hair. She glanced past Devlin to Darcy, an apology of sorts in her expression, then looked at the man demanding the impossible.

"We've been told by the experts that this blizzard is a big one. The biggest of the year. It's rolling in hard from three directions, and we're right in the middle of it."

"Then fly the other way," Devlin argued, brushing snow from his expensive jacket.

"We cannot take responsibility for that," Abigail went on. "Our pilots are not willing to take the risk."

"Then I'll fly it myself," Devlin said. "I have my license."

"I think—"

"My license, my bird," Devlin interrupted her. "You have no power to stop me."

Abigail sighed. "Actually, we do. It's the law — no solo flights over the mountains. A pilot must have a co-pilot, in case of emergencies. And none of our pilots are willing to go with you, Mr Storm."

Devlin growled beneath his breath. He looked at Abigail, then at the balding man, then finally over his shoulder at Darcy.

"I'll take her."

"What?" Darcy exclaimed, shaking her head. "No, that's impossible, not to mention extremely presumptuous. I'm not a co-pilot, I'm a receptionist."

"You're fine. Luckily a co-pilot doesn't need to know what they're doing," he said. "You just need to sit next to me and stay quiet."

"*What?*" Darcy replied, her thoughts swirling like snow.

"Fifty thousand if you'll ride with me, right now."

Darcy's mouth fell open for the second time in ten minutes, and she looked at Abigail. The older woman shrugged.

"It's your call, Miss Wainwright. Technically, Mr Storm is correct. There's no rule to say the co-pilot has to be a trained pilot. There's nothing against it in our rulebook."

"But . . ." Darcy said. "But my job . . . Don't you need me in reception?"

"I'll make sure she flies right back," Devlin interjected. "Or I'll put her in a car. Either way, she'll be back here safely by tonight."

"Sign here, for our insurance," Abigail said, handing the clipboard to Devlin. He ran his eyes over it then signed, handing it back. Darcy realised she was still shaking her head. Devlin glanced at her, his expression as cold and unreadable as ever.

"One hundred thousand," he said in a demanding tone. "Yes or no."

It was more money than she'd earn in five years here, all for going on one helicopter ride over the mountains and down into the airport — half an hour at most. The idea of it terrified her, just like the idea of most things terrified her. Adventures were things to be afraid of, but she knew that the money could change her life. It could get her home.

"Yes," she said, her voice little more than a squeak.

Devlin nodded at her, his mouth curling into the closest thing to a smile she'd seen since she met him. Her heart drummed a little more, and maybe it was the stress of the situation, or maybe it was the way Devlin was looking down at her, his eyes piercing hers, but suddenly Darcy had had enough.

And you're about to spend half an hour alone with him, said her brain. She ordered it to shut up. Abigail was giving instructions to the balding man, and Devlin snatched up his suitcase from the ground. He glanced down at her one last time with an extreme, almost unnerving intensity.

"I'll have you back by nightfall," he said. "That's a promise."

CHAPTER 3

DEVLIN

"Is this the fastest you can go?"

Devlin paced back and forth, checking his watch every thirty seconds. There was still so much to do, and the storm was closer than ever. Every time a gust of wind blew, the whole hangar seemed to tremble, and from the sound of the snow drumming on the tin roof, visibility would already be poor. His heart was pounding in his chest. He did have his pilot's license, and he'd flown helicopters before, but not this one, and not for a long time.

He had to do it, though. So much was riding on this trip.

He glanced to his side, seeing the other reason that his heart was beating so fast. The cute, doe-eyed receptionist stood there, furiously chewing her nails and looking like a rabbit that had been cornered by a fox. Most women would give anything for half an hour with Devlin Storm, but this girl — Darcy — seemed to want nothing more than to get away from him.

There was something unexpectedly attractive about that. Ordinarily, people spoke to him like he was royalty. They complimented him, and sucked up to him, and said whatever they thought he wanted to hear. This girl, though, had stood her ground and told him where to go. That showed a surprising amount of strength for someone so terrified.

She caught him looking and scowled at him, turning her back. He couldn't resist a smile, but it didn't last long. Another fist of wind shook the building and he checked his watch.

"Come on!" he yelled.

"We're moving as fast as we can, Mr. Storm," said Abigail. "Please be patient."

The Bell 525 Relentless was being wheeled towards the hangar doors, piloted by the balding man. Devlin would have done it himself, but Abigail had forbidden him. Another insurance matter, probably. He had a good mind to buy the entire resort just so that he could burn their insurance policy to the ground, but he couldn't be bothered with the hassle. Maybe he'd do it when he got back home.

If he ever got back, that was. This was taking for ever.

"Come with me," he ordered Darcy, striding towards the hangar door. It was open, and drifts of snow poured in on the wind. He'd almost reached it when he heard a strange noise behind him. Turning back, he saw the girl there, her arms folded over her chest and her teeth chattering like castanets. She was dressed in a shirt and a knee-length black skirt, a pair of cheap black pumps on her feet.

Devlin sighed, rolling his eyes. He walked swiftly back the way he'd come, heading for a small room behind the desk. He knew from experience that this is where the pilots kept their kit, and after a quick rummage on the shelves he came out with an armload of gear.

"Here, put this on," he said, handing her a huge, orange thermal jacket and trousers. She did as she was told, zipping the jacket right up to her neck. She looked ridiculous, like an orange snowman. He handed her a wool hat, and some gloves, which she took without a word. Her expression had softened a little, though, which he hoped was gratitude.

By the time he'd reached the main hangar door again the chopper was on the helipad, the rotors spinning lazily. The balding man was climbing out, and Devlin put his head down, charging through the bitterly cold wind.

"You sure you wanna go up there?" the man asked, glancing at the sky. It was as dark as evening now, even though Devlin's watch told him it was only just past four. Threatening clouds rolled over the distant peaks, heavy with snow and coming this way fast. For a moment, he wasn't sure at all. Then he took a deep breath and nodded.

"Radio the airport. I need them to clear a landing space and hold it for me."

The man nodded, then scurried back to the hangar. Darcy was struggling across the open ground to the helipad, and Devlin waved her on impatiently. He climbed into the cockpit, taking his seat. He expected the girl to make her way into the back of the helicopter — where six luxury leather chairs waited, along with a minibar — but she climbed in beside him, brushing snow from her shoulders. He almost asked her to move, but there was no time.

Besides, as she pulled off her hat and smoothed a gloved hand over her chocolate-coloured hair, he felt something inside him stir. It wouldn't be the worst thing in the world to have her next to him to take his mind off the storm.

The girl looked at him, saying something that was lost behind the growl of the engine. Devlin pulled on a pair of headphones and handed another set to her. After a second or two, her sweet voice filtered through into his ears.

"Are you sure it's safe?" she asked.

"Completely," he replied. "Now keep quiet and let me concentrate."

He pulled back the cyclic and the big chopper responded instantly, rocking on its pads. Darcy squeaked, her hands gripping the sides of her seat as the helicopter rose gracefully. Past Devlin's calm exterior, his pulse raced — especially when another gust of wind shook the machine like a child shaking a toy.

"I've never been in a helicopter before," the girl said, her voice trembling with nerves. "I mean, I've flown plenty of times. Well, twice. I flew over here from Wisconsin, for work. That was, like, four years ago now. It was supposed to be an amazing new job, you know, a life-changing experience, but it didn't work out."

Why on earth was she telling him this now? Devlin was focusing too hard on the controls to tell her to be quiet again. They were a hundred feet up now, the resort already like a model village beneath them. Up here the wind was fiercer than ever, but the helicopter was state of the art — it should be, for the price tag it came with — and it felt stable. He lifted them higher, then banked to the side. The girl screamed again, then started talking even faster, like she was a fizzy drink that had been shaken and opened.

"Nothing's worked out, to be honest. Not since I've been here. You see, I spent all my money getting over here, and when the job fell through, I was stuck. I can't afford to get home. My folks aren't around, and none of my friends are rich, and the cost of moving me and my life back to Wisconsin is just too much. I've been working—"

Devlin banked the chopper again and she squealed. The sky was dark in every direction but one, and even though it was the wrong way for the airport, he pushed the chopper east. It roared effortlessly through the sky, still climbing.

"Oh god," the girl went on. "I forgot where I was. Yes, I worked here and there and everywhere. Ski places mainly, although I don't really ski. Climbing places, but I don't climb either. Adventure holidays, although I don't really do adventures. They scare me. Then I found myself at the Royal Alpine last week, when a position opened up on reception. Penny's a friend of mine. She's from London believe it or not. She told me about it and I jumped at the chance. It's about the most exciting thing to happen to me in the last four years, although I have to confess, I'm regretting it a bit now."

She made a funny noise, and Devlin glanced at her. He had never actually seen somebody turn green before, but she was definitely close. He had a sudden urge to comfort her, to rub her back to help ease her nausea.

"Do not throw up in my helicopter," he said instead, fighting another squall. Snow drummed against the windscreen, the chopper's wiper blades sweeping back and forth. The girl nodded.

"Okay," she answered, a hand to her mouth. Amazingly, though, she kept on talking.

"I thought maybe I might make some new friends here," she said. "Friends are helpful, don't you think? We all need friends. Have you got friends? Of course you have, look at you. And there are so many famous people I wanted to spot. Maybe they might want to be my friends too. Probably not. But I haven't even had time to look, and now I won't even get the chance to speak to people at the ball, because I'm stuck in this death trap with you."

At this, Devlin laughed. He managed to conceal it with a cough, scowling at the young woman.

"You want to explain to me why you're telling me your life story?" he asked, hearing the venom in his voice and hating it. It wasn't like the girl was doing anything wrong.

"I'm not," the girl replied, throwing back a scowl of her own. "I just talk when I'm nervous. Nobody asked you to listen to it."

"It's kind of hard with the headphones on," he said.

"Then take them off," she replied. "They make you look ridiculous anyway."

"You're one to talk," he said, trying to ignore her for long enough to focus on the airspace ahead of him. They were still heading east, towards the biggest mountain in the area. Even though they were close to a thousand feet, it still towered above them. If he was hoping to get to the airport, he really needed to turn north now and skim between this peak and the one next to it — easy enough to do.

But he wasn't heading for the airport.

"I'm not going to say anything else," the girl said, pretending to zip her mouth closed. "I'm not going to say another word about how rude you are. It's really uncalled for. If my mum was still around, she'd have something to say about that, about your awful behaviour. Dad, too, God rest his soul."

Devlin had a sudden pang of sympathy that both of her parents had passed on. He risked another look at her, seeing how vulnerable she looked, how fragile. Her eyes were the biggest he'd ever seen — they reminded him of a baby rabbit's. Her whole face was soft and warm and welcoming, and it hurt him a little to know that he had caused such furious words to come out of such a perfect mouth.

"Mum always told me manners don't cost a penny, and they don't, do they? So perhaps you could think about that next time you open that mouth of yours. Maybe you could think about what other people are going through. We don't all live in £11,000-a-night rooms and fly around in million-dollar helicopters."

"Fifteen million," he corrected, gripping the cyclic hard as he steered slightly south into the wind. "This cost fifteen million."

He heard her swallow through his headphones.

"That's just ridiculous," she said. "Think of all the good you could do with that money, all the — Hey, why are you going south-east? The airport is that way."

Devlin raised an eyebrow. The girl was smarter than he'd given her credit for.

"There's something I need to do first," he announced.

"Uh-uh," she replied, shaking her head. "That wasn't the deal. It's too dangerous."

"If you don't like it, you're welcome to get out," he said, increasing their speed and pushing the helicopter closer to the giant mountain. "It won't take long. Just think about how far that fifty grand will take you."

"A hundred," she replied, quickly.

"What?"

"You upped my fee to one hundred thousand, remember?"

Devlin grunted, he had a vague recollection of a double or nothing bribe.

"Whatever. Fifty, a hundred, either would get you all the way to Wisconsin, although who knows why you'd want to go back there."

"You just can't help it, can you?" she said. "You must be a sad man, Mr. Storm, if it takes so much effort to be nice."

That actually stung him. He clamped his mouth shut before he could reply, adjusting their bearing slightly. The mountain took up almost the whole of the windshield now, and the snow was so thick he could barely see. But he thought he could make out a glow right ahead, the bright bulbs of another landing pad.

"Hold on," he said. "This could get bumpy."

The girl was already holding on, her knuckles white. Devlin craned forward in his seat and saw the ground rising beneath them. They were close enough now that he could make out the individual trees. That was definitely a landing pad ahead, and he nudged the helicopter towards it. Another squall rocked them hard, and the girl shrieked.

"You're too close!" she yelled.

"It's fine," he replied, but that was a lie, because just at that moment the engine gave a mighty lurch, and the helicopter's alarm started blaring.

CHAPTER 4

DARCY

It was like something from a nightmare.

In fact, the entire last *half hour* had been like something from a nightmare. First Devlin's unbearable arrogance, then her outburst in reception, which still might cost her the job she'd only just managed to get.

She didn't think things could have got worse, but then she'd practically talked Devlin's ear off while he was trying to fly the chopper. She couldn't help it, she always talked when she was nervous. On the flight over to Europe four years ago she'd spoken nonstop to the little old lady sitting next to her, until the little old lady had pretended to fall asleep — for six hours.

But the embarrassment was disappearing fast, to be replaced with dread. The helicopter ride, which was scary enough to begin with, had become utterly terrifying. Darcy had no idea what was going on because the snow was too thick, and the skies too dark, but it looked like Devlin was flying them right into a mountain. The helicopter was rocking from side to side, and a siren was blasting into the cabin.

That *definitely* wasn't good.

"You're too close!" she said again. Through the door she thought she could see the treetops just yards beneath them. What on earth was he thinking? He'd gone completely the wrong way for the airport, flying them south-east into the biggest of the mountains in the region. There was nothing out here but sheer slopes and thick forests and freezing temperatures... and a wind that rocked them wildly from side to side.

"Trust me," he replied, something she *definitely* wasn't going to do.

Devlin fought with the controls, the helicopter bucking like a rodeo bull. The alarm rang and rang and rang in her ears. There was a sudden crunching noise as the chopper made contact with the branches of a tall spruce, then they were spinning fast.

Please don't let us crash! she pleaded. *I'm so scared!*

She didn't want this to be her last day on earth, and she certainly didn't want Devlin Storm to be the last man she ever saw. She turned to him as they spiralled earthward, seeing an expression of fear cross his own perfect features.

"We're going down," he said. "Brace!"

Then he did something that completely surprised her. He dived across the seats and wrapped his strong arms around her, pulling her close. She gasped into his soft, warm jacket, feeling the hard body beneath. There was no time to appreciate it, because a second later the helicopter thumped into the snow and she was hurled into Devlin as the helicopter slammed into the trunk of a tree. There was an awful wrenching noise as the rotors sheared off, then the machine rocked itself into stillness.

For a moment she just sat there, her heart the loudest thing in the world. Devlin held her tight, his breaths coming hard and fast, and she pushed her head into the folds of his jacket, barely daring to open her eyes.

It felt like an eternity later that he pulled away, and she reluctantly let him go. Devlin sat back in his chair, wincing. He held his right arm with his left, his face a mask of pain. He looked around the controls, then through the window, and finally he turned to Darcy.

"Are you okay?" he asked, taking off his headphones.

She took hers off, too, shaking her head.

"No, I'm not okay!" she said. "You crashed! We never should have gone up."

He opened his mouth as if to reply, but then the helicopter lurched, her side dropping alarmingly. Darcy screamed, looking through the window in her door. It was hard to tell through the swirling snow, but it looked like they had landed right on the edge of a deep ravine.

"Stay calm," Devlin urged, seeing the same thing. "Do exactly as I say."

"The whole reason we're in this mess is because I did exactly what you said," she shot back, clinging onto her chair so hard her knuckles turned white.

"Do you want to argue, or do you want to get out of here in one piece?" he replied. Darcy glared at him, but he turned away from her and grabbed the handle for his door. He grunted in agony as he pushed it, and the door flew open, caught by the wind. Snow and sleet poured into the cabin like water, taking Darcy's breath away. Devlin started to climb out, looking back and offering her his left hand. "Come on."

She shook her head, fear gripping her like a vice. The helicopter shifted in another blast of wind and her heart dropped to her feet like she'd gone over the edge of the big dipper. She reached out and gripped his hand as tightly as her gloves would let her. He pulled her and she clambered over both seats, following him out of the door. He moved his arm to around her waist and she looped hers around his neck, allowing him to lift her to the ground. She was paralysed with the fear of dropping down into a deep ravine, too scared to let him go.

He yelled something to her, but the screaming wind was too loud. Devlin peeled her hands from around his neck and snow battered at her face. It was colder than anything she'd ever known, colder even than when she'd got locked in the walk-in freezer at her first job in a fast-food restaurant. It seemed like her bones were made of ice, and it hurt to breathe. Devlin had let her go and was struggling through the blizzard to the rear of the helicopter. She chased after him, not wanting to let him out of her sight.

"Food," he shouted back. "And medical supplies."

She nodded. He grabbed the door and pulled it, grunting at the effort, and swapping to his left hand. Darcy helped him, and together they slid it open. Devlin grabbed his suitcase, hauling it out into the snow. He was about to pull himself inside when a fist of wind struck the helicopter. It tilted away from them, gravity finally claiming it. With a groan like a wounded bear, it tumbled over the edge of the ravine, Devlin giving it up just in time. Darcy watched it go, the helicopter breaking into pieces as it rolled and crashed to the rocky floor 100 metres beneath them.

"No!" Devlin roared.

Beyond the ravine Darcy couldn't see anything but mountains and snow. No sign of the resort. No sign of *anything*. Behind her, the mountainside rose relentlessly towards the dark sky.

Devlin ducked down on his haunches. He slammed a fist into the snow and glared at Darcy.

"What are we going to do?" she shouted, the wind snatching her words away as soon as they'd left her mouth. She pulled her coat tightly around herself, fumbling with the zipper in her gloves, but it did little to ward away the cold.

Devlin stood up, his face expressionless. He scanned the mountainside, cradling his right arm. Then he nodded past Darcy's shoulder, saying something that was lost in the storm. She shook her head and he walked up to her. He was so tall and broad that he sheltered her against the cold. He leaned in, his lips almost touching her ear. The feel of his words made her shiver, her skin prickling with goosebumps.

"There's a ranger station near here," he said. "It should be manned. It's where I was hoping to land."

"What?" Darcy uttered. "Why? You said you needed to get to the airport."

Devlin nodded.

"I did. I do. But there's something I needed to do first."

"You're insane!" she shouted. "And so selfish! We're stuck in the mountains, in a blizzard, and all because you wanted to make a stopover at a ranger station? What on earth was so important that you'd risk our lives?"

He ignored her, picking up his case in his good hand and walking up the slope. The snow came up to his ankles, making it difficult, and there was definitely something wrong with his right arm. Darcy stayed where she was, a blizzard of panic and confusion blowing inside her skull. The reality of the situation was starting to set in. This wasn't just annoying, this was dangerous. They were stuck on a mountain with no food and no heat and no medical supplies. If they didn't find shelter soon, then the storm would be the end of them.

The falling snow was so thick that Devlin was already almost invisible. Darcy called out to him, ordering him to wait for her, but he pushed on regardless. She put her head down, pulling the hood of the jacket up and clamping it to her head. Despite everything, she was grateful to Devlin for finding her the jacket and trousers — if she'd been out here without them, she wouldn't have lasted five minutes against the freezing temperatures. But her feet were so cold they felt red raw, and that wasn't a good sign.

The ground was rough, the snow deep, and the wind was doing its best to push her back towards the ravine. Her shoes struggled on the ice, her ankles frozen solid. The slope was steep, and after a handful of steps, Darcy was struggling for breath. She wasn't unfit — as much as she hated adventure, she loved her little local gym and worked out there twice a week — but she wasn't used to such wild conditions. Devlin, on the other hand, was. She'd read somewhere, in the millions of articles and interviews written about him, that he loved extreme sports. He was a keen snowboarder and climber, and had even won a couple of medals for cross-country skiing. That fitness was paying off. He strode confidently across the wild terrain, now just a vague outline in the storm.

Why wasn't he waiting for her?

"Devlin!" she shouted. "Wait!"

He didn't hear her, or he didn't care. Probably the latter. As soon as they reached the ranger station she was going to start tearing strips off him. He was by far the least considerate man she had ever met.

She was so busy fuming that she didn't notice he'd stopped, and she walked right into the back of him. It was like walking into a bear, he was so solid. She took a step back, shielding her eyes from the furious snow.

"I think that's it," he called back, nodding up the slope.

Darcy squinted, and saw that the mountain levelled out up ahead. There was a soft glow coming from just beyond the ridge. It didn't seem so far. Her heart seemed to thaw at the sight of it, and she offered him a smile.

"Can you manage?" he asked, and she nodded.

"Of course I can," she said. "Can you?"

He let go of his case for long enough to flex his fingers. He wasn't wearing gloves, she saw, and his skin had turned blue. She thought about offering him hers, but then decided he wouldn't have done the same if their roles were reversed. She was surprised he hadn't asked her to give them to him.

"Try to keep up," he shouted over his shoulder as he picked up his case. Then he was off again, storming up the slope.

Darcy took a deep, chilled breath and marched after him. The snow had soaked through to her feet, which were now completely numb. But the thought of a warm ranger station up ahead, with blankets and maybe even something hot to eat and drink, spurred her on. After a few minutes the ground began to level out, and they crossed the ridge to see the source of the light.

A helicopter landing pad sat in front of them, its four tall, yellow lights almost completely buried by snow. Past them was a squat, square, wooden cabin with absolutely no sign of life.

"Come on!" Devlin yelled. He cut across the landing pad, practically running to the cabin. By the time Darcy had caught up, Devlin was inside. This time he held the door open for her, and she stumbled through it into the cold, dark interior.

CHAPTER 5

DEVLIN

The wind was so strong that it took Devlin all his strength to close the cabin door. His right arm was a ball of agony — every time he moved it a bolt of pain blazed all the way from his wrist to his shoulder. He just didn't have the strength to push the door shut, but Darcy appeared next to him, grunting as she put her shoulder to it. It closed with a solid click.

The building fell quiet, the wind just a forlorn howl from outside. Devlin turned so that his back was to the door, leaning against it and trying to catch his breath. He'd been out on these slopes countless times over the years, but never in weather like this, and never without a team of support staff and a Range Rover on standby. He would have kicked himself, if he hadn't been in so much pain. If the chopper had landed just a few yards to the side, then they both would have plummeted into the ravine. It wasn't just his life he had risked, it was hers, too, and that was unforgivable.

"I hope you're happy," she said. "That was utterly reckless."

He could have argued with her, but what was the point. She was right. It had been reckless and dangerous and selfish.

But that was Devlin Storm all over. He was reckless and dangerous and selfish. This wasn't the first time he'd come close to death. It had happened a dozen times. It had only been a few years ago that he'd almost died climbing a mountain in the Rockies. He'd snapped a tendon in his knee, and suffered from dangerous levels of hypothermia. The only reason he'd made it back alive was because he was on the climb with some of his APEX brothers and they'd carried him back to safety.

He glanced down at his suitcase, wondering if this trip would even be worth it.

Only, it *was* worth it. It was something he had to do.

"Utterly reckless," the girl said again, her teeth chattering. He glanced at her, but it was hard to see anything because the building was so dark. A little snow-bright sun squeezed through the windows, but none of the lights were on. That was weird because ranger stations were usually manned twenty-four hours a day.

Not that this actually looked like a ranger station, he thought once he'd had a chance to glance around.

"If you could stop complaining for a second and give me a chance to think," he said, ignoring the throbbing pain in his arm as he searched the wall for a switch. He found it after a few seconds, flicking it. The bulbs in the ceiling winked on sleepily, revealing a large room that was empty apart from a small stack of wood in one corner and a couple of crates. The walls were peeling, the floor filthy.

"We could have died," she muttered, walking away from the door. She had her arms wrapped around herself, but even in the puffer jacket she looked frozen, and her words chattered with her teeth. "I think that's a valid reason to be complaining, don't you? Don't answer that. It's a rhetorical question that you don't get a say in. Dead. I've done nothing with my life except try to avoid adventure and this is exactly why. Look at me. Frozen. Stuck here with you in . . . what did you say this was? A ranger station?"

"No," Devlin said. "I don't think it is."

"But you said—"

"I said that's what I thought it was," he interrupted, walking across the room. There were two doors on the wall to the right and he walked to the first, opening it up to see a small restroom. "This looks more like a science outpost. A deserted one."

"But the lights are on outside," she argued. "There's a helipad with lights on. That means there's people here, right?"

"Solar lights," he said, closing the restroom door and opening the one next to it. It led into a dark corridor. "They stay on all year, in case of emergencies."

"There has to be something useful here, though," she added, walking past him and switching on the corridor light. Three more doors led off from the narrow space, all closed. "Like a heater or a fire or a radio so we can call someone to come and rescue me. You, too, if you'll let them."

"Of course there will be a radio," he said, ignoring her barbed comment. "This place will have everything we need."

He was making himself sound more confident than he actually was. He had no idea what they would find here. He walked to the nearest door and opened it, seeing a small bedroom with two single beds pushed to opposite sides. There were blankets on both, but other than them, a small desk, and an empty locker, the room was bare. The girl had opened the door next to it, revealing another room that was deserted except for a few old boxes and a stack of toilet paper.

"Sure, everything we need," she said, her voice thick with sarcasm.

Devlin grunted at her, then walked to the final door.

Please. Please have a radio.

He opened the door and flicked on the light. Ahead was what looked like a cosy living room, a corner sofa against two walls, a coffee table, a log-burning stove, and a TV table. There was no TV, though, and certainly no radio or phones. Devlin tried to ignore the sense of dread that was rising inside him. He knew from experience that the supplies they didn't appear to have were essential to surviving this kind of environment. He walked to the sofa and sat down, wincing at the pain in his arm. He'd have to check it soon to see if it was broken, but he was too afraid to find out.

Just like he was too afraid to think about what might happen to them, stranded here on the mountain.

"I don't see a radio," the girl said. "I don't see food. I don't see medicine. All I see is a sofa and some toilet paper, and we can't eat either of them."

"Just give me a minute," he snapped back. "Can you please just shut up and let me think."

"Because you've done such a good job of thinking about everything so far," she replied.

He glared at her, but the anger he felt soon dwindled away. She looked so fragile standing there in the doorway, so vulnerable. Her big eyes were fierce, but they were also full of fear. She knew how close they had come to death, and she was probably in shock. She was also turning a bit blue around the lips.

"Listen, lady," he said, and her mouth fell open in shock.

"*Lady*?" she interrupted. "You don't even remember my name?"

He held up his good hand to try to calm her. But she was right, he didn't know her name. Maybe he was in shock too. Or, more likely, he just hadn't paid attention when she told him back at the resort. Devlin hated himself a little. He could barely see her beneath the puffy jacket bubbling up around her chin, but just her presence in the room was like his own personal pain relief.

"It's *Darcy*," she shot. "Darcy Wainwright. Which you'd have heard perfectly well if you hadn't been so in love with the sound of your own voice."

"This isn't getting us anywhere," he said, trying to stay calm. "Can you please just let me think."

"Sure," she stated. She walked to the arm of the sofa, as far away from him as was possible to be, and perched there, shivering. "Think away."

Devlin sighed.

"Okay," he said. "We need a plan. And the first thing to do is make sure we don't freeze." He looked at Darcy, offering a gentle smile, trying not to let the way her lips were vibrating with the cold distract him. "And at the risk of looking like exactly the kind of womanising monster everyone says I am, the first thing we need to do is get you out of those wet clothes."

CHAPTER 6

DARCY

How dare he!

Darcy couldn't believe what she'd just heard. Not only had Devlin practically thrown her into a helicopter and crashed her into a mountain, but now here he was trying to get her to undress. She threw him a look that she hoped he'd feel like a slap around the face, happy to see that it wounded him. His smug smile vanished.

"I'm sorry," he said. "I just mean that it can be dangerous to sit in wet clothes. It can be fatal. Trust me, I've had hypothermia twice and once it very nearly killed me. I need to change too."

Darcy raised an eyebrow, feeling her cheeks heat. The idea of Devlin undressing made her brain stutter and heat pool in her, fierce enough to melt all the snow in the Alps.

"Uh . . ." she stuttered, hoping he'd blame her hesitation on her chattering teeth. "Change into what? I didn't see any closets."

"I'll do a thorough search in a minute," Devlin suggested. "There must be something we can use. I'll get that fire lit as well. I saw some logs back in the room we came through."

That thought was a welcome one, too, and Darcy nodded.

"I'll have a look for some food," she said. "If this place used to be a science outpost, then there must be something here."

"Good," Devlin replied. "Like I said, we're going to be fine."

She wished she could be as sure as he was. Through the single small window she could see that the storm was even more furious, snow hurling itself against the building as if the mountain had fists. The sound of the wind was like an army of ghosts, and it sent chills through her. With no food, no clothes, a small amount of wood, and no radio, they'd have to head back out there sooner or later.

"The reports we were getting said the storm is a big one," she pointed out, panic bubbling in her chest. "It could be days before it blows over. We could be buried alive in here."

"We won't be," he said. "Trust me."

"I don't trust you as far as I can throw you," she said. "What were you thinking, bringing us up here? Does anybody even know where we are?"

Devlin shook his head, running his good hand through his fair hair.

"The airport will radio when we don't arrive, probably within the hour. The chopper has a tracking beacon which should still be operational."

"Should?" asked Darcy. "This gets better and better."

"If it isn't," he went on, ignoring her. "Then the authorities will realise what's happened and will send out a rescue team. They'll have helicopters in the air tonight."

"No, they won't," Darcy said. "Not in this storm. They wouldn't risk it."

"Not for you, perhaps," he agreed. "But for me they will. You know who I am."

"I know exactly who you are, Devlin Storm," she said. "An arrogant, self-centred, pompous arse, who is one hundred percent an only child."

She bit down on her tongue. It wouldn't do anyone any good to get upset. She needed to conserve her energy for what really mattered: staying alive.

Devlin was grunting in pain as he tried to pull off his jacket. She decided that she wouldn't help him because he certainly wouldn't have helped her. But his face was knotted with agony, and he was really struggling. After thirty seconds of watching him struggle, her resolve melted. She went to him, taking a sleeve and pulling slowly.

"Gently," he groaned.

"I am being gentle," she said. "Can you stop being a baby about it?"

She dropped the snow jacket to the floor, then helped Devlin take off the suit jacket underneath. She offered to help him with his shirt, too, but he shook his head.

"I'll be fine," he said, a shade paler than he was before. "Go check for food."

Darcy arched a brow. The arrogance of this man. She best to ignore it, not even his muscles were worth putting up with that. Walking out of the living room and into the storeroom next door, Darcy counted to ten. It was so cold in there, she was worried her eyeballs were going to frost up, and it took her a moment to remember how her arms should work. There were five boxes — a stack of three on one side of the room and two more by the window. She walked to the nearest box and fumbled at it with her gloves until the flap finally came free. Inside was a bunch of glass beakers, pipettes, and other scientific equipment, all utterly useless under these circumstances. Lifting it off the stack, she opened the next one and found a bundle of linen that looked like it might have been about a hundred years old. She pushed it to the floor then opened the third, finding more cloth.

It was too hard to examine the contents with her gloves on, so she took them off and emptied both boxes. There were clothes inside, a handful of thick, starchy shirts, Gor-Tex-type trousers, woollen jumpers, and a pair of snow boots that clattered loudly to the floor. There were hats and scarves, too, as well as some ancient underwear that she kicked away with a shudder.

Behind her, she heard Devlin muttering to himself as he walked past the door. She left him to whatever he was doing, turning to the last two boxes. Inside one were three huge books about mountain wildlife.

Come on, she said, praying that the final box would be stuffed full of chocolate and coffee. It wasn't, but to her relief, there were some foil-wrapped protein bars and a small, half-empty first-aid kit. She checked the date on the food bars, seeing that they had expired three years ago. She was fairly sure they would still be edible, though, and if not, they'd have to risk it anyway. Taking them out and stuffing them in the pockets of her coat, she scooped up the bundle of clothes and carried them back through to the living room.

She laid the old clothes out on the sofa, shivering uncontrollably as she tried to find the least uncomfortable looking ones. Devlin wasn't there, so she shrugged off her jacket and kicked off her shoes and trousers, her feet red hot and burning. Her shirt was soaked through from the snow that had fallen down the back of her jacket, so she unzipped it and wriggled out of it, standing there in her underwear. She'd just picked up a pair of grey snow trousers and a thick sweater when she heard a noise at the door. Turning to see Devlin standing there, a couple of logs under his good arm, Darcy felt her whole body heat with the strength of the glare he was giving her. He gave a single shake of his head and averted his eyes. Darcy felt it like a slap in the face. She knew she wasn't model material, especially standing sopping wet in old underwear and with bright-red frost-bitten skin, but for Devlin to make it so obvious was just cruel.

"Excuse me," she cried, throwing the dry jumper on as quickly as possible. "A little privacy would be nice."

"I didn't know," he replied, still looking the other way. "A little warning would have been good."

"Says the man who crept down the corridor like a ninja," she said. "Why are you still standing there?"

"I'm going, I'm going," he said, turning. One of the logs dropped out from under his arm and landed on his shoe. "Ow!"

"Go!" Darcy yelled, and he limped out of sight.

She quickly scrambled into the trousers, which were way too big for her. Luckily, they had a drawstring, and she pulled it as tight as it would go. The clothes could have fit a sumo wrestler with room to spare, but they were dry and warm and she shivered contentedly as she pulled on a pair of thick socks.

"Are you decent yet?" Devlin called out. Darcy tied her hair into a bun to stop the water dripping from it. "I'd like to make a fire before I freeze to death out here."

"Yes," she said. "Completely and utterly clothed you'll be pleased to hear. Not a shred of naked skin unless my face is going to cause you discomfort?"

Devlin hobbled back into the room, his own face steely.

"Are you sure? I don't want you adding peeping Tom to your complaint about me."

"I'm sure," she replied, almost smiling. "And peeping Tom makes what you did sound sweet. You're more of a voyeuristic weirdo. I'll add it to the list, along with unhinged and dangerous."

She didn't mean to sound unkind, but the way he had turned so quickly away from her undressed form was still poking her incessantly between the ribs.

He walked past her, opening the door of the wood burner and throwing in the logs. There were firelighters next to it, and he threw a couple in, sparking them up with a lighter he pulled from his pocket. Within seconds, the flames were roaring, the logs crackling. The room filled with soft firelight and welcome warmth, and suddenly the storm outside didn't seem so scary.

Devlin tried to get up, groaning in pain and almost falling. Darcy ran to him, her annoyance momentarily forgotten, taking his good arm and helping him up. His shirt was drenched, patches of skin visible beneath it.

"You can't stay in that," she said. "I found some bits and pieces that should fit you."

"I can manage," he said, his voice cool.

He blatantly couldn't. He was so pale she thought he might fall over. Trying not to think too hard about what she was doing, she unbuttoned his shirt. It took some effort to pull the wet cotton from his skin, and when it finally came free, it was Darcy who felt like she might pass out.

"There you go," she said, not sure where to look. "You know, I once entered a wet T-shirt competition by accident. My shirt looked much like yours just did, all stuck to my skin and see-through. I only wanted to go for a walk in the park — how was I supposed to know there was a film crew from some dodgy cable channel? A guy came running at me with a hose and, bam, soaked right through. If I'd known half the town was going to see my bra that morning, I'd have worn a nice one."

She winced, willing herself to shut up. There was no need to draw Devlin's memory back to the grey monstrosity he'd witnessed moments earlier. Devlin blinked at her, his body tensing at her touch. Or maybe it didn't, maybe it was Darcy's mind playing tricks. She was tired and hungry, and her thoughts were fuzzy around the edges as she tried not to look at Devlin's rounded swimmer's shoulders, or the bulging muscles of his arms, or the wide expanse of his chest, or the clearly defined washboard abs. There wasn't an inch of fat on him, his body as sublime as if it had been sculpted by Michelangelo. Only his right arm looked out of place. The lower part of it had turned an ugly shade of yellowy purple.

"I could have done it," Devlin argued, his voice weaker now. He looked at his arm, and once again she thought she saw a chink in his arrogant exterior.

"It looks broken," she said, and he nodded.

"Wouldn't be the first time."

He was trying to undo his trouser button, and Darcy felt her face burn even hotter. He swayed, looked as if he might fall, and before she could even think about what she was doing, she pulled down on the waist band of his trousers and lowered him onto the sofa. Working the dripping suit legs over his shoes, she tossed them next to the fire and stood there staring at the flames, at the wall, at the sofa, at *anywhere* that wasn't a half-naked Devlin Storm.

"Um . . ." she said, flapping like a landed fish. "Try these."

She grabbed an old grey shirt from the sofa and eased it over his head. He pushed his left hand through, before gingerly manoeuvring his right, billowing the material as large as it would go. The dry trousers were like something from a museum, complete with braces, but she helped him into them, pulling the braces over his shoulders. He winced, then sat back without so much as a thank you.

Darcy ran from the room, ridiculously hot and flustered. Out in the corridor, she pressed a hand to her burning face, exhaling sharply. Devlin Storm, half-dressed and looking like every bad decision she'd ever been tempted to make, was not what she needed right now. She shook out her hands, willing away the heat creeping over her skin. No big deal. Just a man. A very unfairly built, infuriatingly attractive man.

"What are you doing out there?" he called through, some of the strength back in his voice. She didn't reply. All she could think about was that despite the way his body made her feel in heat, it was going to be a long night trapped here with a man as awful as Devlin Storm.

CHAPTER 7

DEVLIN

Of all the people to be stuck here with, he thought, *why did it have to be someone so prone to incessant, distracting chatter?*

Devlin sighed, trying to ignore the agony that pulsed from his right arm. For a second back there, he'd thought he was going to pass out. Luckily, Darcy had helped him change rather than just leaving him in his wet clothes. But the thought of listening to her talk on and on was almost as painful as the thumping in his arm. How was he supposed to get them rescued if he couldn't hear himself think? Why couldn't he have been stuck here with a mountain ranger, or a survival expert? *They* wouldn't get side-tracked by the idea of a wet T-shirt competition.

Instead, he was stranded with a ditsy, fearful, argumentative pain who wouldn't know the meaning of the word silence if it hit her in the butt. Oh, but what a butt it was. He'd seen his fair share of women with minimal clothes on, but from the brief but full-on glimpse he'd been afforded of Darcy, Devlin guessed that unlike the women he usually socialised with there had been no surgical alterations, no fillers, no Botox,

44

or butt-lifts. Darcy was as real as they came, and it had been a refreshing change. And a shocking one, given the way his body had started to react, even though he had been freezing and in a lot of pain.

"Did you check the bedroom?" Darcy called through from the corridor, interrupting his daydream.

"I didn't have time," he shouted back, gruffly. "I was too busy finding firewood, so we wouldn't freeze. You know, important stuff."

"You didn't exactly go out and chop down a tree, *Paul Bunyan*," she said. "We both know you found it in the convenient pile I'm staring at right out here."

She was so infuriating. Devlin sat forward, preparing to stand up, but another wave of dizziness gripped him. Why couldn't he have been stuck here with a doctor? That way, maybe he wouldn't be in so much agony. What he really needed right now was an IV full of pain relief, then he might be able to focus on what to do next.

"Here," said Darcy, reappearing. She had a small, green first-aid kit in her hand, along with a long, sturdy stick that she must have found in the wood pile. Despite himself, Devlin's eyebrows shot up.

"Good find," he said, and she nodded.

"Well, I, for one, am trying to make myself useful."

"I lit the fire," he protested, nodding at the roaring flames in the wood burner.

"Again, you had a convenient pile." She took a roll of bandage from the first-aid kit, carefully pulled up his right sleeve, then got him to hold the stick along the length of his injured arm. Tenderly, she wrapped the bandage around the makeshift splint, her fingers soft on his skin in contrast to the hard unyielding stick. If his mind hadn't been full of white-flashing pain, he might have even enjoyed himself, and paid more attention to the stirring at the base of his stomach. Darcy got to the end of the bandage and tied it tighter than maybe necessary, almost as though she was reading his mind and setting him straight. She pulled out a packet of pain killers, popping two pills free from the blister pack.

"Luckily they're still in date," she said, rolling his sleeve back down over his splint. "Not even someone as impudent as you needs a touch of pain-killer poison to go with their hyperthermia and a broken arm."

He took the pills, tossing them into his mouth.

"Water?" he said.

"Did your mother never teach you how to say please?" she asked.

He swallowed the pills dry.

"No, she was too busy teaching me how to be successful," he replied. That was a lie, his mother had always taught him that money was the least important of life's worries. Devlin sighed, feeling suddenly sad and exhausted, wishing more than anything that he could have a dose of his mum's words of wisdom right now. "Look, arguing is no good for anybody. We need to find some food, then figure out a plan."

Darcy walked to where she'd left her coat and pulled a couple of protein bars from the pocket. Devlin almost smiled. Maybe she wasn't such a bad person to be stranded with after all. She offered him one and he took it, but he didn't open it. Darcy crouched down in front of the fire, laying their wet clothes out in front of the flames and then stretching her delicate hands out to warm her fingers enough to tear open her own bar. He was struck by how beautiful she looked there, the soft firelight dancing on her skin reflected in her big, brown eyes. Her face was soft, yes, but there was a steely determination in her features that was surprising — not to mention attractive.

She must have felt him looking because she turned to him and scowled.

"What are you looking at?" she said, brushing her hands down her face. "Have I got crumbs on me? Is that better?"

"No," he replied, a smile growing on his lips. "Just wondering why you're sitting there instead of searching the other rooms."

Her mouth dropped open, and she rolled her eyes at him, taking his words for a joke. He'd spent so much of his life being Devlin Storm, the arrogant billionaire, with people fearing his reactions, that being with Darcy was a new experience, one he knew he couldn't get too used to. He looked away from her, staring out of the window. The sky was growing even darker now as evening settled in, and the storm showed no sign of slowing down. He hoped the snow would stop soon, otherwise there really was a chance the cabin would be buried by morning. The helipad lights would already be invisible.

"Do you enjoy being an arrogant prick?" Darcy asked, matter-of-factly. "Is it something you do for fun? For sport? Do you add it to your CV when you're boasting about your achievements?"

Devlin didn't reply, because if he ignored her, then he could ignore the niggling doubts that were circling his mind like flurries of snow. He didn't enjoy it. He hated it. He hated the way that people looked at him when he was like this. Not the celebrity hunters, of course, who expected, even wanted, the attitude, but regular people. They all looked at him like they would happily throw him off a cliff, and knowing that made him feel sick.

Not that he would ever share those thoughts with Darcy.

"*My* mum taught *me* a lot of things, too," Darcy went on as the fire crackled behind her. "She taught me that there is no such thing as a small act of kindness. Even the smallest gesture can mean everything to someone if they need it."

He sighed, turning back to the fire. Her mum sounded like a wise woman, the same way his had been. Hadn't she said something similar to him once, recently, in the days before she'd died? *Gentleness and kindness will make our homes a paradise upon earth.* He could see her saying it now, from the bed she had spent most of her last six months in. She'd been so proud of him, of what he'd achieved, but so disappointed too because of everything he'd given up on his way to the top.

"I'm sorry," he whispered, speaking quietly to his mum. Darcy must have heard him, though, because she seemed to relax.

"Oh," she said, as if she had never expected those words to come out of his mouth. "Well, it's just worth thinking about. How's your arm feeling?"

The painkillers had knocked the worst of the pain away, leaving just a dull ache.

"Better," he muttered. "Thank you."

"A sorry *and* a thank you," she replied. "Those painkillers must have been stronger than I thought."

He glared at her, then saw that she was smiling. It lit up her face as if the sun had risen inside the little living room. He laughed softly.

"It must be the shock," he said. "I will retract my thank you and my apology in the morning."

Darcy managed a laugh too.

"You look cold," she said. "Do you want to come closer to the fire?"

He shook his head, but the truth was that the chill was seeping into his bones again. He had no doubt that he was in shock, and the best cure for shock was warmth and comfort and rest. Darcy must have read his mind again because she pushed herself to her feet. Even dressed in baggy trousers and a moth-eaten old sweater, she still had a magnetising look about her that made his heart lurch into his throat.

"Wait here a moment," she said. "I've got an idea."

CHAPTER 8

DARCY

Darcy left Devlin on the sofa and walked out into the corridor. She was shaking, and not just from the cold. The events of the last couple of hours had left her feeling more tired than she had ever felt in her life. The whole thing felt surreal, like a bad dream, and part of her wished she would wake up in her bed back home — in her warm, comfortable, soft, boring bed.

Boring? She wondered where that word had come from. She'd never really thought of her bed as boring before. But it was. Her whole life was warm, comfortable, soft, and boring. She hated adventure, and other than travelling to Europe four years ago to start a new life — a huge leap of an adventure she deeply regretted — she had stayed as far away from them as it was possible to be. Adventures were cold, and uncomfortable, and dangerous, and they certainly weren't for her. The last few hours had cemented that.

So why was her heart drumming so hard? What she was feeling was nerves, sure, and panic, but it was something else, too. If she didn't know better, she'd almost say she felt excited. And as much as part of her wanted to be home, there was a part of her that prayed she wouldn't wake up in her bed, because if this was a dream, then so was Devlin.

Enough, she told herself. It had to be the adrenaline talking, because there was absolutely no part of her that was attracted to Devlin's impossibly handsome face, or his athletic torso, or that infuriating bad-boy facade.

Right? Right?

Pushing the thoughts out of her head, Darcy passed the storeroom and walked all the way to the front of the cabin. She used the bathroom, checking the cabinets to find them all empty, then examined the boxes they'd seen on their way in. There were a few magazines in one, their pages yellowed with age, and in the other were more papers, these ones more official looking. Darcy dug through them until she found a map of the mountains. Pulling it free, she tucked it under her arm then grabbed another two logs for the fire.

"Here," she said, returning to the living room and passing the map to Devlin. "This might help. Map reading is not one of my skills, but I'm sure you know your way around an Ordinance Survey. And if you don't, then we'll have to figure it out together."

He took it without a word, and she dumped the logs by the fire before walking back out of the room. This time she made her way into the bedroom. Both beds were made up, which was a relief. The linen felt cold, but she was pretty sure it wasn't damp. There wasn't much else here, just a handful of personal items like toothbrushes and shaving equipment in the locker. Darcy grabbed the linen from the beds and carried it through, dumping it on the sofa. Then she went back and grabbed the mattress from the closest bed, hefting it down the corridor and putting it in front of the fire. She did the same with the other one, panting with exhaustion and actually sweating by the time she'd manoeuvred it into place. Devlin sat there, one eyebrow raised.

"Thanks for the help," she grunted, collapsing onto one of the mattresses.

"You're welcome," he replied, flashing her an infuriating smile. He held up the map. "You want the good news or the bad news?"

"I can't see how there would be any good news whatsoever," she said. "So, start with the bad."

"We're not where I thought we were," he said, tapping the map. "I was right, this is an old research station. It's marked here in pen. The ranger station I was hoping to find is a couple of miles east of here, and a thousand feet or so over our heads."

Darcy felt a cold trickle of dread in her stomach.

"And the good news?" she asked.

"Well, you were right," he said. "There isn't any, really. We just have to hope the storm clears long enough for somebody to find us."

"And if it doesn't?" Darcy asked. Devlin sighed.

"Then we have two choices. We either make the trek up the mountain in order to find the ranger station. There will be help there, and if not, there will definitely be a radio."

"Or?" she asked.

"Or we try to find our way back to the resort, which is at least ten miles in the other direction. Judging by the map, it's a dangerous route. That ravine we nearly ended up in is just one of dozens."

"Great," said Darcy. "So we really are stuck between a rock and a hard place."

"A cold place," he replied quicky, lifting the map a little and covering what Darcy could have sworn was a blush rising on his cheeks. "A cold snowy place."

"Not a hard place?" she asked, feeling her own cheeks blaze like the fire. "I'm sure that's the saying. A rock and a hard place, no? Am I wrong? I'm probably wrong."

Shut up, Darcy. Stop talking now.

Devlin cleared his throat and shook the map out to reopen the corners. He studied it closely for a beat too long and Darcy wanted the mattress to open up and swallow her whole.

"We'll be okay," Devlin said, eventually. "You just have to trust me, we're going to be okay. We can do this. Just stick with me and I'll get you out of here."

The bubble of embarrassment popped immediately at the idea she could trust this man to get her home safely when he was the one who put her in this position.

"My hero," Darcy said, her voice dripping with sarcasm. She stopped herself before she could say any more, swallowing down her frustrations. Devlin was right, arguing would get them nowhere. Whatever happened next, they had to learn to work together. They had to learn to look after one another. Darcy sighed deeply and patted the mattress next to hers. "Come on, you'll freeze up there."

"You sure?" he asked, and she nodded.

Devlin eased himself onto the mattress, resting back against the sofa. She did the same, so that they were sitting side by side, almost touching. The fire popped and roared at the end of their makeshift bed. For a moment, it was almost possible to forget about the storm, and the fact they were stranded. Darcy had dreamed about moments like this — sitting in front of a blazing fire in the middle of nowhere with a handsome man.

Only in those dreams the man had been kind as well as handsome.

She glanced at Devlin. He was lost in the flickering flames, those green eyes incredibly intense. He still looked powerful, and dangerous, but there was a vulnerability there she hadn't really noticed before. He was a man who was used to being in control, she knew, and right now he looked lost.

"Are you all right?" she asked, and he stirred as if he had been deep in thought.

"What do you think?" he snapped. He took a deep breath. "Sorry, I'm fine. I've been in worse places."

"Really?" she questioned. "Worse than this?"

"That near-death experience in Colorado was worse," he said. "And one time I was jet-skiing in the Maldives and I hit a reef. I had to swim half a mile back through shark-infested waters."

"*Seriously?*" Darcy said. Devlin nodded, looking almost proud for a moment before Darcy went on. "That has to be the stupidest thing I've ever heard."

"Why?" he asked, turning to her.

"Because it's dangerous," she said. "You could have died."

"There's nothing wrong with a little danger," he argued, returning his attention to the fire. "People used to think fire was dangerous, but without it we wouldn't have been able to survive. Maybe it's the same with life. The dangerous moments are the ones that truly make us feel alive."

"I don't believe that," Darcy said. "I think people who chase that danger, chase those extremes, I think they're missing something else in their life. I think they're *scared* of life."

"Says the girl who's scared of everything," he retorted.

"I am not."

"You worked in a ski resort, but you're scared of skiing," he said. "You worked in a climbing place but are scared of climbing. You worked in an adventure trekking place but are scared of adventure. Did I get that right?"

So, he *had* been listening to her on the helicopter. Darcy didn't know whether to be pleased or insulted. She shrugged. There wasn't much point in arguing, because that's exactly what she had said. And it was true. All of the opportunities life had thrown at her, she'd turned them down. Maybe he was right, maybe it was her who was scared of life. She shrugged, pulling the blanket up over her jumper. There was something she wanted to say, but she didn't know how Devlin would react. Clearing her throat, she decided to trust him.

"My dad died when I was a kid," she said. "He was a fisherman. He was the best sailor I knew. He could sail any boat like it was his best friend. He taught me how to sail, too. He was a big man, indestructible. At least, that's what I thought."

"What happened?" Devlin asked when she stopped. Darcy laughed, but there was no humour in it.

"A storm," she said. "Mum begged him not to go out in it, but it was trout season and he didn't listen. Like I said, he was an expert. He knew the lakes like he knew himself. So he went out, he just never came back."

The storm howled outside the window, the cabin rattling in the wind.

"I'm sorry," Devlin said, meeting her eye.

"He loved extremes too," she confessed, her gaze caught in Devlin's. "He loved adventure. And it killed him."

She wiped a tear away, snuggling under the blanket.

"My dad was nothing like that," Devlin said, and she noticed instantly that he spoke about his father in the past tense. "He was a coward. The only time he ever showed any interest in me was when I started to make serious money. That's all he cared about. He sacrificed me and my mum for a few pounds in his pocket."

"He's passed on, too?" Darcy asked. Devlin shook his head.

"No, but he's dead to me."

"What about your mum?" she asked. It seemed utterly bizarre that she was sitting here by the fire, chatting with Devlin Storm. But what else were they supposed to be doing? A liquid warmth filled her belly as Devlin shifted on his mattress and his arm brushed against hers.

"She was . . ." Devlin took a shuddering sigh, and Darcy's heart broke a little bit, thoughts firmly back where they should be. "She was amazing. She was a saint. I owe her everything. She always told me that fear was a good thing, because it showed you that you had something worth fighting for, worth living for. She never cared about money, or fame, or big houses, anything like that. She lived for a smile and a laugh and a good meal. She only passed away recently. Just four weeks ago. I wish . . ." He turned away from Darcy and she could have sworn she saw his eyes glisten with tears. When he turned back his face was closed, all the emotion wiped. "There's no point wishing, though, is there? I can't buy wishes."

Darcy reached out her hand, then pulled it back. Then she reached out again and put it over Devlin's good arm, offering what little comfort she could.

"I still can't believe she's not here anymore," he said. "I'm never going to get used to it."

"I know," she replied, tucking her hand back beneath the blanket. "It's okay to feel all the emotions right now. You have to let yourself grieve."

Devlin nodded, and his eyes once again turned to the fire. She wondered if the conversation was thawing something inside him, the same way heat thawed the ice. Maybe Devlin Storm wasn't just an arrogant billionaire.

There was another thing, too. When the helicopter had been about to crash, Devlin hadn't tried to save himself, he'd tried to save *her*. He'd thrown himself onto her, cushioning her with his own body. She was fairly sure that was the reason he'd broken his arm, but if he hadn't done it, she could have been seriously injured.

"Can I ask you something?" Darcy asked, eyes back on the fire.

"What?" he replied.

"Earlier, when the helicopter went down, did you try to protect me?"

He considered the question, then shook his head.

"I was going for the other controls," he said. "I thought mine might have been damaged, and I wanted to try yours."

She knew a lie when she heard it, even when it was being told by such a well-practised liar. But why wouldn't he tell the truth about this? It wasn't like it was a terrible thing, something to feel ashamed about.

"Well, thank you," she said. He breathed a soft laugh, thawing a little more.

"No problem. As long as you know I wasn't trying to protect you."

"Sure," she said through a smile. "Can I ask you something else?"

"Do you have to?" he asked.

"What was so important, up here in the mountains? What needed doing so much that you were willing to risk your life — *our* lives — to do it?"

Devlin turned away again, resting his head on the sofa. The room suddenly seemed ten degrees colder.

"You ask too many questions," he said, once again turning to ice. "Now please stop talking and get some sleep. Tomorrow is going to be a difficult day."

CHAPTER 9

DEVLIN

Devlin lay there, a fog of confusion disorientating him. Why did Darcy want to know about *him* and not about Devlin Storm the billionaire. Devlin Storm the CEO. Devlin Storm the famous entrepreneur and his penthouse suite and bulging bank balance. He was normally batting away questions about how many zeros he'd added to his wallet that week, or what type of private jet he was flying on that weekend. Darcy was skipping those important questions and hitting straight for the personal, mundane stuff. Devlin didn't get it. He scratched his head like a cartoon and behind him, Darcy sighed.

He wondered if she would lash out at him, if she would ask him more questions or maybe throw some insults his way, but she just rolled over so that her back was to him. He felt terrible for reacting to her questions the way he had, but she'd hit on such a nerve. His mum had passed so recently that it still felt like a raw wound, and the last thing he wanted to do was talk about it. Besides, if she knew the truth about why he was here, why he'd risked their lives, she'd probably laugh at him. The whole world would laugh at him. That's why he had kept it a secret.

The only thing was, now he'd spent time with Darcy, he knew she wouldn't laugh at him, not even a little. Darcy seemed genuinely kind and caring. She was annoyingly argumentative, sure, and quick to defend herself — not exactly a bad quality — but beneath all that, there was a deep compassion. *There's no such thing as a small act of kindness*, she'd said. *Every kindness is a great act, and can change a life for ever.* She'd gone out of her way to help him ever since they arrived at the cabin — splinting his arm, and finding him clothes, pain relief, and the map — and she'd shown none of the false affection and clinginess that he got from other women. He had no doubt that if she found out the truth of why they'd crashed on the mountain, she'd be perfectly kind about it.

But he wasn't going to tell her ... not yet. Not until he'd thought of a plan to get them home. The truth was, he had no idea what to do next, and if he didn't think fast then they could be in serious trouble. He screwed his eyes shut, feeling the pain start to ebb back into his arm. Darcy had splinted it well, and the painkillers had been effective, but a broken arm was a broken arm, and it was excruciating. He couldn't think straight. It would be better to get some rest, then try to figure things out in the morning.

Besides, how was he supposed to think about escape when all he really wanted to do was roll over and look at the woman who lay beside him? Although the conversation had taken an unfortunate turn, and the conditions weren't exactly ideal, he'd enjoyed talking with her. In fact, he couldn't remember the last time he'd spoken so freely about anything to anyone — and he was sure he had never come close to breaking down with anyone else before. Usually, he clammed up when people asked him about his life, or he gave a flippant, scripted reply that made him look like the shitty rich man the world knew him to be and he didn't care. But there was something about Darcy that made him feel like he could open up to her, like he could tell her anything.

It's the endorphins from the near-death experience talking, he told himself. *There's nothing special about her.*

Then why couldn't he stop thinking about her? He moved carefully onto his back and glanced over at her. She was so close he could smell her hair — a hint of coconut that made him feel like he was lying on a tropical island, not in a cabin on the mountainside. What he wouldn't give to curl himself into her, to bury his face in her hair and his hand on her waist and . . .

"If I die first, you have my permission to eat me if you need to." Darcy's sudden statement was so out of the blue it made Devlin bark out a laugh.

He coughed to try and hide it, bending his good arm behind his head and resting back onto his hand.

"Noted."

Darcy shuffled around onto her back, too, the movement tugging at the covers and making Devlin's skin fizz as they brushed against his clothes. He stared at the ceiling, trying not to think about eating Darcy. Why had she said that? Now all he could think about was catching her standing almost naked, shivering in her underwear. He wanted to eat her, to run his tongue along her collarbone, to dip his fingers and taste her. Something stirred deep inside him, and he shifted his hips, trying to focus on the patch of damp that looked like a map of Australia blooming above his head. The covers were heavy, but not heavy enough to disguise how his thoughts were making him feel.

She sighed, and the sound made his head spin.

"Well?" she asked, expectantly.

Devlin froze. Was Darcy feeling the same way he was? Did she want him to taste her now? He cast his eyes sideways. Her profile was like the Alps, peaks and troughs forming her perfect nose and lips. Lips that he bet tasted as sweet as the rest of her would. A heat buried itself deep in his stomach, pulsing through his body enough for him to forget his broken arm.

"Are . . . are you sure?" he stuttered. He didn't know what had come over him. Put him in bed with a gorgeous woman and he was never lost for words or moves. Darcy, though, she was something else.

"Well, I'm not sure I am anymore," she said, and Devlin silently cursed his hesitancy. "I offer myself up as a meal in the worst-case scenario and you don't return the favour. I mean, I get that it's not the easiest decision to make, but you could offer me a finger to chew on or some ribs."

She drew silent for a moment and the reality of what she had actually been offering sank in. Devlin felt like an idiot. Of course she didn't want him to devour her in the same way he wanted to.

"Though maybe it is an easy decision for you," she went on. "Given that you're a survival expert and I'm a loser who doesn't like adventure. It would be best if I go first anyway, there's not an inch of fat on you. I'd have to rely on gristly muscle. Whereas my backside could feed you for a week."

Devlin lifted the pillow and buried his face in it, groaning. This woman had no idea what effect she was having on him and it was more painful than the break in his bones.

"I know, I know," she continued. "Stop talking and get some sleep because tomorrow is going to be hard. But I'm still cold and my feet feel damp and I'm sharing a bed with a man who flew a helicopter into a mountain after promising to keep me safe. It's not conducive to forty winks, let alone a great night's sleep. And I normally wear an eye mask."

Devlin answered with a grunt, trying not to picture Darcy in a blindfold. She was right, though, he was cold, too, and his arm ached, and at the end of the day they were stranded because he'd been reckless. Darcy shuffled again beside him, turning onto her side and curling into a little ball, her back brushing his hip.

"Not even a little toe," she mumbled, before her breathing settled into the unmistakable rhythm of sleep.

Devlin pulled the covers up to his chin, watching Darcy's back rise and fall through the blankets. When was the last time he'd shared a moment like that with a woman? It had been years. For all his reputation as a womanising playboy, he was actually terrified of relationships — especially after the way his father had treated his mother. He'd always been better off on his own. Devlin Storm the island, Devlin Storm the *mountain*, aloof and indifferent.

So what was it about Darcy that made him feel so different? What was it about her that made him feel like he was at risk of coming undone?

As if trying to answer him, the wind rattled the cabin, throwing sleet and snow against the window. Devlin shuddered, glancing at the fire. The logs they'd thrown on were burned away, so reluctantly, he cast off the blankets and walked through to the room at the front of the cabin. He tucked one log underneath his throbbing right arm, then managed to scoop another two in his left. He was halfway through the door again when he paused, looking across the room.

His suitcase sat there, by the front door. He wished he'd had the foresight to fill it with equipment, the same supplies he would have taken with him if he was going out on a cross-country ski run: a flare gun, utility tools, emergency food, foil blankets, and of course, a satellite phone for emergencies. But they all lay at the bottom of the ravine along with the helicopter and mobile phones that would be useless up here anyway. Instead, other than his passport, the case held only one thing.

"I'm sorry," he said. "I'll make it right."

Feeling the sharp pains of grief and regret, he walked back into the living room, threw the logs on the fire, then lay down and tried to sleep.

CHAPTER 10

DARCY

Darcy stirred, lost in dreams of making snowmen in her backyard in Wisconsin. She shivered, rolling over in her bed and snuggling up to the shape next to her.

Then she frowned.

Where on earth was she? The mattress beneath her felt unfamiliar and uncomfortable, and the blankets were cold and musty. There was no noise but the howling of the wind and the creaking of wood — those and the murmurs of the man lying beside her.

Her eyes shot open and, just like that, it came rushing back as fast and loud as an avalanche. The helicopter ride. The blizzard. The crash. And Devlin Storm.

She was cuddling up to Devlin Storm.

Gritting her teeth, she slid her arm free and wriggled away from him. He stirred again, an expression of pain crossing his features for a moment before flitting away. He licked his lips, and Darcy found herself licking hers too.

"Don't leave," Devlin mumbled in his sleep. "You're the most beautiful woman I've ever met."

A burst of laughter escaped Darcy and she covered her mouth with her hand so she didn't wake him. The infamous Devlin Storm, the bad-boy billionaire, and here he was telling her she was the most beautiful women he'd ever met. Maybe he was delirious from his injury. He didn't look like he had a temperature, but looks could be deceiving.

Darcy rolled slowly onto her back, careful not to jostle his bad arm. The laugh was short lived, because all she could think about was how long it had been since anyone had told her that — asleep or awake. Of course, she'd had boyfriends back in Wisconsin but nothing serious. They'd all been fun while they lasted, but the problem was they never lasted. Darcy was so busy looking after her mum and the house that the men she seemed to pick took issue with where she placed them in her priorities.

None of them would have believed where she was now and who she was with. Darcy Wainwright was not an adventurer. No. She was timid, cute, quiet, a mouse. One date she'd been with had even questioned if she was a selective mute.

He was one of the many reasons she'd flown to Europe four years ago. After her mum died, Darcy had wanted to find comfort with a partner, someone who could help her see the way through the grief. But instead she'd found more hurt and knew that there was nothing left to keep her in Lancaster. That comment had really upset her, and she'd jumped at the chance of moving halfway around the world to get away from judgemental men, and maybe show them she was more adventurous than they'd thought.

Weirdly, though, Darcy felt more secure with the sleeping man beside her than she had with any of those dates. Even though the sleeping man was a great hulking sack of grumpiness who didn't really care about her. Darcy stifled another giggle. That didn't really bode well for her love life, did it?

Why are you thinking about love? she asked herself, rubbing sleep from her eyes. She looked at Devlin. There was no way she could ever feel attracted to somebody as selfish and as mean as he was. It just wasn't in her nature to be with a man like that. She needed somebody thoughtful, and kind, and compassionate, somebody who didn't try to put her down or insult her or order her about with every word.

No, Devlin Storm was definitely not the man for her.

Definitely not.

He shifted in his sleep, wincing with pain as he moved onto his back. Even in the simplicity of sleep with his muscles slack, his face was the most offensively perfect thing she'd ever seen. Gone was the hot-blooded broody look. The alpha male whose intense green eyes could bed whichever ladies he took fancy to. Instead, he was a sleeping Adonis with cheekbones and a jawline that could cut through the snowdrift. And a cupid's bow so perfect she wanted to reach out a finger and trace the lines. His hair had mussed a little on top, a bird's nest that was thick enough for Darcy to imagine running her hands through and . . .

Darcy. She chastised herself silently. Devlin Storm might not have been the man for her, but the way he looked was playing havoc with her hormones.

She was running hot and cold, and if she wasn't careful, she'd give herself a fever and start saying delirious things back to him. As though making a point, a giant shiver ran through her body and as quietly as she could, she crept to the fire and threw on another log. Settling at the foot of the mattress for a moment, listening to the howling wind and the gentle snores from Devlin. Two sounds so incongruous with each other, yet they seemed to be in sync.

Then she gathered a couple of sofa cushions and rested them between her and Devlin so that she wouldn't roll over in her sleep again. She couldn't imagine anything worse than resting her hand on his stomach, stealing her fingers up under his jumper, following the trail of hair down to his waistband, putting her lips on his lips, his hands on her . . .

Enough!

Darcy rolled over to face the wall, her cheeks aflame, pulling the blankets up to her chin and listening to the storm batter the cabin. Devlin Storm would have to wait. The only thing that mattered at the moment was surviving.

***

"Rise and shine, Miss Wainwright!"

Darcy stirred, stretching like a cat and almost purring beneath the covers. Then she snapped her eyes open, remembering once again where she was. She was surprised to see that the cabin was drenched in fierce sunlight and muffled by an eerie quiet. She sat up, massaging a crick out of her neck and blinking the fuzziness from her eyes until she made out Devlin standing in the doorway. He was holding something in his good hand, and he carried it into the room. He looked at her, tilting his head, an almost smile crossing his lips. The way his eyes studied Darcy, the intensity of them made her skin prickle.

"What time is it?" she asked, trying to smooth back her hair.

"Six," he said.

"Six?" she replied. How on earth had she managed to sleep for so long? The fire was still going, radiating heat, and the old mattress beneath her had become strangely comfortable. If she tried hard, she could almost convince herself that this was a luxury suite at the Royal Alpine, and that the man standing over her was her boyfriend.

If Devlin noticed her blush, he didn't show it. He stretched out his hand and she saw that he was using one of the nature books as a tray. On it was a petri dish with a broken-up protein bar, and two beakers full of water.

"Your champagne breakfast is served, madam," Devlin said, still grinning. "Our luxury spa opens at seven, where you will find a team of masseuses waiting for you to treat you the way APEX Club members should be treated. None of this shack in the mountains rubbish."

Darcy laughed, wondering if she was still asleep.

"The APEX Club?" she said, leaning back against the sofa and picking up the beaker. "They're the ones who booked out the resort. I want in."

Devlin coughed and looked down at his own filled petri dish.

"You probably don't, to be honest. It's mostly just me and my friends messing around." His protein bar was holding his attention.

Darcy guessed why he was putting her off the club that she was 100 percent not nearly rich enough to join, but she felt he was in a good enough mood to press him on it.

"And these friends of yours, are they infamously brooding, bad-boy billionaires too?" she teased.

"No," Devlin shook his head, the corners of his lips twitching. "I think you'll find some of them are more than approachable. Annoyingly so."

He sat down on the mattress next to her, grinning.

"Hold up," Darcy said. She was slightly distracted when Devlin shifted closer and she noticed just how good he smelled. How someone who'd hiked up a mountain after crashing a helicopter and sleeping in a cabin could smell so fresh was beyond her. "Hold up. The APEX Club is just you and all your billionaire friends? So it's the APEX *Billionaire's* Club. You're a member of a club called the APEX *Billionaire's* Club?"

She peeled with laughter, enjoying the way Devlin's perfect lips pursed.

"Wait, I never said we were called that," Devlin protested. "The APEX Club—"

"Is that to remind yourselves how rich you are every time you go there?" Darcy teased again. "The APEX *Billionaire's* Club." Darcy let out a honk of a laugh. "Well, my club is a lot more exclusive. I don't need to brag about my wealth."

"The Darcy Wainwright Club? So exclusive I'd double the member numbers by joining that one." Devlin scooted sideways and out the way of the back of Darcy's hand.

"It's a good job I slept well, mister," Darcy said, grinning. "And talking of which, what's got into you this morning?"

"The storm's blown over," he answered, shuffling back towards her. "It must have worn itself out. Blue skies and no wind. We stand a good chance of getting rescued today."

Relief flooded through Darcy.

"That's great," she said. "I thought it was supposed to last for days."

"The weather up here is so unpredictable," he pointed out, taking a bite of his energy bar. He swallowed. "Storms come and go. But there's nothing to say it won't charge itself back up, so we need to move fast."

Darcy nodded, taking a deep drink of water. It was freezing cold and had a strange aftertaste.

"You did wash this, right?" she asked, looking at the beaker. He shook his head.

"Take a walk on the wild side, Darcy. Live a little."

"I'm more worried about dying a little," she said. "What if they were conducting experiments in these? What if they were, you know, storing *urine* in them or something?"

Devlin's smile wavered.

"Yeah, I probably should have washed them," he admitted. He took a gulp from his. "But never mind. It's snow water, as fresh as it's possible to get."

Darcy took another sip, trying not to worry. It wasn't champagne, but it was still one of the most amazing things she'd ever tasted. She picked up a piece of protein bar, chewing its peanut-buttery goodness as Devlin spoke.

"I peeked outside this morning. The snow is deep, but not as bad as I'd feared. We should still be able to walk on it. I'm too worried about the ravines to head down, so I suggest we make our way up. It will be harder, but it's a shorter walk and far less dangerous."

Darcy nodded. The protein bar tasted pretty gross, but she was grateful for it.

"The ranger station is two miles or so away, and from there we'll be able to radio for help. If conditions stay like this, we'll be home in time for lunch."

Darcy paused. Home. Back at the resort, then to her tiny apartment. Her tiny, *empty* apartment. She looked at Devlin, knowing that after today she would never see him again.

"Great," she said, but she didn't really mean it. For a while she sat in silence, watching the last of the flames.

"Penny for your thoughts?" Devlin asked.

"Oh, um, nothing really," she replied, floundering. "I was just happy, you know, that the storm is over."

"Me too. Once we've eaten, we'll pack some supplies and head out. You good with that?"

"Sounds great," she said. "I can't wait to get out of here."

She wondered whether Devlin would notice the lie.

CHAPTER 11

DEVLIN

Devlin finished the last of the protein bar, using his fingers to mop up the crumbs. His right arm still ached, but he'd taken more pain killers when he'd woken and they were fighting off the worst. It helped that his mood was a million times better than it had been last night. With the storm long gone, and the day as bright as anything, the helicopters would be out in force looking for him. By noon at the latest he'd be sitting in the bar with his friends drinking champagne and flirting with the waitresses.

He smiled at the thought. This little trip to the mountains would be nothing more than a bad memory, a story to tell at dinner parties. He'd buy another helicopter, and life would go on just as it had before.

He wasn't sure why the thought filled him with sadness. Once again, he'd be Devlin Storm, and the world would be his oyster. What did he have to feel down about?

"Thanks for breakfast," Darcy said, placing the makeshift tray on the floor and stretching again. She was dressed in that ridiculous sweater, and her hair resembled some kind of haystack, but she was still tantalisingly beautiful. She caught him looking and frowned, putting a hand on her head. "It does this. I don't suppose you've got a bottle of conditioner in that case of yours? Is that something your club promotes? APEX conditioner?"

He raised an eyebrow as he shook his head, then pushed himself to his feet.

"We should leave as soon as possible," he said. "In case there's another storm moving in. I'll double check the map, and leave a note here in case anyone finds the place."

"I'll do another sweep of the cabin for food," she said. "Just in case we missed anything."

"Good," replied Devlin, nodding. They were turning out to be a fairly good team. He started to go, then hesitated. He didn't remember much about last night — he'd been so exhausted he'd pretty much passed out. But he had a vague memory in his head, something that might just have been a dream. "Darcy, did I say anything to you while I was asleep?"

Darcy laughed, but she shook her head.

"You were as quiet as a mouse," she said, but she was smiling in a way that made him unsure whether he believed her or not.

"That's a relief," he said, with a little smile of his own. "By the way, you cuddle like a python when you're asleep. I thought you were trying to crush me."

Her mouth dropped open in embarrassment, and she picked up a cushion and hurled it at him.

"I do not!" she yelled.

Devlin laughed, escaping out of the room as a second cushion came flying towards him. He was still laughing as he walked into the small bedroom. He laid the map on one of the stripped beds, and double-checked the route he'd drawn in pencil. It was going to be a tough climb up the mountain to the ranger's station, especially with his arm out of action, and especially with Darcy in tow, but he was almost 100 percent sure they could manage it. They didn't have a choice. If they stayed here, with no way of contacting the world, then they risked never being found.

Besides, heading up the mountain was where he needed to go to finish what he'd started. It was the whole reason he was here in the first place.

He heard Darcy humming to herself as she walked out of the living room and past the door. She had such a sweet voice, even when she was hurling insults at him. It hurt his heart a little bit to hear her singing — in a good way. Although he'd deny this in front of the world's press, who all thought he was a devilish womaniser, it had been a long, long time since he'd woken up with a woman beside him. The last time it had happened, in fact, was the morning he'd split up with his last girlfriend — nearly a year ago.

The memory of it, of Claudia packing her things and walking out of the door, was still painful — not because he regretted her leaving, but because he regretted so much of the time they had spent together, the time he had wasted on her. Devlin focused instead on the soft and gentle voice he could hear from the other room. Darcy was everything that Claudia wasn't. Claudia had been a model, as beautiful as they came, but her beauty had felt so artificial. Claudia had been cold, and selfish, and unkind, whereas Darcy was compassionate and considerate and generous.

Come on, he said to himself. *You don't even know her.*

That was true. They'd met just over twelve hours ago, and the circumstances weren't exactly normal. But maybe that was it — strange things happened under extreme conditions. It was pressure that turned trees into diamonds, after all.

He folded the map and slotted it into his pocket, then he tore a page from one of the textbooks they'd found and scribbled a note onto it, struggling to shape the letters with his injured arm.

This is Devlin Storm. Me and the girl are alive. We spent the night here and are now en route to the ranger station via the pass. Look for us there.

He added the coordinates of the station, then gave it one last read through, feeling something twang in his stomach. He quickly crossed out where he'd written *the girl* and added Darcy's name instead. Feeling better about it, he left the note where anyone entering the research cabin would see it. Walking back to the living room, he found Darcy there. She was pulling her jacket over her thick sweater and doing a good job of tying herself in knots.

"Need a little help?" he asked. She stopped, her arms out like a scarecrow, then nodded.

"I don't think I've ever worn so many clothes in my life," she said.

"You'll need them," he replied, walking to her. He held the jacket while she pushed her arms into the sleeves, then he zipped it up for her. "It'll be pushing minus ten in the shade, but it will warm up later in the day."

She shuffled, trying to pull her loose trousers back into place.

"Shall I . . . ?" he asked.

"What?" she said.

"Your trousers."

"What about them?" she replied.

"You know, shall I fix them."

"You want to fix my pants?" she asked, and her cheeks turned the most delightful shade of pink. "Do they need fixing? Is there something wrong with them?"

"Not if you want them to drop to the ground halfway up the mountain," he said, and her blush deepened even further. "That didn't come out quite the way I intended it to," he went on, feeling his own cheeks heat a little as well. "But when you're climbing an ice shelf, the last thing you want is to lose your trousers. May I?"

"Uh . . . I guess so," she said, lifting her arms. Devlin grabbed the waistline of her trousers and, ignoring the pain in his arm, folded it over, then again, tying the drawstring as tight as he could. He knotted it twice more, then stood back, noting she'd swapped out her dress shoes for the boots she'd found.

"Better?" he asked. She nodded, doing a little jig.

"Much," she said. "Although I probably should have used the loo first."

They laughed together, their eyes grazing each other's, snagging and holding for a beat, then another. Devlin's mind went completely blank, like an untouched field of heavy snow. All he could think about was those huge eyes, those full lips, and that sweet, innocent voice. His brain was caught in a hamster wheel of where it had gone last night, flashes of his indecent thoughts making him buzz. Thoughts of a hand on her waist and his fingers tracing her curves, and he felt his trousers tighten across his groin. She was something else.

"Right!" Darcy squeaked, dragging her eyes away from his. "We should probably make a move!"

"Definitely," he replied, his voice gravelly. "Absolutely."

He tried to walk past her, just as she tried to walk past him, and they bumped together. And for a sweet moment Devlin's fantasies were coming to life. His strong fingers closed around her waist, and they ended up closer than he intended. At least, that's what he was telling himself as her front rubbed against his. He felt everything. The softness of her body through her layers, the heat of her skin through her hands, the tingling in his lower belly.

Let her go you idiot.

"Sorry," he said, dropping his hands like lead weights and standing to the side, offering her the right of way. "After you."

"Thank you," she said, bolting through the door.

Devlin couldn't help but smile as he watched her waddle away in her giant coat. Then he walked to the fire, emptied snow over the rumbling ashes, and picked up his own clothes. They were bone dry, and he carefully slid on the suit jacket first, then the thermal coat, clumsily buttoning everything up as tightly as it would go. Darcy had found some hats and gloves in the storeroom and even though they were a little small he managed to wrestle them on, along with a pair of battered boots that were ugly but, thankfully, toasty warm. It wasn't exactly the right sort of kit for conditions like this, but all in all it wasn't too bad.

He walked from the room, pausing by the door to look back. The two mattresses still sat between the sofa and the newly doused fire, blankets bundled on top. He wasn't sure why, but he felt sad at the thought of leaving here. This little cabin had stood here for who knows how long, and for years now it had been empty. Yet it had provided shelter and warmth and food for him and Darcy. It had kept them alive, without a doubt.

And it had brought him and Darcy closer. No matter how he'd felt about her back at the Royal Alpine, spending last night in her company had shifted something in him. Yes, she was frustratingly talkative and often a little daft, but she had been fearsome and capable in the storm. And she seemed to genuinely care about him. Not about his wealth or his position. Him. Devlin.

As difficult as the day was going to be, he felt glad that he wasn't on his own — and gladder still that it was Darcy who was with him. At least, with her, he wouldn't get bored, and she was smarter and hardier than he'd given her credit for.

He was *almost* enjoying spending time with her.

Stop being a fool! he told himself. And that's exactly what he was being, a fool.

Darcy was there for one reason and one reason only, or maybe one hundred thousand reasons. Devlin had almost let himself forget about the money he'd bribed her with. But he knew, deep down, that was the only reason Darcy was seeming to be genuinely lovely. It had to be. Why else would someone as kind as Darcy be interested in someone like him?

One of the reasons he'd been so successful, especially in the years he and Claudia had been together, was that he'd put matters of the heart so far behind him that they couldn't get in his way. He was ruthless, and determined, and heartless, and that's the way it had to stay if he was to keep his position as one of the richest and most famous men in the world.

Yet standing here, in this modest little building, he wasn't even sure if that's what he wanted anymore. He felt more at home here than he had done in any of his houses and apartments, any of his hotel suites. He felt like he *belonged*.

"You ready?" called a voice from the other end of the cabin.

"I am," he said.

He left the room and made his way down the corridor, walking into the front room with a steely determination to not get carried away. Darcy was by the front door, his suitcase open in front of her. She was putting something inside it, and a red-hot fear exploded inside him, uncontrollable.

"What do you think you're doing?" he shouted. She jumped up, shocked, and he stormed towards her so fast that she jumped away from him.

"I was just putting these in the case," she said, holding up another protein bar and what might have been an extra pair of gloves. "I thought we could carry everything we needed in—"

"You don't think," he said, his voice a low and frightening growl. "That's my suitcase. You have no business opening it."

Darcy's face screwed up as she glared back at him.

"I was trying to help," she said.

"Then don't," he spat back. "Don't do anything unless I tell you to. Don't speak, don't think. If you want to get out of here as much as I do, then you'll do exactly what I say. And stay away from my stuff."

He grabbed the case as best as he was able with his bad arm, then opened the door. Behind him, he heard Darcy stutter an apology. But he ignored her, and marched out into the snow.

CHAPTER 12

DARCY

The last thing Darcy wanted to do was cry, but she literally couldn't stop herself. The tears came like meltwater, spilling out of her, and the sobs racked her whole body.

Devlin's rage had come out of nowhere. The way he had spoken to her was as bad as a physical blow. Why had he got so angry at her for putting something in his suitcase? It wasn't like he had much in there, just an old tin and his passport. There had been plenty of room. He'd had no right to attack her so fiercely, especially after being so nice to her this morning. His moods were as unpredictable as the mountain weather, a storm that could come and go in a flash.

It wasn't just that, though. It was everything that had happened in the last twenty-four hours. The shock was still catching up with her, and even though she'd been trying to put a brave face on everything, she was an emotional wreck. Devlin's outburst had tipped her over the edge — she was the helicopter falling into the ravine — and it was all she could do not to curl up in a ball in the corner of the room and stay there.

No, she said to herself. *You're stronger than that. Don't let him get to you.*

She took a deep breath, smudging the tears from her eyes with her gloved hands. She felt like she wanted to burn down the mountain with a flame-thrower, but she'd settle for not letting Devlin get away with taking his yo-yo emotions out on her. He wasn't the only one feeling scared. He'd said it himself that they had to work together. It wasn't her fault he had the emotional intelligence of a toddler who'd skipped their afternoon nap.

Placing the protein bar and the spare gloves in the pocket of her jacket, she stepped out of the cabin. The cold hit her instantly, stinging the exposed skin of her face. It didn't feel as freezing as it had the previous night, though, because there was hardly any wind, and the sun was just peeking over the smaller slopes to the east. The snow came up to her shins, perfectly crisp and white. She'd had the good sense to wrap the boots she'd found in old pieces of cloth, then in plastic bags, so even though they weren't exactly ideal, and they might have been abandoned because they were holey, at least they felt warm and dry.

Devlin was already a dozen yards away, struggling through the snow with his case clutched in his good hand. He was moving fast, without so much as a glance back. Darcy looked past the cabin to where the mountainside dropped away. She thought she might have been able to see the distant resort, or maybe a town or something, but there was just rock and snow for miles, with the occasional scrap of forest poking through. Part of her thought about heading down the mountain anyway. Who needed Devlin? She could find her own way back. Then she thought about those ravines, hidden by the snow, and the shudder that passed through her was enough to put a stop to that idea.

She considered staying right where she was, too. The cabin roof was covered in six inches of snow, and the helipad was nowhere to be seen. She could spend the morning clearing the helipad lights, though, and she could probably find enough rocks to spell out SOS. Any helicopter flying overhead would be able to find her. She laughed, a billowing cloud of breath hanging in the air in front of her as she imagined a rescue team dropping her back at the resort while Devlin clambered up the mountainside in the cold and the dark.

No, for a start, Darcy was pretty sure that if the rescue team got to Devlin first and they weren't together, he'd be likely to just leave her stranded and head back down the mountain to get his stupid, perfect face on the front covers of all the papers as quickly as he could. Secondly, she wanted to prove she could climb this bloody mountain. Prove it to Devlin. Yes, that would shut him up. But also, as she lifted her face to the sun, she wanted to prove it to herself.

Stupid Devlin and his stupid man bag.

Steeling herself as best she could, she closed the cabin door behind her and set off after him. She trod in his giant footsteps, but even then it was difficult because the snow was so deep. She was panting for breath after the first ten paces, her feet already numb, and Devlin still showed no sign of waiting for her.

"Hey, you want to stop a minute?" she yelled, her voice both weirdly muffled and amplified by the thick snow. It was so quiet up here — just the crunch of their feet and the thump of her pulse in her ears.

"No," Devlin shot back. "Keep up."

Darcy roared into the mountain, all of a sudden realising what people meant when they saw red. The snow turned a deep shade of merlot through the veil of anger. How dare he talk to her like that. Her fury pulsed through her veins, powering her legs and closing the distance between them. Darcy had no idea what she was going to do when she caught up to Devlin, all she could focus on was each individual step. The mountain above stretched higher than she could see, and the drop away was spectacular. Maybe Devlin could have a helping hand over the edge. Or a sharp boot to his backside.

She let out a laugh. Barely able to lift her feet high enough to tread in his footprints, she was unlikely to be able to reach his bum. And it was so muscly that her foot would just bounce right off it and she'd be the one tumbling down the mountain, gathering snow like a snowman. The idea was so ridiculous it took the edge off her anger. Just.

Up ahead, Devlin was carefully navigating a pile of boulders blocking their way. It looked like it was hard going for him, especially with the case in one hand and his other arm broken. Darcy waded through the snow until she finally caught up to him.

"Do you want me to carry it?" she asked, swallowing her anger.

"So you can look inside again?" he shouted down. His foot slipped and pebbles rained down around her feet.

"Are you kidding me, right now?" she shouted, placing a foot on one boulder and using another to haul herself up. Stars pulsed in the corner of her vision and she wasn't sure if it was from anger or exertion. "I offer to help even though you were awful to me and you're accusing me of what? Spying? Who cares about your stupid case? As much as you seem to love your own life, I don't find it remotely interesting. Maybe I shouldn't have gone into it without asking, no, but I just wanted to put something in it. Bring along some protein bars to help us BOTH on the way up this stupid mountain."

"You're infuriating," he grunted, pulling himself up to the boulder next to Darcy.

The heat radiating from him was like a lit firework. She pushed her hair from her face with a gloved hand.

"Me?" she shouted, inching closer and pressing her glove to his chest. "I'm infuriating?"

His eyes blazed at her, but he stayed quiet.

"I'm not the one acting like a child." She stepped back, thinking about the shoe-box-sized tin and passport in his bag with rage. "For what reason? None, that's what. I am not one of your minions, Devlin. I'm not here to be shouted at or spoken down to or left to die out here because you're too much of an idiot to wait for me. Out here on this bloody huge mountain we are equals, you hear me. We're both in danger of storms and avalanches and ravines. The mountain doesn't care who you are. It's not going to save you. It doesn't care about your empire or your fleet of helicopters or the servants you have tending to your every whiny whim. This mountain cares for your money about as much as I do."

She poked his chest again and turned clumsily in her bag-covered boots and thick coat, staring at the climb ahead with tears stinging in her eyes. A sharp thought flashed across her mind and she turned back, blinking away her emotion before postulating just in case he got the wrong idea.

"Which is Not. At. All."

Devlin looked down, his expression still dark.

He was silent, unmoved, but Darcy didn't want to waste valuable time waiting for him to develop feelings, so she set off on the climb ahead. Carefully, she manoeuvred her way up the boulders, trying to count to ten and recalibrate her breathing so she didn't accidentally fall off in a fit of anger. Hauling herself up the last rock, she found herself on a wide, open plateau. There was a gentle breeze here and it picked up swirls of snow, making them dance like angels in the morning light. Darcy could feel them on her tongue as she stopped for breath. She scooped up a handful of snow, letting it melt on her tongue and then swallowed the cool water.

Devlin had stopped, too, looking a little worse for wear. He rested his case by his feet and clamped his broken arm to his chest. Darcy looked at him, the angel and devil on her shoulders unable to fight for victor. She was angry at him, but she also needed him to be okay so they'd make it to the ranger's station. The angel winning out, she walked to him, her feet slipping in the snow.

"Look, Devlin," she said, forcing her tone to stay civil. "We need to stick together. I'm offering to help you. Please just accept my help and let me carry the case for you."

He sighed out a steaming breath, staring at the floor. Then he turned to her, his green eyes shining in the fierce light.

"No," he said, with a voice that made Darcy flip.

Counting to ten was out of the window now. Darcy could count to infinity and still not understand the man standing in front of her.

"You're standing there all cold and unapproachable," she scoffed. "I guess I must have misread nearly every single one of our interactions back in that research hut, then, because all I'm asking you to do right now is trust me. And if you don't trust me, then what chance do we have out here?"

"Darcy—"

"What?" she asked. "What have I done wrong now?"

"Darcy," he said again, eyes fixed on hers. "I trust you."

Darcy felt his words like an untimely shove. Or maybe a warm hug. She couldn't quite decide.

She lifted a brow in response, no easy feat in the freezing cold temperatures.

"It's me," he said. "I don't . . . I don't cope very well with other people. I don't cope very well with being helped. I've been on my own too long."

"I find that hard to believe," replied Darcy, pulling the collar of her coat tight around her neck. "Aren't you around people all the time? Supermodels and actresses?"

"Yeah, sure," he said. "If you believe what you read in the newspapers."

"It's not true?" she asked, taking a step towards him, so close she could see the flecks of emerald in his green eyes. Devlin shook his head. "Is the first rule of billionaire club, do not display weakness? That's sad, Devlin."

"It's just me." He gritted his teeth.

She wasn't exactly sure what he meant by that, but she could tell by his expression how much he was hurting — and not just his arm.

"You can talk to me, you know," Darcy said. "I know I'm not a model, or rich, or famous. I'm just me. And you're right, I'm scared of most things. I'm scared of adventures. But you know, my mum always told me the greatest gift you can give in life is listening to people, and one thing I definitely am good at is listening."

Devlin looked at her, *really* looked at her, as if she was a rare and fascinating plant he had discovered on the mountainside. He opened his mouth as if to speak, then closed it again, turning away.

"There's a gentle climb ahead," he said. "Not exactly easy, but the terrain isn't too treacherous. I'll carry my case just fine. But . . ." He swallowed, as if about to do the most difficult thing he'd ever done. "But after that there's a patch of harder ground to get past. I'd be grateful for the help then, if the offer is still there."

"It will be," she said. "Providing I actually make it that far. It's so cold!"

He smiled, then picked up his case.

"The faster you walk, the warmer you'll be."

CHAPTER 13

DEVLIN

The slope wasn't quite as gentle as he'd hoped, and the thick carpet of snow hid countless loose rocks and craters, but he took it one step at a time, testing the ground before committing himself. He kept the pace slow for safety, but also for Darcy. He felt bad for what had happened as they'd been leaving the cabin, and for marching off and leaving her behind. She had been right, it was the kind of thing a child did, not a grown man.

Glancing back, he saw her just behind him. She was still putting her feet exactly where his had been, like it was a game. It was a sensible move, though, and once again he found himself impressed at how smart she was. Her makeshift shoes were a stroke of genius — her feet were most certainly warmer and drier than his were.

He was impressed with how she had stood up to him, too. Darcy Wainwright was proving herself to be more of a firecracker than she gave herself credit for. Devlin could count on one hand the number of people who would dare to talk to him the way she had back there, and the memory of it made his stomach somersault. He also didn't know a single other person who would be that kind and magnanimous while also flying into a rage at him. It was obvious she disliked him, understandably given the way he'd treated her back at the research hut, but she still offered to help him *and* he hadn't needed to bribe her with more money in order to do so. Devlin scrunched up his forehead. That was what he was finding most difficult, he realised. Accepting help when he wasn't paying for or demanding it.

He turned back to the plateau, working his way around a shark's fin of snow-covered rock. The ground dropped away sharply to the side, and he could see the line of their footsteps leading down to the distant cabin. It was almost invisible in the snow, but anyone flying overhead would probably see them, and see their prints too — unless another storm hit, of course.

That thought concerned him. He'd spent enough time in the mountains to know that bad weather could hit any time. Usually he had his phone and his sat nav on hand, so that he would get plenty of warning. But all he had to go on now was his own senses and experience. The sky was clear, though, perfectly blue in every direction.

Please stay like this, he pleaded, silently.

If it didn't, if it turned, then he and Darcy would be in serious trouble.

He glanced back over his shoulder again, slowing down to let Darcy catch up. He felt a strange and unexpected feeling of protectiveness over the young woman, and a huge pang of regret for what he'd said to her. The thought of anything bad happening to her out here was painful. He couldn't remember the last time he'd felt that way about anyone — even with Claudia he'd kept his distance.

Although that hadn't always been the case, had it? It was almost too hurtful to think about, but he forced himself to — if only to get a grip on the feelings that ran through his head, and his heart. He remembered one night he and Claudia had been dining out on the terrace of his villa in Tuscany. It had been an incredible evening, and he'd been so relaxed that he'd started telling Claudia about his childhood, about what it had been like growing up in a poor and unhappy family. It had felt great to be able to open up to her, to *anyone*.

Claudia had held his hand across the table, nodding as he spoke, her eyes soft with understanding.

But when he ended things months later, that very story was the first thing she sold to the press.

Her betrayal had cut way deeper than the breakup ever did and he'd never spoken to anyone about his private life after that.

Devlin Storm the island, he thought to himself. *Devlin Storm the mountain.*

Darcy hadn't been too far off when she had joked about the first rule of the billionaire club being *do not display any weaknesses*. Only, it wasn't the rule for any club he was a member of, especially not the APEX Club. It was a rule Devlin had built around himself like a protective forcefield.

He turned to Darcy again, and she smiled up at him with the same fierce determination.

"Are you okay?" she asked, and he nodded. "The offer's still there if your arm's getting tired."

A good listener, she'd said. A good person. Darcy wouldn't have sold his story. Would she?

"I'm good for the moment, thanks," he said, slowing more and letting Darcy walk beside him.

The snow was hardened here, their footsteps not so deep and draining. They walked on in companionable silence, punctured by the occasional wheezy groan from Darcy.

"I wouldn't have left you behind," he offered, cautiously.

"What?" Darcy's voice came in a breathless whisper.

"Back there, you said I'd left you to die." Devlin went on. "I didn't. I wouldn't do that. I sometimes act without thinking—"

"No shit," Darcy interrupted.

Devlin ignored the pop, but a smile grew on his lips.

"I could see you at all times — I knew where you were."

He left the words hanging in the air. They were true.

"Thank you," Darcy said, so quietly her words were whipped away by a flurry of windy snow.

Devlin smiled, ducked his chin down, and pushed forward up the steep slope. His arm throbbed, a new burning sensation was trickling down his skin and he knew that wasn't a good sign. A break he could deal with, infection was a whole other ball game. He really needed to get a look at it, but they had a long way to go to the ranger's station yet.

"Devlin," Darcy's voice was a welcome distraction from the pain. "I know you said you'd never leave me behind, but what would happen if a mountain lion started running for us? Would you run off and leave me then? That would be exceptional circumstances, so I'm not saying I'd mind, but—"

"The Alps doesn't have mountain lions," he interrupted.

Darcy seemed to ponder that fact for a moment, as she trudged silently through the snow.

"That's a bit of a cop-out answer," she said, eventually. "What if it was a bear then?"

"Nope," Devlin replied, steering them around a crop of large boulders.

"Nope you wouldn't run, or nope there's no bears?"

Devlin laughed, feeling a bubble of happiness burst unexpectedly in his chest.

"There are bears, but they're not this high up. Not this time of year."

"Hmm," muttered Darcy, scratching the top of her hat with her gloves. Devlin remembered the way she'd pushed at his chest, and the heat that had been radiating from her cheeks had set his insides alight. "That's still a bit of a cop-out. So I'm taking from your lack of answer, you'd run. That's okay. It's important we have a bit of survival instinct in us all."

"Darcy, I don't know if I'd jump in front of a bear if it was lumbering towards us. I might do. But maybe trust me enough to know I'd not take you where the bears could be . . . if I could help it."

The look she gave him froze his heart. In the same way she'd asked him to trust her, that look said she wouldn't trust him as far as she could throw him.

"Do you not feel safe with me?" he asked quickly, the idea burning hot like the infection growing in his arm.

Darcy's eyes widened. "Oh no," she said. "It's not that I don't feel safe with you. I'm just trying to picture you jumping in front of a bear to save me."

Her lips lifted in a smile that defrosted the panic at the thought that he scared her.

"You seem to have forgotten quite quickly how I protected you in the helicopter crash."

Darcy scoffed, adjusting the scarf around her neck to cover her chin and lips too. Devlin was sad not to be able to watch them moving anymore.

"Protecting the controls, weren't you?" she asked, eyes glinting.

The mountain path narrowed again, a steep drop off giving way to the tips of snow-covered trees. Devlin took the lead, slowly navigating the terrain, each step being tested before he put his weight through his feet. He could feel sweat trickling down his neck by the time they got to a solid, wide section of snow again. And he was pleased to feel Darcy catch up and walk alongside him.

"Do you know what animals we're most likely to see here?" he asked, noticing how pale she'd gone and the way her was brow knitted between her soft eyes.

She shook her head.

"Hares."

"Really?" She gazed up at him. "Hares as in giant rabbits? Up here?"

"The very same," he said. "They're mountain hares, and they live up here in the snowy climes. They change colour throughout the year. White in winter, brown in the summer.

I'd definitely throw myself in front of you if one of those charged at us."

Darcy laughed, the sound like melting ice.

"I'd be elbowing you out of the way if you did. I love rabbits," she said.

"Hares."

"Whatever," she replied, grinning. "I always wanted a pet rabbit growing up. Used to be on my birthday and Christmas list every single year. And every year I was disappointed. Mum said we couldn't afford to keep a pet because they always get broken and vets bills are higher than our medical bills. We didn't have insurance. So if we see a snowy hare up here, I'm grabbing it and taking it home with me. I'll keep it in the reception desk at work if I have to."

Devlin didn't doubt for a second that Darcy would race after a hare if she saw one. He was enjoying hearing about her life. Enjoying being in the quieter moments of their conversation and slowly realising that not everything had to be fireworks and raise blood pressure in order to be meaningful.

Darcy was teaching him a lot about himself and he wanted to show her he was learning.

CHAPTER 14

DARCY

The higher they climbed, the harder it was to breathe.

Darcy had been expecting this. Although she'd never been climbing before in her life, she'd had to attend a health and safety seminar when she'd started working at the resort. Abigail Lamb, the boss, had walked her through all the advice she needed to pass on to guests — things like which areas of the mountains were out of bounds, the warning signs of avalanches, and how to avoid frostbite. There had been a whole section on altitude sickness — when there simply wasn't enough oxygen in the air to keep your body working. She didn't remember the ins and outs of it, but she did remember that one of the symptoms was a terrible headache.

A terrible headache like the one she was getting now.

She rubbed her temples, stopping for a moment and closing her eyes. The headache was probably just because of the cold, and because of the blindingly bright light. They'd been walking for nearly two hours now and the sun was above the peaks, its light bouncing off the snow in every direction. It felt like being in a tanning booth, but with your eyes open.

"You all right?" Devlin asked. She squinted at him, seeing that he'd come to a stop too. He dropped the case, stretching his good arm.

"Just a headache," she said. "Probably nothing."

A look of concern crossed his features, but only for a moment. He looked down the slope, then craned his neck up at the mountain that towered over them.

"How high are we?" she asked.

"The ranger station's at about 9,000 feet," he said. "I'm guessing we're over 8,000 now. Are you feeling sick? Tired? Dizzy?"

Darcy nodded.

"Tired, sure," she answered. "But that might have something to do with, you know, crashing in a helicopter and sleeping in a cabin. Dizzy, a little, but only from exhaustion. And I'm more hungry than sick."

She was, although she was so hungry it was making her feel nauseous. Her stomach felt like an empty bag, and the sound of it growling had been the loudest thing on the mountainside besides than their crunching footsteps.

"Let's take a break," Devlin suggested, picking up the case and walking to her side. "Why don't you eat something?"

"We've only got one protein bar left," she said. "We need to save it."

"Have a bite," he urged. "Go on, it will give you a boost."

She nodded, pulling the bar from her jacket pocket. She used her teeth to tear it open, then took the smallest of nibbles from the top.

"You can have more than that," Devlin said.

"I don't want to," she replied, grimacing. "It tastes like an old sock."

He laughed, and she held it out to him.

"Your turn."

"No, thank you." He shook his head. "I'm okay."

"Hey, have you forgotten our last conversation already. Come on, we're a team."

"I thought we were talking about rabbits," he said, considering the protein bar. "Oh man, I could eat rabbit stew right about now."

"Oy, you leave Nibbles out of this conversation," she hurled back, lifting the bar to his face as his good hand was full.

"Nibbles?"

"And Norman," she added. "I'm capturing two."

Nodding thoughtfully, he opened his mouth and took a bite.

"Thanks," he said, chewing then swallowing.

"Don't get used to me feeding you," she replied. "I know your APEX *Billionaire's* Club must have an army of servants who do that, but I'm not one of them."

He laughed, and the cloud of his breath drifted up into the sky. He looked different when he laughed, his eyes crinkling. Unreserved, unharried, like when he was sleeping. A dangerous tingling warmed her belly and she looked away.

"Is that what you think my life is like?" he said. "Servants feeding me? Getting me dressed?"

"Isn't it?" she asked, smiling. "I bet you have somebody to tie your shoe laces."

"Of course," he said, smiling back at her. "His name is Jim, and I pay him a million quid a year to make sure my shoes are on properly."

He shook his head.

"My life isn't any different to yours," he said. "Not really, not when you boil away all the other stuff. I get up, I go to work, I go to the gym, I watch TV, I read, I eat, and I go to bed."

"But you get up in a mansion, you drive to work in a Porsche, you have a personal gym, you're *on* the TV, and your bed is probably made of gold. If you need something, you buy it. If you need someone, you buy them too."

Devlin shrugged, the smile dropping away.

"That's not true," he said.

"You bought me," she replied. "One hundred thousand, wasn't it?"

"It's not like that," he said, again. "I was desperate, and the money felt like a necessity. I needed to get up to the mountain and you were my only hope."

"But there's the difference," Darcy added, not unkindly. "A huge difference. You were desperate for my help so you paid me because you had the finances to be able to do that."

Devlin closed his eyes in exasperation.

"I grew up with nothing," he said, eyes firmly shut. "We were so poor, my dad was useless, he was in prison half the time. Mum did her best, she was amazing, but we never had anything. I earned every penny I've got, and I'm not ashamed of it."

"I'm sorry," she said.

She looked at his face, studying the worry lines on his forehead so closely she didn't realise he'd opened his eyes. He gave her a silent look that made her chest constrict and the skin on her neck prickle with heat.

He breathed deeply, then nodded.

"If your head gets worse, or you feel severely dizzy or sick, then tell me," he said. "High altitude pulmonary or cerebral oedemas are no joke. They can be fatal."

He pulled the packet of pain relief from his pocket and offered her two pills.

"This will help, wash it down with some snow."

She did as he told her, removing a glove and scooping up some scratchy snow, dissolving it in her mouth. It lifted her mood a little. Her snow scooping hand soon started to sting with the cold and wet, but as she tried to pull her glove back on, it stuck to all her fingers and hung off them like the branches of a willow tree. Devlin pressed his lips together and put down the case.

"Here," he said. "Let me help."

Darcy watched as Devlin pulled off the glove from his good hand with his teeth and started to tug at hers. He sighed as the glove slid easily, his chest rising and falling, his Adam's apple bobbing. His fingers brushed the skin of her wrist, and for a moment it was like he was holding her hand. Darcy's breath caught in her throat. Her skin tingled. And she was almost certain the sharp intake of breath came from Devlin and his realisation of how it looked. He dropped his hand like Darcy had electrocuted him, turning to pull back on his own glove.

"Thanks," Darcy said, her voice husky. Devlin gave her a nod and they started back on their way, walking side by side.

Every so often Darcy would feel Devlin turn and inspect her, as though she was about to fall or faint. She could see the concern even from the corner of her eyes and it made heat pool in all her softness. She was suddenly too hot in her layers of clothing, and she tugged at her collar in a futile attempt to cool down, grateful that Devlin didn't mention her rosy cheeks. The quiet of the mountain pressed too hard — she needed to fill it.

"You're good at this."

"Good at what?" he asked.

"Walking," she replied. "Through snow. You're a cross-country skier, right?"

"Yeah," he said. "I love it."

"You're crazy," she said, out of breath again. "Why would you do this for fun?"

He laughed.

"I like the challenge of it," he said. "It's good to test yourself. Cross-country skiing is one of the hardest things you can do, but you *can* do it. There's really nothing as exhilarating as pushing yourself to your limits, and nothing as rewarding as crossing the finish line. I've competed a few times, mainly in Canada, but Scandinavia too. Cross-country skiing, and marksmanship."

"I heard you were competitive," she said, her foot slipping on a loose rock beneath the snow. Devlin was beside her in an instant. "Like, *really* competitive."

"I am," he said, stepping back into line as Darcy walked on. "But it's not like that. I don't care if I win or lose. It doesn't matter where you come in the ranks, as it's not about who you beat. The only person you should be competing with is yourself. Do better. Be better."

"Are you actually Devlin Storm?" Darcy asked, smiling. "I remember reading an interview with you where you said you enjoyed nothing more than crushing your opponents."

Devlin shook his head. "Yeah, that sounds like something I'd say. Pompous and ridiculous and self-aggrandising."

"But that's not you," Darcy said. Devlin stopped walking, turning to her and fixing her with his intense gaze.

"Can I tell you something?" he asked, speaking more quietly now that they were face to face. "Something you probably won't have read in many interviews."

"Sure," she said, following his lead as he walked on again, his arm brushing hers as they went. It was a solid contact that felt good in this wide expanse of pure, white nothingness.

"I wasn't called Devlin Storm growing up. Devlin, yes, but I had my dad's name, Priestley. I hated it because I hated him. He was the least priestly person you could ever meet. His name was a joke. Mum had his name, too, and her maiden name was Smith, which felt far too dull."

"How did you end up with Storm?" Darcy asked. She'd heard the name Priestley before, it was a common fact that he'd changed his name, but she had never heard the reason why.

"Mum was a quiet woman," he went on, his voice even softer now, so that she had to lean closer to him to hear it over the sound of their crunching feet. "That's why dad liked her, I think, because he could order her around. She used to do everything for him, and I never once heard him ask nicely, or say thank you. He was the same with everyone. He just had a way of making you feel small, small enough that he could boss you around, use you. I used to hate it so much, the way he was."

He took a moment to think about his own words, his green eyes seeing something that Darcy could not.

"I hate how like him I am," he said eventually. "I hate that I can see him in me every single day — that arrogance, that selfishness."

"Why are you like it, then?" Darcy replied. "Why not change?"

"Because I saw what happens when you don't keep people at arm's length" he said. "I'm not going to be at the mercy of someone just because I fall in love with them. If I start letting them in, I might lose everything."

"You might gain a lot more," said Darcy.

"That's a risk I'm not going to take," he snapped back.

She could feel the anger pulsing off him in waves, but there was something else — a flicker of regret, as if he were lost in a moment from his past. Sensing the shift, she kept quiet, giving him space. They both trudged up the steep slope in silence. It was a few minutes before he started speaking again.

"Mum was kind and loving all her life," he said. "She could never stand up to dad, because he would use his physical strength against her. Except once. I still remember it so clearly. I was twelve, I'd just had a growth spurt, and I was in the wrestling club at school. All my life I'd been afraid of Dad, but for the first time I was bigger than him, stronger. He was just out of prison, and I think he wanted to show me that he was still the man of the family. One night, drunk and angry, he raised his fist to me and Mum . . ."

He took a deep breath, a cloud of it billowing out of his pursed lips.

"Mum changed. In that instant, she became something else. There was a sudden strength in her, a fury. It was like a storm was raging behind her eyes, and she ran in front of me and pushed Dad as hard as she could. He went down like a ton of bricks, and she just stood over him and ordered him never to touch me, never to even lift his fist to me again. And he never did, not once. For all Dad's meanness, his anger, for all the times he made my mum feel like garbage, he never once threatened me again."

"A storm," Darcy said. "That's where your name came from?"

Devlin nodded.

"I took that piece of her, that strength, that storm I saw in her eyes, and I made it part of me, for ever. She's with me. She's always with me."

"I'm sorry you lost her," said Darcy.

"Thank you. It still doesn't feel real, you know? I still think I can just pick up the phone and . . ."

Whatever he was about to say became stuck in his throat and Darcy's heart melted like snow in the sun. She reached out and touched his arm, as tenderly as she could, pulling him to a halt. He stood there, facing away from her, and when she finally coaxed his head around, she saw that his amazing, green eyes were swimming with tears.

"Come here," she said, and he shook his head. She opened her arms. "Just for a moment. I promise I won't tell anyone."

He let her embrace him, and she pulled his head onto her shoulder, putting her other arm around his waist and hugging him as hard as she was able to in her layers of clothes. She felt his body shudder, but whatever sadness was there must have been quickly locked away because after a moment, his body tensed and he pulled back.

"It's the air," he croaked, clearing his throat. "It's too thin. Makes my eyes water."

"It's okay, Devlin," she replied. "There's nothing wrong with being human. There's nothing wrong with needing help or with asking for some compassion. Your mum saved you that day because she acted out of love for you. If you want to be like her and to keep a bit of her with you, like you say you do, then maybe you need to open your heart to receiving it to. I bet you've never truly been in love, have you? Never fought for someone who meant the whole world to you?"

He scrunched up his nose.

"We need to keep going," he said, hefting up his case. "All talking does is slow us down. All it does is make us vulnerable to the mountain."

Darcy felt foolish for trying to get him to open up. All too often she'd read that men like Devlin didn't share their feelings. They were solitary, and closed, because they believed that any attempt to open up would be a chink in their armour.

But the thing was, she hadn't tried to get him to talk. He'd done it all himself. Sure, she'd asked a few questions, but it was him who'd steered the conversation into the past, and towards his parents. She got the feeling that Devlin's emotions were like a core of ice, buried deep inside him and kept guarded at all times. But that ice water heated up sometimes, it came to a boil, and he just couldn't stop it from bubbling over.

The world knew Devlin Storm as a cold, uncaring, emotionless man, but in the short time she'd spent with him, Darcy was starting to understand just how fragile he actually was.

But she had no desire to be shouted at again, so she stayed where she was, walking beside Devlin as they marched up the slope. She rubbed her hands together, trying to flex her numb fingers. They'd made good progress, climbing the mountain faster than she'd thought. If the weather held, and there were no catastrophes, then they'd reach the ranger station in another two hours or so.

They had reached a small rocky outcrop and Devlin went first, scrambling up it. Darcy waited until he was at the top then took her turn, heaving her exhausted body up over the rocks until her arms and legs screamed at her to stop. But she made it, and despite her heart rate soaring through her hat, Darcy was proud of her climb. She looked to Devlin for recognition of her hard work, but he simply started walking again.

She followed a little behind, watching Devlin as he strode on ahead with a sense of determination. As she walked, she thought about everything that Devlin had said to her — his poor childhood, his drunken father who had been in and out of prison, his loving mum. It was so different to the Devlin Storm she'd read about in the papers, so different to the picture of himself he presented to the world.

That Devlin was the very definition of a spoilt brat. That Devlin had claimed to come from a long line of wealthy people, the crème de la crème of British life. That Devlin had driven a new sports car every week, had lived in a new penthouse or mansion every month, and had spent millions of pounds every year on parties for him and his friends. The Devlin with her here today was a different man entirely. But which one was real?

She would never know. In a few hours they would be flown off the mountain. Darcy would be taken to the local hospital, and Devlin would no doubt be transported to a private clinic somewhere. Their worlds were so far apart that they would never see each other again.

Good, she said to herself. *I'll never have to be at the wrong end of a Devlin Storm piercing glare again.*

The thought of it, though, the thought of never finding a way through Devlin's icy shields and into the truth of him, made her head pound and her heart race.

Ahead, she heard a clatter of rocks, and another angry shout from Devlin.

"Come on!" he yelled.

How infuriating could he be? One moment he was telling her to stay back, the next he was ordering her to catch up. She ignored him, purposefully slowing down and taking a moment to breathe. Beneath her the world shone, the brightest thing she had ever seen in her life, and as much as she hated adventures, she couldn't help but be mesmerised by the sights it brought to life.

It was only when Devlin cried out again that she realised he didn't sound angry at all.

He sounded scared.

CHAPTER 15

DEVLIN

He felt the snow give way beneath him, and suddenly there was no ground. It was like the mountain had swallowed him whole, the blazing sun giving way to absolute darkness. He dropped into the black heart of the ice, reaching out with both arms even though the pain was unbearable. His left hand snagged a rock and he grabbed it, arresting his fall. Scrabbling with his legs, he found a ledge, hearing rocks and pebbles drop into the bottomless pit beneath him. It was a crevasse, a deep, narrow one concealed by snow.

Devlin Storm was trapped.

His heart raced as he clung to the rock, the freezing air stabbing at his lungs. He yelled out Darcy's name, his voice barely carrying over the gusting wind. Panic clawed at him as his mind screamed that he should never have let her out of his sight. He hadn't even heard her steps behind him. She could be anywhere — or worse, she could fall too. Was she even following him anymore? How could he have been so stupid? The first rule of survival was to stick together. By losing his temper with Darcy he may have just condemned them both.

"Darcy!" he cried out again. One of his feet slipped and he fought to secure it again. His heart was battering his ribs like a tiger in a cage, and his fingers were numbing fast. In minutes they would cramp, and it would all be over. "Darcy, please!"

She was gone, she couldn't hear him, she—

"Devlin?"

He almost cried at the sound of her voice.

"Darcy, be careful. There's a crevasse."

He had a sudden image of her falling into it, falling past him, screaming into darkness.

"Please be careful," he cried out.

"I see it," she replied, her voice even closer now. A flurry of fresh snow fell onto his upturned face, and by the time he'd blinked it away, she was there, leaning over cautiously. Her eyes were huge with fear.

"Thank goodness," he said.

Her eyes were wide with fear, but they steadied when they met his. "What do I do?" she asked, panic creeping into her voice.

The honest, awful truth was he didn't know. His mind was a hissing mess of white noise, too full of pain to be able to think straight.

"I've got an idea," she said, disappearing from the gap at the top of the crevasse.

Devlin took a breath, waiting for Darcy to reappear. What had he been thinking? He had walked on, not wanting to deliberate too hard about what Darcy had said. She was right, had hit the nail on the head. He hadn't ever been in love because losing himself to someone was a sure-fire way to losing control. She was getting too close and Devlin had no idea what she wanted from him and why she was so curious about his life. He wasn't used to opening up and sharing, and Darcy had this knack of making him feel it was okay. But it wasn't.

The sunlight pierced his eyes but Devlin felt as frozen solid as the ice around him. He squinted, feeling his fingers start to twitch and cramp. His foot slipped again, sending a wash of ice flurry down into the gaping void. There was no noise as it hit the bottom and Devlin knew with sickening clarity that the bottom of the crevasse was so far down that he wouldn't hear it even if it made it all the way down. They were metres deep sometimes, taller than his penthouse on the ninth floor. He gripped tighter, his life flashing before his eyes.

"Please, Darcy" he cried out. "Hurry."

She did, appearing again and dangling something down to him. It was the sleeve of her jacket — the heavy-duty Gore-Tex was easily strong enough to hold his weight.

But would she be strong enough to hold him?

"I'll brace myself on a boulder," she said, as if reading his mind. "There's one right here. Just tell me when you're ready and I'll pull."

There was no way he'd ever be ready for this. He stared down into the impenetrable darkness of the ravine. All the billions in the world wouldn't help recover his body. And it hit him, right then and there. It hit him, just how pointless his wealth was. He'd faced death before, yes, but his wealth had saved him because those trips had been pre-planned down to the last minutiae. Now he just had Darcy, and he knew that at this moment in time, Darcy was all that he needed. None of it mattered. Not the cars, not the houses, not the watches and the helicopters and the holidays. None of it mattered, and none of it made sense.

"You can do this," Darcy said. She'd vanished, but she was close by, the sleeve of the jacket still hanging there. "I know you, you're the strongest person I've ever met. But you have to believe in yourself. Just fight past the pain, past the fear. You can do it."

Right there was something that made perfect sense to him. Darcy. He gripped the rock with his bad arm, groaning at the sickening wave of pain that rolled through him. He fished for the jacket sleeve, wrapping it around his wrist twice and then clutching it hard. Then he took a breath and called up.

"I'm ready."

"I'm ready," she called back.

He crouched slightly, his knees grazing the rock. Then he jumped. He felt the jacket tighten around his wrist and he pummelled the rock wall with his feet, scrabbling up into the light of day. He managed to grab the edge of the crevasse with his bad hand, screaming as he planted his other hand down, too, but he didn't have the strength to hold on. He felt himself slipping, then Darcy was there, her hands on his, pinning them to the rock. He managed to dig his toes into a crack, pushing with everything he had. Darcy pulled, screaming with the effort of it. He got his stomach over, then his legs, then he was wrapping his good arm around Darcy and holding on to her as though she was a karabiner and the only thing keeping him safe.

For what seemed like for ever, he lay there, Darcy wrapped up in his terrified hug, on the mountain that had almost killed him.

The mountain that still might if he didn't get a proper hold on himself. Devlin knew he had made a fatal error. He'd been blindsided by pride and shame and all the other emotions that he kept in a locked box inside his chest. He was ashamed of his past, of his abusive dad, and his caring but permanently frightened mum. He didn't want people to know, because if they thought badly of his life, then they would think badly of him too. They would think that he was somehow weak, somehow scared. Darcy knew all of this and that put him at a disadvantage. She could use it against him.

It was better to be a mountain, to be strong and unmoving. Sure, it meant you had to build a rock wall between yourself and other people. You had to stay aloof and uncaring. But so long as you didn't let people in, then there was no way they could hurt you.

But look at where that got me.

He'd been an idiot. He hadn't been able to hear Darcy's steps behind him and he knew she was probably fuming and staying as far away as possible. Why on earth would she want to be near him after the way he'd behaved? He'd acted like a child, like a baby.

In other words, he'd acted just like Devlin Storm.

But he'd heard a noise. That's what had distracted him. He'd been studying the map when he had heard something overhead, a deep, distant throbbing that had pulsed through the air.

A helicopter.

He had squinted into the sun, seeing a black speck between two neighbouring peaks. It had been flying right towards them, and even though it was too far away to possibly see him, he had jumped up and down, dropping the case so that he could wave his arm. He had been standing on rocks, in a grey coat, practically invisible, so he'd been reckless and dashed onto the slope, his feet crunching in the snow as he waved furiously at the chopper, shouting for it to see him. And then he had fallen. He'd been so focused on the helicopter that he hadn't seen the ravine.

For the first time in what felt like an eternity, Devlin allowed himself to breathe. The rush of fear and adrenaline slowly ebbed away, to be replaced by a warmth he hadn't expected. He was okay now. Safe. After what felt like for ever, Devlin loosened his grip, pressing his lips to the top of Darcy's head.

"Thank you," he whispered, his voice full of emotion he hadn't let himself feel until now.

But something was wrong. Darcy wasn't moving. Her body, still in his arms, was cold. Too cold.

Panic flooded him as he pulled back, looking down at her pale face. "Darcy?" he whispered, fear lancing through him.

CHAPTER 16

DARCY

It was Devlin's voice that brought her back.

She stirred, her mind as numb as her feet, as numb as her fingers. She was so exhausted, and the last few minutes had taken every last ounce of energy and strength from her. There wasn't a fibre of her body or mind that didn't ache from the effort of pulling Devlin up from the crevasse.

But she *had* pulled him up. She had done it.

He'd rolled over and laid beside her, his eyes closed, his mouth open as he sucked in breath after breath. He clutched his bad arm with his good one, his forehead creased with pain. When he opened his eyes, though, it was relief that she saw there. Relief and an intense, moving gratitude.

"Are you okay," he said, his voice little more than a whisper. "You saved my life." Darcy shook her head.

"I'm fine. You didn't need me. You would have got out of there."

"No, I wouldn't," he said.

He groaned as he tried to sit up, and she helped him. He was shaking uncontrollably, his teeth chattering. She was, too, she realised. She looked for her coat but couldn't see it, wondering if Devlin had accidentally kicked it down into the ravine as he was escaping. She hoped not. Without it, she would freeze.

"What happened?" she asked, getting to her feet, and scanning the nearby snow. Her coat was nowhere to be seen and she tried not to let the panic grip her too hard.

Devlin stared at the sky, the rise and fall of his chest slowing.

"I saw a helicopter," he said, blowing out a puff of air that floated up into the blueness.

"Oh thank god, really?" she followed his line of sight, but the sky was clear. "Has it come for us? Where is it? Did it land?"

Devlin didn't look down from the sky. His lips were moving and he looked as though he was trying to summon the helicopter back into view with dark magic. Darcy thought about doing the same and then remembered she wasn't a witch and it would serve her better to try and find her coat.

"It's gone, it didn't see me," Devlin said, catching Darcy's eye as she walked in front of him.

"Probably because you were in a crevasse," she joked without thinking, looking away flushed when she realised what she'd said.

For a moment she thought the joke was horribly timed, because Devlin's expression was grave, but as she glanced back she saw his lips tugging into a smile as he hummed sceptically. His eyes snagged on hers, twinkling alpine green, and he burst into laughter. Darcy felt her heart soar.

"You got me there," he said, cocking his head. "Next time, I'll try to be less inconspicuous."

"Do you think you'll manage to be more high profile? Could be tough for you," she replied. "Maybe I should flag down the helicopter when it comes back."

And it would come back, wouldn't it? Darcy felt her ribs ache as the coldness seeped into her clothes. Devlin's smiling eyes warmed her a little.

"I could write my name in the snow," Devlin suggested.

"Like the Bat Signal," Darcy agreed, rubbing her arms. "Surely, for someone like you, it would summon help with a dash of psychological intimidation thrown in for good measure. Why didn't I think of that yesterday? We could have been back in the resort by now."

Her teeth were chattering so hard that Darcy was finding it difficult to get the words out and there was no chance her lips could crack a smile. But she felt like smiling. It filled her insides like warm treacle.

"You're unbelievable," he said, shaking his head. The corner of his mouth lifted and dimpled his cheek.

"So I've been told," she replied, so cold her brain wasn't finding the words as quickly as it should have been.

"Your coat," Devlin said, the humour evaporating from his features as he seemed to notice how low her temperature had dropped.

"You threw it down the ravine," Darcy chattered. "A . . . a . . . after it saved your life. B . . . b . . . bit mean if you ask me."

Devlin grimaced, and struggled up to his feet, taking the hand Darcy offered. It took him a while because of his bad arm, but eventually he managed to unzip his own thermal jacket.

"I don't need it," she protested, as he shrugged it off. "You're the one who fell in a big hole. You're probably in shock."

But when he held it to her, she could feel the heat radiating from it and she took it gladly, sliding it on. It carried his warmth with it, and his clean, minty scent, and she felt like she could cosy up right here and stay warm for ever. Devlin, on the other hand, looked absolutely freezing — dressed in nothing but two shirts and his suit jacket.

"Maybe we could share it?" Darcy suggested, lifting the coat flaps open and studying the inside lining.

Devlin pulled his hat down, a flop of hair poking out of the front, bothering his eyes. He tucked it away with his good hand and Darcy found herself wanting it to pop back out.

"Kind of you to offer," he said, his lips twitching, "but I don't think we'd both fit in it. And it would be hard to walk pressed up against you. You know, because one of us would have to go backwards or something."

He looked away, flustered. Darcy thought he looked cute when he was embarrassed. It broke the wall around him. Turned him from all-round, ice-frosted sex god to cinnamon-roll boy next door.

Where did that thought come from?

"I didn't mean at the same time," she said, pulling her own hat down and wishing she could cover her whole face. "I meant take turns."

Devlin's eyes widened and he cleared his throat.

"Right," he said, looking at the climb ahead of them. "Yeah, that probably makes more sense than . . ."

He didn't finish his sentence. Instead he wiggled his hand and then tugged at his suit jacket, popping his lips.

"Let me know when you want a go," Darcy said. "And I'll make some room."

She pushed gently against him, brushing his good arm with hers.

"Noted," he said, nodding once.

It was his tick, Darcy had noticed. Whenever Devlin found something he wasn't sure about, he'd go all hard-faced at it. Noted and a nod. But she was breaking through, because when he said it to her just then, his cheek dimpled in a smile.

"Come on then," she told him. "Lead the way. Where are we going?"

"It's not far," he said. "They're already out there looking for us. They might have found the helicopter wreckage, which means they can trace us. There could be a team already at the ranger station waiting for us with warm clothes and some brandy."

"Then we'd better go meet them," she said as they set off.

But as they were rounding the lip of the crevasse, Devlin stopped suddenly. He looked up and his expression turned to one of panic.

"My case," he cried, the whites of his eyes flashing in the snow. "Oh no, did it fall? Please no, please don't let it have fallen down there."

"Hey," Darcy said, placing a hand on his arm. "Hey, it's okay, it's back there. It's fine."

He took a huge breath of relief, walking over to it and picking it up. For all his strength, and all his toughness, he looked unbearably fragile.

"I know I shouldn't ask you," he said. "I know you've done more than enough for me already. You've saved my life. But could you possibly . . ."

Darcy laughed, taking the case from him.

"It would be my pleasure," she said.

CHAPTER 17

DEVLIN

He'd spoken the truth. It really wasn't far.

But it was hard work, and slow. Every step he took, Devlin expected the ground to open up beneath him again. He tested every inch of snow, poking the toe of his shoe in until he felt solid rock. It got harder with every passing minute because his feet were like blocks of ice. In fact, his entire body felt frozen solid, especially with no coat to keep him warm. Not that he was complaining about having to give it away.

He kept looking at Darcy as he walked. He couldn't take his eyes off her. There was no doubt about the fact that she'd saved his life. He never would have been able to pull himself out of the crevasse, not with his broken arm. If it hadn't been for her, he would have hung there until his strength gave out, and even now he'd be lost in the darkness of the mountain. The thought terrified him more than anything else in his entire life — not just dying, because there had been plenty of times he'd come close to that doing extreme sports around the world. No, Devlin couldn't quite put his finger on what felt different this time. Only that it might have something to do with Darcy and the sudden urge he had to kiss her.

He snuck another look at her. Her face was fierce with concentration, her lips moving in an unspoken conversation. She looked incredible. It was such a ridiculous thought that he almost laughed. But he didn't, because he knew it was true. Something had happened to him in the last twenty-four hours — a fundamental change in the way he saw himself and the world. Yes, part of that was to do with his near-death experience of crashing in the mountains, but part of it was to do with something else, too.

It was to do with Darcy.

"Whoa, careful," she said, and he stopped dead in his tracks. Ahead of him was another crack in the rock, this one too narrow to fall down, but wide enough to get a foot stuck in.

Pay attention, you idiot, he told himself. He really needed to stop thinking about Darcy and start thinking about getting to the ranger station alive. But it was impossible. Right then, she was the only thing grounding him. The sound of her bubbly laugh, her wide smile, the size of the heart she was carrying around with kindness and compassion for everyone. Even him. He felt himself smiling at the very idea.

Stepping over the crack, they continued up the slope. Now that the sun was out, the top layer of snow had started to melt. That was a good thing because the bigger crevasses in the ice were now visible — yawning mouths in the rock that wanted nothing more than to swallow them both. They stayed well clear of them, making good progress upwards.

"You really think that helicopter was looking for us?" Darcy asked, her cheeks a sweet pink with the cold and exertion.

"I'm sure of it," he replied. "I'm surprised there haven't been more of them."

"There might have been," she said. "But they'll be concentrating the search on the area between the Royal Alpine and the airport, thinking we went down there. Seeing as that's what you told them we were doing."

He nodded. That was a smart observation, and one he hadn't thought of. Of course they wouldn't be looking here. Who in their right mind would fly onto one of the biggest mountains in the country in the middle of one of the fiercest storms of the year?

"Can you tell me why?" Darcy asked, as if reading his mind. She seemed to have an uncanny ability to do that. "Why did you head here, knowing it was so dangerous?"

Devlin felt the familiar hollow feeling eating away inside him at the reason he'd been so reckless. He opened his mouth to tell her to stop asking him so many questions. Then he stopped. She deserved more than that, and not just because of what she'd just done. She deserved more than that because she was a good person. And, truth be told, he was starting to enjoy Darcy's questions. He liked the way they popped out of her mouth and how she sometimes looked as surprised at them as he felt. Devlin was feeling more open to answering them too.

But he wasn't quite ready to share this secret yet.

"There's something I needed to do," he said. "Something I still need to do. It's . . . it's incredibly important to me."

He expected her to ask more questions, to hunt for the truth like a journalist. Instead, she just nodded, and said nothing else. It was that silence, more than anything else — that silence, and the kind little smile she gave him — that made him feel like he was rolling right back down the mountain they were climbing. A freefall that scared him.

They walked side by side, swapping the jacket between them when they felt the cold biting, occasionally reaching out for one another and holding hands to help each other when they reached a crack in the rock, or a hillock of loose stones. They kept pace, step for step, working in such perfect harmony that it was as if they'd been climbing mountains together their whole lives. Darcy carried his case without once complaining about it, and on the three occasions he offered to take it back, she refused to even acknowledge him. It was just as well, because between his broken arm, and the ache in his other hand from holding onto the side of the ravine, he didn't think he'd have been able to carry it another dozen yards.

"I feel like a goat," Darcy said, taking the jacket back from Devlin and snuggling into it as they clambered across another rocky section.

She let out a cute little bleat and Devlin couldn't help but laugh.

"A goat?" he asked. "Not Nibbles or Norman the rabbit."

Darcy cocked her head at him.

"Hmm," she replied. "Maybe more my style, I suppose. Timid."

"But with a hefty kick on them," Devlin added, pointedly, not wanting Darcy to see what he'd said as an insult. "And the way you moved your legs when you were sleeping last night, I'd say you'd give them a run for their money."

The flush on Darcy's cheeks deepened and she massaged her neck with her gloved hand.

"You know," Devlin went on, digging himself into a ravine all of his own making. "I just mean that you moved in bed a lot, not that you kicked me."

He was making it worse, and now all he could think about was Darcy asleep next to him on that uncomfortable mattress and the way she'd muttered in her sleep as she'd shuffled closer.

"Anyway, a goat you say?" He thought if he stopped talking then he might not melt into the snow like the bumbling fool he seemed to have turned into.

"Yep," Darcy said, jumping down from a large rock and landing in the snow with a puff. "A sure-footed mountain goat. Like you see stuck to the sides of cliffs because they're perched on a teeny tiny ledge. Darwinism at its finest."

Devlin thought Darcy was Darwinism at its finest, but he kept that morsel to himself, watching as she trod ahead, still bleating like a baby goat, her arms outstretched for balance.

Half an hour passed in a heartbeat, and it was only then, as they began to round the side of the mountain, that Devlin noticed the sky growing dark. He'd been so focused on the route they were taking — and who was he kidding, Darcy too — that he hadn't glanced upwards for some time. When he did, he saw the dark clouds gathering around the mountains at the horizon. His heart tumbled into his boots with the same speed he'd tumbled into the crevasse.

"That's bad, right?" asked Darcy, noticing where he was looking. "A big cloud like that isn't bringing good things with it."

"Not necessarily," he said, shivering hard. "It might not come this way."

Darcy hummed sceptically and she was right to, because it did. Twenty minutes later and the stormfront was so close he could smell it, the air coppery and sharp and weirdly electric. He had no idea what the time was, and he couldn't see the sun any more through the heavy, yellow-black clouds. They were bloated with snow, and judging by the fact he couldn't see the farthest mountains anymore, either, he knew it was already falling hard.

"The ranger's outpost station should be right around the corner," he said, a sudden wind lifting his words away. It kicked up powder from the ground and threw it at him, and he felt the temperature of his body slip another few degrees.

The first flakes of snow were beginning to fall from the ever-darkening sky, but as they passed a giant fist of rock that protruded from the mountainside, Devlin spotted lights up ahead.

"There," he called out, and Darcy whooped with joy.

The ranger's station sat on a ledge of rock between two jutting trunks of mountain, light blazing from its windows. Three giant radio antennae stood to attention on the roof. Devlin had a moment to feel hopeful before he noticed that the landing pad was empty.

"You think there's somebody there?" Darcy asked, waving snow away from her face.

"I don't know," he replied. "It doesn't matter. It's warm, there will be food, and most importantly, a working radio. Come on, one last push."

He put his head down, holding Darcy's hand as they stumbled through the last of the snow and onto the natural stone staircase that rose to the station. He felt Darcy slowing down, her hand pulling at his as the snow started falling thick and deep, the wind snatching at their clothes. Giving her hand a squeeze of encouragement, he nodded at her through the quickly diminishing visibility. A silent push. He knew she could do it — she just needed to believe it herself. He got to the door, grabbing the handle and pushing it open.

"After you," he shouted, holding himself strong against the battering winds and snow.

Darcy tucked herself into him, and her body angled against the strength of the winds, she almost fell through the doorway to safety. He followed, pushing the door against the growing storm with his whole body weight until he heard it click shut. It was warm and quiet away from the winds. They were safe.

And, it would seem, alone.

CHAPTER 18

DARCY

It felt *amazing*. The moment Devlin closed the door a wave of relief poured over her like she was standing in a warm shower. The building wasn't exactly tropical, but it was well insulated, and certainly more comfortable than the brutal mountain climate outside. They stood in a small, bright hallway, the scent of mint and something inherently masculine flooded her nose as Devlin shook off the halo of snow from his hair. She turned and angled her head to see his face. This close, she had a face full of his broad shoulders.

"Do you think there's anyone here?" she asked. "How does this work?"

Devlin's teeth were chattering so hard he couldn't speak so he simply shrugged.

"Hello?" Darcy called out, wishing with all her heart that a bunch of rangers would come pouring through one of the two doors leading from the hallway, wrapping them in blankets and feeding them gallons of hot chocolate as they whisked them into a helicopter bound for home.

There was no reply. The building wasn't exactly big, so if somebody was here they would have heard her call. Still, she tried again, opening the door to the right to see a large, open living quarters complete with kitchen and lounge area. There was even a pool table and a TV.

"Hello?" she called again.

"Hey, is anyone here?" Devlin shouted, his teeth still chattering wildly. He opened the other door into a garage, but when she peered over his shoulder, she saw that it was empty.

"Maybe they're out looking for us?" she said, but Devlin shook his head.

"I didn't see any tracks," he said, shivering. "They'd have been visible in the snow. No, I think this place is empty. Solar lights, they stay on all year."

The building didn't have that same neglected air as the research hut had. This room felt like it had breathed in the last year at least. Devlin walked around her, and Darcy followed him into the living area. The sofa called to her with its comfortable, if dated-looking cushions, but she willed her legs to keep going. An open door led to a bunkroom, with a toilet and shower, and another, through the kitchen, led into an office. They walked into the office, and Devlin burst out laughing when he saw the huge, modern radio set sitting on the desk. Darcy felt another giant wave of relief.

"Thank goodness," he said. "We're going to be okay."

He reached up and tucked a stray lock of her hair out of her eyes and back under her hat. The action was so simple, yet Darcy felt her whole body tingle at the touch of his cold fingers on her skin. Their eyes caught. Neither of them in a hurry to look away and Darcy's belly flooded with warmth.

"We're going to be okay." Her mouth was dry.

In the quiet, and stillness, and calm, she found herself leaning towards Devlin. He mirrored her, until they were so close she could feel his breath on her lips. She felt her own lips part, a pulse of electricity running between them, static energising every part of her that was touching him.

Then Devlin shuddered violently, his teeth clacking together like castanets.

"I'm so sorry," he said. "I'm just really, really c-cold."

"Oh, man, sorry," Darcy said, stepping back. Her cheeks lit up like a furnace, and she grew so hot she had to unzip her coat. "I'm going to go in search of some warm clothes, you see what you can do with this radio. Deal?"

He nodded and she left the office, running into the bunkroom and opening one of half a dozen lockers that ran along one wall. They were stuffed full of brand-new clothes and thermal equipment, and she rooted through them until she found something in Devlin's size. Large. Scooping it up, she returned to the office to see him sitting at the desk, his sore arm hanging limply at his side. In his good arm he held the radio receiver in gripped fingers, his thumb on the button shaking so wildly with the coldness that had seeped into his bones, it didn't stay active. He let it go, growling.

Darcy skipped over to him and placed the down-filled jacket over his shoulders, careful not to touch his broken arm. He shrugged it on further and tucked his chin into the high funnel neck that looked like it was lined with rabbit fur. Darcy was almost 100 percent sure it was fake, or she might have thrown it out of the window.

"Thank you," he said, his voice muffled. "I just need a minute to melt the iceberg that's formed around my brain, then I'll get us rescued."

Darcy tugged at her hat.

"Do you want me to . . . go?"

"Stay," Devlin answered without taking a beat.

Darcy had been about to offer to look for food or a first-aid kit that was higher tech than a stick and some bandage, but his order took her words from her lips.

"Please," he added, the rumble of his voice a tonic. "Stay."

Darcy nodded, for once lost for words. She drew her lips into her mouth, dropped silently into the seat next to him, and watched patiently as Devlin's shivers subsided.

After a minute, or maybe ten, he emerged from the cocoon of his (faux) fur collar and huffed out a breath.

"Thank you," he said again, staring at the receiver. He picked it up and pressed the button. "Hello, can anyone hear me? This is Devlin Storm, and Darcy Wainwright. We flew out of the Royal Alpine yesterday evening and crashed on the mountain. We are both okay, and currently located at . . ."

He looked around, and so did Darcy. She spotted a piece of paper pinned to a drawing board with a fire escape plan on it. It had the station code written at the top.

"Four, eleven, F, T," she read.

"Four-eleven, foxtrot, tango," Devlin said. "That's four-eleven, foxtrot, tango, over."

He let go of the button and the radio hissed with static.

"Come on," he pleaded. "Come on."

"Please," said Darcy. "Please let somebody hear us."

The radio bleeped, then a voice broke through the white noise.

"Mr Storm, this is Officer Allaman of Mountain Rescue," it said in a French accent. "We hear you, loud and clear. Over."

Devlin whooped, punching his good hand into the air. Darcy did the same, laughing and crying at the same time. Devlin grinned from ear to ear at her as he spoke into the radio again, his cheeks dimpled, his eyes crinkling.

"I can't tell you how good it is to hear your voice," he said. "For a little while there we were starting to think . . ."

He paused, shivering, although Darcy wasn't sure if it was the cold that did it, or just the thought of what might have happened to them.

"For a little while there, we were starting to think we weren't going to make it," he went on. "We're here, we're safe, and awaiting rescue. Over."

The radio hissed. Devlin sat back. His lips were still a deep shade of blue. She pulled his jacket from her own body, hushing him when he protested.

"I'm really fine," he said. "I don't need—"

"I won't have you come all this way just to die of hypothermia," she scolded. "Come on. Just until we've finished here and you can get out of your own clothes and dry off."

But before she could take off the coat to use as an extra layer for Devlin, the radio bleeped again.

"Mr Storm, that's a negative on rescue."

Darcy and Devlin froze.

"What?" Darcy mouthed. "They can't just leave us here for ever, can they? You'll be missed, you've got . . . fans?"

Devlin looked at Darcy curiously as the radio came to life again.

"There's another storm moving in. It's probably already reached you. All our birds are grounded. We had teams out all day, but they were way off track. I can't risk sending my people out in this. But the ranger station should have everything you need. They're kept fully equipped at all times, and there are instructions for heat and water. My advice is make yourself at home, keep warm, keep fed, play some pool. We'll get to you when we can. Over."

Darcy saw Devlin's brow furrow, and she knew what was about to happen. He was going to start tearing strips off the man on the other end of the radio. He was going to demand immediate rescue at any cost, because he was Devlin Storm, and nothing else would be good enough.

Instead, though, he nodded.

"Thank you," he said, his eyes catching again on Darcy's. "We'll bed in and wait it out. And Officer, please don't risk a rescue trip unless it's safe. There's no emergency here. We're not in any hurry. Over."

"Received," said the voice. "Over and out, Mr Storm."

Devlin placed the radio receiver back in its cradle, and Darcy's heart felt like it was escaping out of her rib cage.

"We're not in any hurry?" she asked.

He shrugged, still shivering slightly. His eyes darkened as they studied her face.

"I'm not in a hurry," he said. "Are you?"

Darcy shook her head. She stared at him and stared at him, then stared at him a little more. No, she wasn't in any hurry to be rescued at all.

CHAPTER 19

DEVLIN

The living quarters weren't up to APEX Club standards, or even up to Royal Alpine standards. Devlin's arm felt like it was about to fall off, though maybe that would give him a sweet release from the pain. In fact, Devlin felt terrible through and through, but at the same time he didn't really mind any of it because Darcy was unpeeling his coats from around his shoulders and this close he could see the dusting of freckles on her nose.

He averted his eyes and bit his lip, trying to think of anything other than the way she had the tip of her tongue poking out between her lips as she concentrated. And how he'd like to reach out and lick it. He needed to remind himself that she was here because he'd paid her to be.

"Arm up," said Darcy, and he obeyed her. She tugged at his wet, frozen outer shirt until it slid free, then she walked to the other side and worked the sleeve over his splint. The ache nearly knocked him out, but he gritted his teeth until it came off. Darcy did the same with his other shirt, tossing it to the floor with a splat.

It was the second time she'd undressed him, and he could get used to it. It was weird, because ordinarily he hated any kind of help. He actually detested people doing things for him. He wasn't really sure why, other than the fact that he hated being in debt to anyone, in any way. He didn't like people to think he wasn't capable of looking after himself, either. There was nothing worse than people looking down on him.

But that was Devlin the island speaking. That was Devlin the mountain.

It was different with Darcy. It was different because *she* was different. She didn't look down on him, but she didn't look up to him either. She looked at him as if they were on exactly the same level, as if they were equals, and he was enjoying the feeling. Nobody had spoken to him the way she had back there on the mountain. She'd been so angry at him and the way she'd called out his awful behaviours was a breath of fresh air. People were scared of him, keeping him at arm's length — or maybe it was the other way around — and Darcy had flattened those arms to his side and put him in his place probably for the first time since he'd made his first million.

He hadn't realised it until now, but the fact that people had only seen him as Devlin Storm the billionaire was one of the reasons that he'd closed himself off from the world. If people didn't see a real man, a genuine person with real feelings and emotions, then why should he *be* a real man? Better to be tough, to be emotionless, unfeeling, fake. That way they couldn't see how much he was hurting.

And he *had* been hurting. He'd been hurting without even knowing it. Darcy had shown him that.

"Here," said Darcy. She carefully patted him dry with a big, fluffy white towel she'd found and then wrapped him in a giant bath robe, which seemed a ridiculous luxury in a place like this. Leaving his broken arm out, she began to unwrap the bandages around the splint. He winced, but she was gentle, pulling the linen strips free, then the stick.

"Oh god," she gasped, and he looked down and gasped too. "That's not good, is it? It looks like an egg plant."

"Aubergine," he deadpanned a reply.

But either way, she was right. His arm had turned an ugly shade of purple, the bruise so dark it didn't look real. The skin felt numb from the elbow down, and he knew that if he didn't get it seen to soon, then it might never heal.

"Is it going to fall off?" she asked, stroking his purple-ombre fingers so gently that he felt a ball of pent-up tension gather deep in his stomach.

"I've got another one." He was joking because he was scared at the idea of losing his arm. He'd seen mountaineers lose limbs for much less.

"Right." She looked at him, eyes searching his face as though reading his mind in that uncanny way she'd developed over the last twenty-four hours. "Well, let's sort that one out then, so you'll at least have one working set of fingers."

Her eyes grew wide when she realised what she'd said and she dropped her chin and focused on his other arm, pulling the glove from his good hand. Well, what *used* to be his good hand. His fingertips were blue and covered with scratches from where he'd clung on to the side of the crevasse. He flexed them gently, wincing.

"It's not so bad," he said. "I think I'll be okay. They're both still attached."

"For the time being," she said. "But if we don't get you warm and dry then I can't guarantee it will stay that way. And you need both arms. Stand up."

"Please, Darcy," he protested, but she pulled insistently, and he grumbled back to his feet. "This is ridiculous. I've been dressing and undressing myself perfectly well since I was three."

She took off his expensive lace-ups, then pulled down his suit trousers, helping him to step out of them. That was as far as she was willing to go, though, and Devlin was grateful when she stood up and changed her eye level. A familiar stirring throbbed dully in his belly, and he had to shift his stance to release it. Losing control now was not a good idea.

"There's a shower," she said, little pink spots growing in the middle of her cheeks as she helped him properly into the fluffy robe, eyes averted from the burgeoning excitement he had no control over. "Why don't you go and get under the hot water? Thaw yourself out a little?"

He nodded, feeling a blossom of warmth in his chest.

"What about you?" he said. "You look as cold as I do, Darcy."

"My clothes are dry and I'm not shivering enough to start an avalanche." She turned and wouldn't take another word on the matter.

The bathroom was spotless and surprisingly big. What was more surprising still was the fact that as well as the giant walk-in shower, there was a bath. Devlin sidestepped it, stripped out of his boxers, and headed straight for the shower to defrost. The controls were self-explanatory and soon he was standing under a wash of warm water that made his skin prickle as it came back to life. He'd known better than to set the temperature too high, but he felt a flame inside his chest that was warm enough to melt the Alps.

He washed as quickly as his sore arm would let him, and then stood under the electric heater as it puffed warm air at the top of his head and over his naked body.

There was a window in the bathroom. It looked out over the slopes they'd climbed to get here — the whole world lying before him, looking almost like a giant wedding cake. The skies were dark again, the snow falling hard, but it didn't scare him now. The storm couldn't hurt him here.

In fact, he couldn't remember a time he'd felt so safe, and so at home.

"Everything okay in there?" he heard Darcy call. He wrapped his arms around himself, realising that he hadn't even shut the bathroom door.

"I'm okay!" he said, searching the room for the giant robe. "Don't come in!"

"I'm far too much of a gentleman for that," she said, and he laughed. "Unlike you."

"Well, don't believe everything you read." He pulled his sore arm into the sleeve and then wrapped himself up until he was decent.

"I just wanted to say the heat is working — it's like an oven back here. It's not quite the Maldives, but it's a heck of a lot better than it was. I might even need to take off my jumper. I feel a million times better already."

"Me too," he said, dragging oxygen into his lungs at the idea that Darcy was stripping just outside the door. "I won't be long, then it's all yours."

He was going to need to wait until the feeling had passed by as his dressing gown wouldn't be the best disguise. Picking up his boxers, he knew they'd be no help, soaking wet from the snow.

"Take all the time you need," Darcy replied. "I'm going to fire up the kettle. You might not believe it, but they've got four different types of hot chocolate."

Devlin smiled at Darcy's apparent excitement at the idea of hot chocolate when really they should be replenishing lost fluids and salts with body temperature water mixed with high energy powders. But he kept his mouth shut and let Darcy revel in her excitement.

"Do you have a favourite flavour?" she asked.

"Surprise me," he said.

He heard her laughing as she walked away and felt his chest expand at the sound.

CHAPTER 20

DEVLIN

Resting on a small sofa at the far end of the living quarters, Devlin took a sip of hot chocolate and felt it melt in his mouth. He may very well know that it wasn't the most conventional way to recuperate, but the sweetness of the drink made that thought fly right on out into the mountains. He'd strapped his arm up in a sling he'd found in the medical box and taken some more pain killers to dull the ache. He'd also finished his share of a meal of rehydrated noodles and was starting to feel more human.

Sweet things aside, he was infinitely grateful to be here. He couldn't stop thinking about how close he'd come to falling into the crevasse, and the spectre of death still haunted him. Of course, he was no stranger to extreme sports, and there had been countless occasions he'd had to sign an indemnity waiver just in case something terrible happened to him on the ocean or the slopes or in the sky. But in those situations he'd been surrounded by friends, professionals who knew what they were doing and equipment to keep him safe, so he'd never really felt like he was in danger. He'd always been in control of his own life, and his own fate.

Today had been very different. He hadn't been in control of anything. If Darcy hadn't been there, if she hadn't had the idea of using her jacket to pull him up, then there would be no more Devlin Storm.

No more Devlin Storm. The idea wasn't as awful as he'd thought it might be. Not the idea of dying, of course, but the idea that the man the world knew as Devlin Storm wasn't around anymore. That man didn't care about anyone but himself, and he wasn't afraid of people knowing it. Sure, people wanted to be with him, but only because he was famous, and handsome. But take away the money and the looks, and nobody would want anything to do with him.

He thought back to when he'd been a kid. His dad had been all the things that Devlin was now, but Devlin hadn't wanted to be like him. He'd always wanted to be like his mum, who would have given the shirt from her back if somebody asked her to. He couldn't think of a single time she'd done anything purely for herself, or anything out of greed. She had been the most selfless person he'd ever known. She'd hated the way the world saw her only son, and had hated the way that Devlin had behaved.

But maybe there is no changing now, he thought. *This is me. This is who I am.*

Groaning, he leaned back into the sofa and closed his eyes. He'd never been in this much pain before. The agony wasn't just in his arm, but in every single cell inside his body. He knew it would be worse in the morning, too, when his battered muscles woke up.

But he was alive. He was still here.

"Penny for your thoughts," said Darcy as she walked out of the bunkroom. She was wearing a bath robe, too, a towel wrapped around her hair.

"Oh, you're going to need a lot more than that," he said, patting the space beside him on the sofa even though it made his eyes water with the pain. "How was your bath?"

"Divine," she said, sitting down. Her cheeks were rosy, her skin glowing as if she'd spent the weekend at a spa. Her huge eyes regarded him with such intensity that he had to turn away. The heat in the building had kicked in, but he wasn't sure if that was the reason he felt roasting hot, even in just a bath robe.

But he didn't move. He wasn't sure if he could. He was so exhausted and there was a magnetism with Darcy that he had no strength to pull away from. Not that he wanted to. She smiled at him, a smile that melted his heart and lit a furnace a little further south.

"This is nice," he said, trying to think of something to say to take his mind off the way his lungs didn't seem to be working properly. He shifted on the sofa, adjusting his position. Darcy didn't need to be scared away by his uncontrollable urges.

"Really?" she said with a laugh. "Crashing a helicopter, spending the night in the ruin of a cabin, falling into a ravine, almost dying in not one but two storms. But you might have stopped hating me somewhere along the way, which *is* nice, I guess."

"That's not really what I meant," he said, trying not to stare at her lips, wondering if they would taste like the hot chocolate she was drinking or something even sweeter. "And I never hated you."

"Really?" she raised a brow at him. "Well, I certainly got the feeling you hated me at least a little to start with."

"That's unfair," he said, though she had a point. He hadn't hated her. He'd hated the situation he'd found himself in. And when he was annoyed, he made sure everyone knew about it.

Darcy sipped her drink and peered at him over the top of her mug.

"Well, can I say I hated you a little bit?" she said.

Devlin turned that thought over in his head and decided he didn't like it.

"Did you?" he asked. "Hate me, I mean?"

Darcy didn't reply, not feeling the need to placate him, maybe. And when she did reply, her answer surprised him.

"Perhaps," she said.

They sat there in silence for a moment, the wind howling, fistfuls of snow hitting the windows like grit.

"Just perhaps? I thought I was the most awful man you'd ever met," he said, his lips tugging into a smile.

"Oh, you were," she replied, a little too quickly. "Are . . . Without a doubt. But . . . but at the same time, you're not. I'm still trying to figure out which one is the real you."

This one, he thought, although the truth was he was still trying to figure it out too.

"Do you want to know what I really think?" she said.

He looked at her, and she leaned into him, bringing a scent of coconut shampoo and something a little more dangerous. She was close enough to touch, close enough to kiss, and the thought of it was so loud inside his head that he almost didn't hear her when she started talking again.

"I think you're like a frozen lake," she said. "Back in Wisconsin everything used to freeze over in winter. We lived a way out of the city, and the farms around us all had lakes that would freeze solid. At least, you thought they were solid. We used to skate on them. I remember one time one of our neighbours even rode their truck on the ice, it was that thick. When I was a kid, we used to think there was nothing in those lakes but ice."

She paused, obviously thinking back to her childhood. It sounded happy, he thought. It sounded a world away from his own.

"Then one day we were out on the ice and I saw something moving beneath it. I couldn't believe it, these little flashes of colour darting in the dark. They were fish, and I couldn't understand how they were alive in the ice. I asked my dad and he just smiled at me. He told me the water doesn't freeze all the way down, there's this little core of heat that keeps it liquid. He told me that the ice actually insulates the water, keeping those little fish alive in the winter, stopping them from being picked off by predators too."

"You're saying I'm a fish?" Devlin said, smiling.

"No," she replied. "I'm saying you're a lake."

"I'm not sure if that's any better."

She laughed, the sound like a playlist of his favourite songs.

"You had a bad run of things when you were younger," she said. "At least, that's what it sounds like. You went through some cold, dark times, and you froze over. That's what the world sees now, this cold, unfeeling guy frozen inside his own never-ending winter. People don't like you because you make them feel cold."

"People do like me," he said, but his voice was quiet.

"People like the *idea* of you," she went on. "And I'm not saying this because I want you to feel bad. I'm saying it because I think it might help you. You're frozen, but you're not frozen solid. There's something in those depths — I can see those little flashes of colour darting in the dark. You're still in there, Devlin, and that ice is keeping you safe, keeping you warm."

He thought about this for a while, chewing on her words.

"If that's the case," he said eventually, pulling away from the heat of her. "Then isn't it best to stay cold, stay frozen for ever?"

"No," she said, shaking her head. "Because if you do that, then it will be the end of you. Those lakes thawed every spring, and those fish went on to live their lives. The really cold years, when the water stayed frozen for month after month after month, those poor creatures suffocated. The ice killed them."

Devlin took a deep, shaky breath.

"How did you get so wise?" he asked.

She shrugged.

"I don't know. I just lived, I guess." A tiny laugh escaped her. "Not that I've really done much living."

"Hey, that's not true," Devlin said, angling his body towards her. "You're an American girl living in Europe. What's that if it's not an adventure?"

"It's less exciting than it sounds," she said, sighing. "I was an idiot for coming here. It was a job, one that sounded too good to be true. It *was* too good to be true. It was a brand-new company set up to help promote women's businesses, to help give women the confidence to set up on their own, to do something amazing."

"That sounds great," he said.

"It was, it really was. I was so excited. I thought that working someplace like that might give me the confidence to do something amazing with my life, too. It might help me feel less scared about everything."

"So what happened?"

"Nothing," Darcy said. "I got the job, used all my money to fly me and my life over here. When I arrived at the place we were supposed to be working they were boarding it up. Turned out the woman who founded it had decided to use the cash for a permanent holiday in Hawaii. I was stuck here, no money, no family to call on. Luckily, I knew some people on Heartbook who put me up in Geneva while I sorted out enough cash for a place of my own. I've been drifting ever since."

"I'm sorry that happened to you," Devlin said. "That was a very unfair and cruel thing to do to somebody."

Darcy shrugged.

"I'm used to it," she said. "Life can be unfair, and it can certainly be cruel. But I survived. Just like this." She gestured at the window, where the storm raged. "It hurt, but I survived. *We* survived."

"You could do a lot of good with £100,000," Devlin said, but she waved him away.

"I don't need your money," she replied. He was about to argue with her, then decided not to. He intended to give her every penny of the money he'd promised, but he didn't want to make her feel bad about it. Not here, and not now.

"Tell me something about yourself, Devlin," she said, tucking her legs up under her and fixing him with those amazing eyes. "Something that I won't have read in the papers."

He drew breath. The story he was going to tell her came straight to mind.

"I only started designing clothes because of my Mum. I was sixteen, and she had a job interview. Dad had just been sent to prison again, for trying to steal a car. We were broke, and Mum went for a job at a supermarket chain. All she had to wear was this moth-eaten corduroy suit that looked like it was older than she was. I remember seeing her in our kitchen, just standing there, trying to get in the right frame of mind for this interview. But she looked beat. She looked like she'd already accepted she wouldn't get it."

"I know that feeling," Darcy said when he paused. "The right clothes make you a different person, don't they?"

"Not quite," he said. "It's the *wrong* clothes that make you a different person. They stop you from being you."

"So you made her something else to wear?" she asked.

"No, I was just a kid. I didn't know the first thing about designing, or making clothes. But that's the moment I decided I was going to do it. Mum didn't get the job, and we stayed poor. But I spent my schooldays in the library reading about tailoring, about stitching and cutting, about the history of fashion. I immersed myself in it."

He smiled, but the happiness of the memory was tinged with an inescapable sadness.

"And I started making something for Mum. I didn't have much to work with, but I took that suit and altered it, and dyed it jet black. I stitched designs into the collar and hems with silver thread that I'd pulled out of Mum's wire dishwashing brush."

"Seriously?" Darcy asked, wide-eyed. He nodded, still smiling.

"Oh, yeah, seriously. The librarian at our school, Mrs Wallis, was this amazing woman who'd been watching me learn about all this stuff. She had this little jar of antique buttons, all shapes and sizes, all different colours and materials. She gave it to me, bless her heart, and I replaced the frumpy brown buttons of Mum's suit with these new ones. Little mother-of-pearl fasteners, and these silver buttons on the sleeves. I mean it was such a mix of different styles it never should have worked, but it did."

"Did she like it?" Darcy asked, leaning even closer. Her hand hovered close to his, like a butterfly about to land on a blossoming flower.

"She was . . . she was blown away," Devlin said, remembering her face, the way it had opened up in delight and surprise. "I gave it to her one morning — six months and goodness knows how many job interviews after I'd had the idea. She couldn't believe I was giving it to her. She couldn't even speak. She thought I'd bought it, and it was only when I told her I'd made it that she really started to cry. She couldn't accept that anyone could just make something like that. I had to show her the dishwashing brush before she believed me." He laughed again. "She was mad about the brush, though. She had wondered what had happened to it."

Darcy laughed, too, and this time her fingers brushed against his hand. It was light, barely there, but it may as well have been a livewire straight to his bloodstream and other places he had no control over. His pulse spiked, heat sliding over his skin. She didn't pull away. Neither did he. Instead, he felt the ghost of her fingertips against his, teasing and tentative.

And then she did it again. This time, more deliberate.

A slow, delicious ache uncurled in his stomach, spreading lower, the kind of heat he hadn't expected tonight, not with her, not like this. He let out a quiet breath, his fingers twitching before he made a decision and opened his hand.

She laced her fingers through his, the movement so natural, so intimate, that it knocked the breath right out of him. She didn't say anything, just studied their joined hands with those amazing eyes, as if trying to decide whether or not this was real.

Adorable. Except adorable wasn't the word anymore. Not with the way her thumb brushed against his, sending another shiver rushing through his body, not with the way her smaller hand fit so perfectly in his, like it had always belonged there.

This felt different from the last time he'd held hands with a woman, because this time, he wanted more. Craved it.

Maybe he really had fallen down that crevasse, bumping his head hard enough to cause a wave of welcome hallucinations.

"What is it?" Darcy asked him.

"I just . . ." He swallowed. He didn't really know how to explain it. "I feel . . . I don't know."

"Like maybe you're starting to thaw?"

She smiled such a big, beautiful, kind smile that it was as if the storm outside had cleared. He couldn't help himself. He moved towards that smile like a frozen man moving towards the warmth of the sun. Darcy leaned in, too, her lips parted, her tongue wetting them.

"You're good with words." His voice was husky. "Or maybe I'm just finding it hard to think with you so close."

Darcy opened her mouth as if to speak, then quickly shut it again. She shook her head, leaning away.

"We should go to bed." She stood up from the sofa, dressing gown flashing Devlin a whole lot of leg. "I mean, *I* should go to bed. It's been a day. We're tired. It's bedtime. I should sleep."

And she darted from the room like one of her favourite rabbits caught in the headlights.

Devlin sat back, resting his head on the back of the sofa. He'd scared her away. He'd been too much. Darcy wasn't here for a holiday. She'd been forced into a trip she didn't want to take. She didn't want him, she'd made that clear. And as he shut his eyes and let the quiet of the outpost envelop him, he wished she'd come back out and fill it with her wonderfully cute, and only a little bit annoying, chatter. He missed it.

CHAPTER 21

DARCY

You're an idiot. Pure bone fide, first class idiot. Devlin freaking Storm tried to kiss you and you ran away.

Darcy paced the bunkroom. Back and forth. Back and forth. If nothing else, it was keeping her warm. Not that she needed to be any warmer with the heating on and the fire of shame burning through her heart. She clamped her eyes shut, but the image of Devlin watching her babble on about going to bed was for ever etched on her memory. Like a dog watching its owner abandon it by the side of the road, realisation slowly dawning.

She sat heavily on one of the bunks, head in her hands, feeling tiredness wash over her. And instead of mulling over what an ungrateful little gremlin she was in turning down Devlin Storm — Devlin Storm — because she thought she wasn't good enough for him, Darcy lay her head down on the pillow, lifted her legs, and proceeded to fall sound asleep.

***

It was the sound of the wind trying to take the glass out of the bunkroom window that woke her what felt like moments later. Darcy groaned, rolled onto her back, and rubbed her face. She groaned again when she remembered where she was. The room was empty. Devlin must be out in the living quarters, making himself useful instead of sleeping like she was.

Darcy swung her legs around and sat up, brushing her hands through her hair and freeing it of knots. There was a strange light to the room — blue tinted, like Devlin had a load of screens on. It was only when Darcy stood up and went to check the glass was secure and not at risk of being blown from its frame, that she realised it was the sunlight trying to burst through the snow at the window.

It was morning. And the other bed hadn't been slept in.

Darcy grabbed her bathrobe and ran to the door of the bunkroom with images of Devlin passed out on the floor by the pool table in the living quarters. She'd been selfish to leave him. No matter how embarrassed she'd felt at turning down his advances, she should have stayed to make sure he was okay. He had a broken arm, and possibly hypothermia. Fearing the worst, Darcy burst through the door, daring not to look. Was he hurt? Would it be worse?

She caught sight of a mop of dark blond hair poking out of the side of the sofa. It wasn't moving. Darcy threw a hand to her mouth and ran to him, her bare feet squeaking on the lino. Poised to do mouth to mouth and chest compressions, Darcy screeched to a halt to find Devlin sleeping peacefully, not a worry on his face. She watched him, regret snaking in her. At some point between her running away from him and his falling asleep, Devlin had made a little bed for himself on the dated sofa cushions. Covered in a blanket, he looked angelic, his hair mussed and his lips gently parted. A little snore escaped every other breath, not a great hulking rattle, just a reminder that he was there, and he was breathing.

With her own heart still hammering, Darcy edged away slowly. She didn't want to wake him, couldn't face how he'd treat her rejection, not yet anyway. After a quick shower, Darcy wrapped herself back in her snuggly robe and snuck through to the kitchen to scavenge for some breakfast. Devlin had rehydrated them both some noodles the night before, but after too long with just snow water and protein bars, she was craving a tonne of fresh fruit and, weirdly, a giant, bloody steak.

"The body knows what it wants," she whispered to herself, filling the kettle and switching it on to boil.

Did it though? Darcy spooned instant coffee into a mug, staring out of the window at the snow drift the storm had brought in. They were buried quite deep — it was at least waist height out there now — and the winds and snow were still battering the outpost, relentlessly.

Her body had certainly wanted to kiss Devlin last night. And more. She could feel her hormones reacting to the idea of him, even as she stood waiting for the water to heat up. Yet she'd run away at the first sign he felt the same. Why?

The kettle came to the boil and she poured water over the coffee, inhaling the liquid gold smell. Opening cupboard doors, Darcy found the long-life milk portions. Peeling the lids from five of them, she tipped them in her mug and turned her coffee a more digestible colour. Pausing, she heard the rhythmic patter of Devlin's sleeping breaths and held off making him a drink too. He needed to rest and recover. She wanted to help him heal. And not just physically.

Opening and closing more cupboards as quietly as possible, Darcy found a tin of fruit cocktail, a bowl, and a spoon. Clicking the lid open and peeling it away, she tipped the fruit and syrup out into the bowl and went to sit at the table by the window. Outside was as muddled as her brain. Her thoughts were whirling with Devlin Storm, the man who up to a few days ago, was just a great bundle of ego wrapped in a pretty gorgeous exterior.

Relishing the sweet cherries, peach, and pear segments, the calories and caffeine kickstarted her brain back to life. Darcy ate in comfortable silence, listening to the wind whip around the cabin. She imagined her family and friends laughing at the idea she was here, stranded in a mountain lodge with a world-famous bad boy. Not only would they not believe she would have gone up a mountain in the first place, but Darcy was so far removed from the idea of being with a bad boy, they'd protest that she was hallucinating. Because Darcy Wainwright did not choose the bad boy. In fact, Darcy Wainwright chose which ever option would provide peace and comfort and most of all, a steady blood pressure.

She finished her fruit and drank the juice from the bowl as there was no one around to tell her not to. Watching her mum deal with the loss of her dad had taught Darcy that reckless men led to heartbreak. Why would she choose to put herself in that very situation when she'd seen the damage it did to those innocent bystanders?

Her dad had been reckless, and he'd broken their family. Devlin was reckless and had nearly killed them both. So why was she drawn to him? Why did she feel the need to help him? Why did her body let her down in every single way imaginable when she was anywhere near him?

There was a shuffling sound by the door. Darcy looked up, the bowl still at her lips, to see Devlin standing there in a pair of cotton pyjama bottoms and not much else. He ran his good hand through his hair as the bowl clattered to the table with an ear-shattering clang. A small trickle of fruit syrup dripped from Darcy's chin, and she wiped it away quickly with the back of her hand.

"Here, sit down," she said, flustered. "I'll get you something to eat. Coffee?"

She got up and waved her arms pointedly at the chair she'd been sitting in. Devlin looked winded, his chest rising and falling. The bruising, now fully blossomed on his broken arm, should have been pulling all of Darcy's attention, but she couldn't tear her eyes away from the perfect definition of his chest and his stomach muscles, and the trail of hair that led down to the top of his trousers that were hanging on his hips for dear life.

Darcy licked her lips and tried to focus, drawing her gaze back to his face. His eyes were ablaze.

"Sorry," he said, his throat bobbing. "I didn't realise you'd be in here. I just came to get some water. I'll let you finish."

Darcy's throat constricted, her stomach twisting. Then she surprised herself by stepping closer to him. Closing the gap so they weren't quite touching.

"No, please don't go," she said. "Sit, please. Sit down."

Devlin looked bemused, but he walked silently to the chair and perched on the edge of it, ready to run if needed.

Darcy bustled around the kitchen, noisily filling the kettle, and setting out coffee in a mug for Devlin.

"You need to keep your strength up," she said. "To make sure your bones can heal, and your body is probably still getting over the shock of the ravine and the hypothermia and all the other crazy stuff it's been through. I'll get you some coffee and how about a bowl of fruit? It's tinned, obviously, otherwise it would probably have grown legs and walked out of the door given how long it's been empty here. But it's yummy. I wanted a steak, can you believe that? I don't even really eat a lot of meat, but my mouth was crying out for a nice bit of rump when I woke up."

Darcy knew she was babbling, but she couldn't be silent in case Devlin filled it with cold, hard truths about how she'd acted last night. Or worse, pretended it never happened.

"They only had fruit, though," she went on. "Or tinned cannelloni, which is nice but not really a breakfast treat. And the coffee isn't bad if you hold your nose while you drink it."

The tin Darcy was holding slipped from her fingers as she tried to pull the tab, skittering across the worksurface of the kitchen and hitting the floor. She watched as it rolled slowly across the lino and came to rest at Devlin's foot. Traitorous tin of fruit.

"Darcy." Devlin bent to pick it up as Darcy sped across the kitchen to get it.

He held it out to her, his eyes an undecipherable green. And as she took it, he wrapped his fingers gently around her wrist and didn't let go.

"Darcy," he said, again. "It's okay. I'm not going to try anything. I'm sorry. Last night was a mistake. We were both tired and probably a little bit out of it with the thin oxygen up here. I'm sorry, I never meant to make you feel awkward."

Of course it was a mistake. There's no way he'd like me. He's Devlin Storm. This is what happens when I throw myself headlong into adventure. Luckily, I avoided getting hurt. Almost. Darcy's mind was working nineteen to the dozen.

"Darcy, are you okay?" Devlin was still looking at her. "You look like you're trying to work out the quickest way out of here. I don't want you to feel awkward — there's no need. We're adults, right? We can deal with this."

Darcy nodded, feeling herself deflate. Relishing the feeling of his fingers wrapped around her wrist because she was sure once he realised they were still there, he'd drop them like she was a hot potato.

"We are," she said, her throat tingling as she fought the tears. "Sensible adults who can hang out together until someone comes to rescue us. We can be grown-ups about this."

CHAPTER 22

DEVLIN

It seemed that they could be grown-ups about it. Boring, polite, sensible grown-ups who skirted around each other and found the floor interesting to look at, and spent a lot of time talking about the weather when they found themselves in the same space.

The morning passed in a fit of uncomfortable silences and too many comments on the way the storm wasn't letting up. Devlin moped around in a pair of joggers and a T-shirt he'd found in the bunkroom cupboard, muttering to himself about what an idiot he was and then wondering why he felt so weird about it all. Devlin Storm wasn't a man who cared about other people's feelings, was he? So why, all of a sudden, did he seem to have developed a conscience about Darcy?

He'd eaten her tin of fruit and drunk the world's worst coffee and watched as she'd slunk out of the room in a fluffy robe that was wrapped so tightly around her waist that it clung to her curves like a second skin. Then he'd taken up residence in the little office room and pretended the radio was in need of a companion.

And yet, every single second Devlin was prodding the buttons or swinging around on the office chair, all he could concentrate on was the thought of Darcy Wainwright and the hold she had over him. From the moment she'd told him *no* back at the Royal Alpine, Darcy had done nothing but treat him like a normal human being. Yes, one who seemed to annoy the heck out of her, but a human all the same. Devlin was so used to people meeting his every ridiculous request and pandering to him that this had been a nice surprise. He felt like he could drop the pretence around Darcy and in doing so, snap free the iron chain that had been taut around his chest for so long. He felt like the real Devlin, breaking free from the captive of the persona he'd built around him.

And then he'd ruined it by trying to kiss the one person who allowed him that freedom.

Not everyone who's nice to you wants to kiss you, Devlin! Only, as Devlin thought it, he realised it actually might be true. Most of the women, and some of the men, who dared to approach him did just want one thing from him. The chance to tell their friends they'd kissed the famous Storm. The chance to sell their story to the papers. With Darcy, though, he'd mistaken her kindness for something else. He must have done. It wasn't often he was so blindsided.

"Urgh." Devlin sighed into his hands and dropped his head on the desk. Of all the weird, crazy risks he'd taken in the last few days, he hadn't been expecting a kiss to be the one to finally floor him. Hypothermia, maybe. Frostbite, definitely. Darcy Wainwright, not even on the list.

And he knew that was where he'd gone wrong.

"Is everything okay?" Darcy peeked around the door to the office. "Only, I heard you groaning and you're sitting by the one means of communication we have with the outside world. Is help going to take longer? Are they leaving us here for an indefinite amount of time and you're worried about being here with me for any longer than you have to?"

Devlin shook his head. "No. Nothing to worry about. The radio is fine and there's been no more contact yet. Not surprising given the way the storm isn't abating. I was just—"

"You're worried we're going to run out of things to say about the snow before we get rescued?" Darcy asked, her gorgeous lips spreading into a smile. "Oh, and I was bringing you some lunch by the way, not eavesdropping on you."

"It never crossed my mind," Devlin said, sitting upright. "Come in."

She stepped into the room, a bowl in one hand, cup in the other.

"It's another tinned beauty," she said, holding out the bowl. Steam rose from it, despite the heat of the room. "And some tea."

Devlin took the food with thanks, peering into the bowl at a pile of filled pasta covered in a red sauce.

"Not bad," he admitted, his stomach grumbling at the smell of hot food. "They sure know how to treat their guests at this place, don't they? Thank you, Darcy."

"I just heated it in a saucepan, the tin did the rest." Darcy nodded and skittered back out to the living room. Devlin followed, forking in a mouthful of food as he went. There was a place setting on the table by the window and Devlin took the seat next to it as Darcy dished her own portion from the pan to her plate.

Through the glass, the visibility was worse than it had been since they arrived. Devlin could feel the coldness of the snow seeping through the window, even though it was sealed tightly shut. He watched Darcy's fluid movements, her too-big joggers hanging by her hips, her jumper sleeves rolled up so they didn't swamp her hands. She was perfect. He had to remind himself that she had said no, in so many words, and he respected that, but it didn't mean he couldn't appreciate her from afar.

"It's not a steak, but I think there might be meat inside the little pasta shapes," Darcy said, sitting down and tucking in.

"I dreamt of my mum's roast dinner last night," said Devlin, his mouth watering. "Crispy potatoes and a rare cut of beef."

"I'm surprised you slept enough to dream at all on that sofa," Darcy said. "It looks older than me."

Devlin looked down at his food, poking a pasta with his fork.

"You could have come in to the bunks, you know," Darcy added. "There was no need for you to sleep out here."

"Honestly, Darcy?" Devlin said. "I did come through and when I heard you snoring, I grabbed a blanket and decided on the sofa."

Darcy was mid-chew so she rolled her eyes at him and pouted, the pillow of her lips doing strange things to Devlin's stomach. He pinched his nose and carried on with his lunch.

She doesn't like you like that. Have some control.

"My snoring is cute," she protested when she'd finished, brow raised. "So I've been told."

"Told by whom? The racoons who live in the trees by the lodge?" Devlin teased, not wanting to picture the lucky man who had once gotten to listen to Darcy's snoring every night.

"My mum actually," Darcy said, her chin pointing at him in defiance.

"Well in that case . . ." Devlin left his sentence open, shrugging.

Darcy smiled at him, and their eyes hooked for a beat. And another. She was so beautiful it made his whole body ache. He needed to remove himself from the room. He needed to go outside and throw himself into the snow to cool off.

Standing abruptly, Devlin knocked the fork from his food onto the table where it clattered loudly. Darcy stood, too, eyes wide.

"Devlin—"

"Darcy—"

They spoke over each other, Devlin closing the gap between them until he could see the galaxy in the sprinkling of freckles on her nose. The tension between them was pulled so tight, that even this close, it felt as though Darcy was a whole world away. Devlin couldn't breathe.

"Are you going to kiss me?" she whispered.

Devlin shook his head. "I didn't think you wanted me to." The words squeezed out despite the malfunctioning of his chest muscles.

"I think I actually might do," she breathed, and Devlin felt himself unravel as she carried on talking. "I'm so sorry about last night. I panicked. You're Devlin Storm, a man who has adventure running through his veins. I'm Darcy Wainwright, a woman who runs the other way when faced with it. You're the biggest adventure I've ever faced and I guess . . . well, I'm scared Devlin. I'm scared that you're going to kiss me and realise that I'm different to the rest of the women you've kissed. And then you'll leave and I'll never see you ag—"

Devlin didn't let her finish. He hooked his good arm around her waist and lifted her up so she was sitting on the table. He pushed her legs apart and stood between them, dropping his head and pressing his lips against hers. She groaned into his mouth and tasted of basil and sweetness. Devlin couldn't hold back, kissing her hard and fast, his hand in her hair. Her hands snaked around his back, pulling him closer to her, nails raking down the back of his T-shirt. He grunted and saw flashes of colour swimming to the surface of his icy shackles. Fire exploded in his abdomen.

"Darcy," he breathed into her mouth and felt her body press into his, trying to get as close as she could.

Her cheeks were pink, her breathing faster than even Devlin's was. He stepped closer, pushing her legs further apart, sliding his hand down her back and under her jumper to hitch her up to him. He needed no air between them. He needed friction, his skin on hers. She wore nothing under her giant jumper and as his fingers stroked her spine, she moaned into his mouth and arched her back.

"You're . . . something . . . else," he whispered. Each word dotted between kisses on her lips, her cheeks, her neck.

Devlin explored the skin in the dimple of her collar bone, trailing a tongue over the gap and back up her throat to her mouth. He couldn't get enough. She was perfect. She tasted just how he imagined. Her skin was so soft under his calloused palm. He dipped his head and met her lips with his again, tentatively exploring between them with his tongue. When she answered with her own, Devlin felt his heart hammer against his rib cage.

He felt Darcy's breath hitch, her lips parting as Devlin's tongue teased hers, sending shivers down his spine. Her hands fisted the fabric of his T-shirt, pulling him even closer, desperate for more. His lips moved hungrily, and he struggled to slow himself down, be more deliberate, memorising every curve, every taste of her mouth. The rhythm of their kiss shifted, deepening with each passing second, until the world outside of them ceased to exist.

Darcy's legs wrapped around his waist instinctively, pulling him even closer. His good hand roamed her sides, slipping again beneath the hem of her jumper, warm against her bare skin. She gasped, breaking the kiss for the briefest of moments.

"Darcy?" Devlin murmured, voice hoarse with restraint, her breath hot and rapid against his lips. "Are you okay?"

"I'm not going anywhere," she whispered back, her voice shaky but certain. "Not this time."

Their eyes locked again, and for a heartbeat, there was only silence. Devlin's thumb traced the line of her jaw, his touch gentle, tender, in stark contrast to the passion of their kiss. His gaze flickered over her, from her flushed cheeks to her swollen lips, before he leaned in again, sealing her promise with one final, slow kiss that left her trembling.

The heat between them was undeniable, blazing and relentless, but beneath it was something deeper — something that threatened to consume them both. And as Devlin finally pulled away, their lips parting with a soft gasp, they both knew they had crossed a line. One that couldn't be undone.

But neither of them cared.

CHAPTER 23

DARCY

Darcy's heart was still racing. She could feel it pounding in her throat as she pressed her lips together, trying to regain some semblance of composure while sitting on the table. Devlin's warmth lingered on her skin, the taste of him still fresh on her lips, and she swore she could still feel his fingers tracing lazy patterns along her spine. An ache pooled in her and she wanted release from it, but she needed to show some restraint.

It had been overwhelming, intoxicating — everything she had feared and everything she had secretly longed for.

She swallowed, her hands gripping the edge of the table beneath her as if the world would tilt at any moment. This was real. He had kissed her. No, *they* had kissed each other. Devlin Storm, the man who seemed to belong more to the wilderness than to any woman, had lifted her from the floor and kissed her like he needed her more than air.

And she had kissed him back. Hard.

The realisation came like a wave crashing over her, pulling her deeper into the whirlpool of emotions she had been so desperately trying to avoid. What had she done? She had let herself fall, let herself give in to something she wasn't sure she was ready for. This was Devlin, after all — the man who chased adventure with reckless abandon, while she clung to the safety of routine and predictability.

But for the first time, that didn't seem to matter.

Darcy glanced up, catching a glimpse of him standing there, his chest still rising and falling, his emerald eyes glassy and unreadable as they lingered on her. He hadn't said anything since their lips had parted, and the silence between them felt fragile, like it might shatter if either of them spoke. The air was thick with unspoken words, with feelings neither of them had dared admit until now. Maybe they still didn't.

Her heart screamed at her to do something, to break the tension, to say anything that might give her back control of the situation, but her body refused to move. She had no idea what to say. How do you talk to a man who had just set your world on fire with a single kiss?

You're scared, she reminded herself. *You've always been scared.*

But maybe she didn't want to be any more.

Before she could find the courage to speak, Devlin's hand reached for hers, his fingers gently brushing against her skin, and she felt that same electric spark shoot through her veins. He moved closer, his eyes never leaving hers, and Darcy's breath caught in her throat.

"Are you all right?" he asked, his voice low, rough around the edges.

Was she? Darcy wasn't sure. She had no idea how to be all right when her entire body was still humming from his touch, her mind racing with the implications of what had just happened. But she nodded anyway, her fingers closing around his, because despite everything — despite her fears and uncertainties — she knew one thing for sure: this was an adventure she wasn't running from.

Darcy took a deep breath, steadying herself, and looked up at Devlin, her fingers still intertwined with his. There was something she needed to say, something that had been tugging at her since the moment their lips had parted. She licked her lips, tasting the remnants of their kiss, before speaking.

"Maybe we could make each other a promise," she said, softly, her voice barely above a whisper. Devlin's gaze locked onto hers, and the intensity of it made her feel as though the room had shrunk around them.

"A promise?" he repeated, his thumb lightly grazing her knuckles.

Darcy nodded, her heart hammering in her chest. "I'll . . . I'll go on more adventures. I'll try to stop running from everything that scares me."

Devlin's expression softened, and for a moment, she thought she saw something vulnerable flash in his eyes.

"And I'll try to be a kinder person," he said, his voice still rough but filled with sincerity. "The man who doesn't shout when things get tough. Who doesn't make ridiculous demands."

"Ridiculously *dangerous* demands," she added. "Like taking a helicopter into a snowstorm against everyone's better wishes."

She smiled at him, small and hesitant, but it felt like the start of something bigger. He raised his hand between them, offering it to her like an unspoken vow and she took it and shook it.

"That's a deal, my brave adventurer," he said quietly, the nickname holding a weight that made her chest tighten.

"That's a deal, my reformed daredevil," she replied, uncertainly.

"Not sure I'd go that far," Devlin laughed.

"Man I can just about tolerate?" she teased.

"How about work in progress?"

Darcy nodded. "Work in progress. I like it."

They shook on it, neither of them dropping the other's hand when it was done. For a moment, they stayed there, hands clasped, the promise hanging between them like a fragile thread.

But then Darcy pulled him to her, closing the distance between them in one swift movement. Their lips met again, but this time the kiss was slower, more certain. It wasn't filled with urgency or fear, but with the quiet understanding that they were beginning something new. That the kiss they'd already shared hadn't been a one-off. It had been something real.

A loud gust of wind howled outside, rattling the windows, breaking their magic. The snowstorm was still raging around them.

"Looks like we're stuck here for a little while longer," Darcy said, a mischievous grin growing on her face. "I found something earlier that I think will help pass the time."

Devlin's eyebrow quirked and Darcy shook her head.

"Don't get any ideas, Romeo," she laughed. "I meant a pack of cards."

"Cards?"

Darcy shifted to the edge of the table and jumped down.

"What?" she said. "Afraid I'll beat you?" she called back over her shoulder as she ducked down to the console cupboard by the pool table and pulled out a pack of well-used playing cards.

"As if!" Devlin said. "I used to play with Mum all the time and she was a hard taskmaster."

"Oh, fighting talk."

She sat back on her chair at the table and took the cards from their sleeve, shuffling them and giving Devlin her best poker face. He was trying his hardest not to laugh, but when the cards toppled from Darcy's hands the floodgates opened.

She grinned, scooping the cards from the floor, unbothered by Devlin's laughter.

"Okay, okay," she said, tapping the cards back into some semblance of order. "Maybe I need to work on my shuffling skills, but that doesn't mean you're going to win. What's your game?"

"Snap?"

Darcy laughed.

"Snap? What are you, five?" She shuffled as she spoke, eyes on Devlin, feeling the tension start to build again between them. "I thought you'd be more of a Poker guy, given your face is devoid of emotion most of the time."

Devlin hit a hand to his chest, clutching dramatically at his heart.

"Oof, you're killing me." He dropped his chin and gazed at Darcy. "If Snap is too fast-paced for you and Poker is a bit hardcore for a first date, then I think we should go with Go Fish, if you're au fait with the rules? First one to 'book' wins."

If Darcy knew the rules of Go Fish then they'd flown out of her head as soon as Devlin had said the words *first* and *date*.

"You want to cut the cards?" Darcy croaked.

Devlin nodded, taking the deck from her hands and brushing his fingers along the inside of her wrist. The sensation travelled all the way up her arm and spread through her body like a warm rush.

"That's cheating," she whispered, watching as he cut the cards in two and stacked them again.

Devlin was silent as he dealt them seven cards each and placed the deck in the middle of the table. He took his time. Whether it was because he could only use one arm or because he was so focused on her, Darcy wasn't sure. But it was maddening, the tension simmering between them, hovering just beneath the surface like an unspoken challenge.

"Give me your Kings, Devlin," she said, trying and failing to sound casual.

"Go fish," Devlin replied, holding steady. "Tell me, Darcy, do you play cards with all your dates?"

Darcy grinned, picking up a card from the pile and adding it to her hand.

"Only the ones up to the challenge," she said.

"I'm honoured," Devlin said.

"I'm already planning my victory dance," she replied.

"Don't get too cocky, Wainwright. I'm full of surprises."

"I'll believe it when I see it," Darcy teased, but her pulse quickened at the way his eyes sparkled with amusement.

After the last few days, Darcy could tell Devlin was starting to relax. His arm was strapped to keep it from hurting so much, his jaw unclenched, his whole persona a world away from the man who'd demanded she get ready for his helicopter. She could tell he was enjoying this — their little back-and-forth — the way they were dancing around the inevitable pull between them. She ignored a niggling doubt that what had happened between them was a result of his adrenaline pumping and clouding the reasoning part of his brain.

They played in near silence for a few minutes, saving themselves for card requests and Go Fish commands. But Darcy couldn't stand how the air was growing thick with unspoken words, so she glanced at him over the top of her cards.

"What does a man like Devlin Storm do in his spare time?" she asked.

Devlin chuckled, studying the cards in his hand. He'd worked out a way to play with just one working arm, it took him a bit longer but he'd done so without complaining that Darcy had picked a game where he was quite obviously at an immediate disadvantage.

"What's this 'spare time' you talk of?" he said. "Show me your Queens."

"Go Fish," Darcy replied. "And I don't believe you work 24/7. So I'm going to fill in the gaps if you don't do it for me."

She watched as he placed his cards face down on the table and then drew one from the deck.

"So," she went on, "I'm picturing you finishing work, heading to the gym and working out until you've released all that pent-up aggression because your assistant brought you the wrong stapler. Once you've run a ten-minute five-mile run and pounded that treadmill like it's the face of your mortal enemy—"

"Okay, okay, jeez," he interrupted. "I see I've got a long way to go to win you over still. So, I'm not sure I should be telling you this, actually."

Darcy arched an eyebrow, trying not to smile.

"When I get home after a long day in the office, I sit in my pants and eat cereal while watching reruns of *Succession*."

The laugh that burst from Darcy surprised even herself.

"You're telling me you watch power-hungry billionaires stab each other in the back while shovelling Cheerios onto a spoon? All in a pair of boxers?"

"What can I say?" He shrugged. "Though they're Calvins, before you start imagining me in a pair of saggy, paisley prints."

Darcy felt her cheeks heat as she pictured Devlin in a pair of Calvins. "Is that not a kind of busman's-holiday show for you?"

"What about you, Darcy?" He ignored her question, watching her for a beat. "What's your show?"

"Am I a total cliché if I say *Gilmore Girls*?"

"Yes," Devlin said with a grin. "But I won't hold it against you."

"It's a comfort," she said. "The small town where everyone knows each other. The quirky characters. The romance. It's my go-to when I want to escape."

Devlin watched her for a beat, his expression softening. "I get that," he said, quietly. "We all need to escape sometimes."

His words hung in the air and Darcy felt like if she grabbed them and tugged, she'd get something deeper than banter. An insight into his real life, past the bravado and the teasing.

She laid down her cards, the game suddenly feeling secondary to whatever else was building between them. "You feel like that? Like you want to just step away from everything for a while?"

Devlin's gaze flickered over her face before he looked back down at his cards. "Yeah, more than I'd like to admit."

Darcy's breath caught in her throat and for a moment they just stared at each other, the game of cards forgotten. She could feel the tension thickening between them again, the undeniable pull drawing her closer to him. She swallowed hard, her voice barely a whisper as she spoke.

"I think it's your turn, Storm."

Devlin blinked as if coming back to the moment. He glanced at his hand again and then pulled out four cards. Darcy could see the corners of his mouth tugging into a smile as he laid down each of the Queens in turn.

"Wait, what?" she said, her eyes widening. "Already?"

"I told you I was full of surprises," he said, grinning.

Darcy threw her cards down in a play huff. "You are such a cheat."

"I won that hand fair and square," he said, eyes on her. The air between them was crackling with unspoken desire.

Darcy stood up, pushing her chair back with a grin. She leaned her hands on the table and bent her face towards Devlin.

"Fine, I guess I'll have to win the next book."

But before she could step away, Devlin had reached out and taken her hand in his. The touch sent a jolt of electricity through her and when she looked at him, his expression was serious.

"Or," he said softly, his thumb grazing her skin, "we could forget about the cards for a while."

Darcy's breath hitched. The way he was looking at her, she felt like he was daring her to close the gap between them, to give in to the fire that had been smouldering all day. Her heart pounded in her chest, and she couldn't find the words to respond.

Instead, she walked around the corner of the table, her fingers resting on Devlin's wrist, feeling the steady thrum of his pulse beneath them. He slipped his hand from hers and moved it to her waist and around to the small of her back, pulling her closer until she was standing between his legs.

The game. The storm. The world outside — they all faded away as he stood up and his lips found hers again, and this time, there was no holding back.

CHAPTER 24

DEVLIN

If the last kiss had been spectacular, then this one was a drug. A drug that Devlin knew was going to take hold of him and never let go. He'd thought about nothing other than kissing Darcy all the way through their card game. Surprised himself, even, when he'd won the first book. Without breaking the kiss he moved them both to the sofa, the soft cushions breaking their fall as they tumbled down.

Pleasure hummed through him with every touch.

"You're going to need to slow down," he growled, shifting his gaze to Darcy, whose eyes were so dark and intense he nearly lost control there and then. "You have a way of making me forget everything. I want to remember this."

He slid his hand beneath her jumper, fingers skimming her bare skin. Darcy moaned softly, leaning into him as he found her breast, gently stroking her hard nipple.

She was perfect. So perfect. There was something about her that was so honest and pure. Kissing her ignited all his senses, as if bells were ringing in his head with pleasure.

Suddenly Darcy pulled away, ending their kiss and bringing Devlin back to reality. The bells were louder. No, not bells. Beeping.

The radio.

Devlin slowly drew his hand away and groaned, leaning his head on her shoulder in frustration.

"Devlin? Darcy?" the static-filled voice came from the office. "It's Officer Alleman. Over."

Letting out a frustrated sigh, Devlin pulled back, resting his hand on Darcy's waist, reluctant to let go. The radio beeped again.

"Okay, okay," he muttered, getting up slowly and running a hand through his hair. He shifted his hips, tugging the material away, trying to make himself more comfortable.

Darcy looked into his eyes as he helped her up, breathing just as heavily, as the unfinished kisses hung between them. He needed more. They both needed more. But they also needed to be rescued so Devlin gripped her hand in his as they both headed to the office and the radio.

"This is Devlin, reading you loud and clear. Over."

Static, then the same voice. The storm was obviously still making itself known because the voice faded in and out, almost swallowed by the howl of the wind outside.

"Just an update," said Alleman, and Devlin found himself thinking *please don't be on your way, not tonight. Maybe not even tomorrow.* "The storm is bad, but it's moving fast. We estimate that it will burn out by 3 a.m. Currently our weather systems show fair skies in the morning, which means we should be able to get a crew out to you by daybreak. It will be no later than seven. Over."

Devlin felt his heart thrum, and judging by the way Darcy looked at him she felt the same way. He turned back to the radio.

"That's great news," he said, flatly. "We can't wait to see you. Over."

"We feel the same way," replied Alleman. "You've given us all a fright. You'll find half the world's news teams waiting for you when you get back. Be safe, get some rest, we'll see you in the morning. Over and out."

Devlin replaced the handset with a sigh.

"Back to normal, eh?" Darcy said, her pupils huge.

"I hope not," he replied.

"I hope not too," she whispered.

The air grew still. Devlin dropped the mic and curled his fingers around Darcy's, tugging her towards him in one swift move.

"No more distractions," he murmured, his voice thick with desire. "You heard: we have all night on our own. I don't want to wait any more, Darcy."

She leaned into him, tilting her head up until their lips were inches apart, the heat between them unbearable.

"Me neither."

Her lips looked good enough to eat. "Come with me."

Darcy didn't need to be asked twice. Without another word, Devlin took her hand and led her through to the living quarters and straight on to the bunkroom. As soon as he closed the door behind them, he turned and pushed Darcy's back against the wood, crashing his lips into hers. The kiss was hungry, needy. Darcy's hands were in his hair as she responded with equal intensity.

The small room felt even smaller now, the heat between them almost overwhelming. Devlin's hands moved to the hem of Darcy's sweater, lifting it just enough for his fingers to skim the soft skin on her stomach. Darcy gasped. Her body arched into him, desperate for more.

"Is this okay?" he whispered against her lips.

"Yes, Devlin, please."

The sound of his name on her lips sent a shiver down his spine and he pulled her closer.

Each touch, each kiss was like fuel to the fire burning between them. Their movements became a blur as he pulled off her sweater, her naked body nearly tipping him over the edge as he trailed kisses down her neck. He lifted each of her perfect breasts to his mouth licking her swollen nipples. Darcy's hands were gripped in his hair, pulling him as close as she could, her breathing coming in tiny gasps.

Unable to wait a moment longer, Devlin scooped her up in his good arm as though she was a featherweight, and carried her to the bunk. They tumbled onto it, kissing and touching with a sense of desperation, as Devlin pulled off Darcy's joggers and, together, they lifted off his T-shirt. He dropped to his knees at the edge of the bed. They were both sweaty and gasping as Devlin took a moment to savour the sight of Darcy — sweet and seductive — until he couldn't take it any longer. He dipped his head and lifted her leg to his shoulder, as he brought his lips to her core, listening to Darcy's soft murmurs of pleasure. Their connection was undeniable, the chemistry between them explosive. Devlin had never felt this kind of urgency, the need to have her and make her feel all of the things he was feeling.

"Devlin," Darcy's voice was trembling.

Devlin licked and stroked until he felt her quiver around him and, as he felt her let go, Darcy cried out his name. A sound Devlin had never heard so perfectly on anyone's lips.

Pulling himself up to lie beside her he wrapped her in his arms, pressing his forehead against hers until her breathing slowed.

He stroked her stomach, idly, feeling the muscles ripple under his fingers. He moved to her rib cage, stroking the side of her breast and her arms. Darcy's head lolled back on the pillow and he kissed her neck and the line of her jaw. He knew he had already had the same thought a million times that day, but she really was perfect.

Outside, the wind and storm still raged, but Devlin knew the storm raging inside him was calming. Darcy was good for him. The softness she exuded was a tonic to the way his emotions sometimes bubbled over. It wasn't that she stopped him acting like the fool he knew he could be, it was more that she allowed him to act the way he wanted to, and the anger dissipated the more he relaxed into the real him.

She had given herself over to him. They had given themselves to each other. A thought nagged at the base of his skull, but he batted it away with a constellation of kisses dotted on her jaw and neck. Feeling like a teenager again, Devlin was awash with nervous excitement. He trailed his fingers over her skin until it bumped with goose pimples.

"Cold?" he whispered, blowing a thin stream of air onto her chest.

Darcy laughed, twisting around on the bed to face him.

"Not in the slightest," she said, smiling. "I think this might be the warmest I've been since we left the Royal Alpine. Thank you."

"Happy to oblige," he said, kissing her again.

He couldn't keep away. She was the drug, not the kisses.

"How's your arm?" Darcy asked, stroking his shoulder. "Lifting me might not have been the best idea."

Devlin felt his skin tighten around her touch, the tension building in him again.

"I used my good arm for that, and you're lighter than my cat," he said.

"You've got a cat?" Darcy's brows shot up. "I would have pictured you with a tiger on a leash. Or maybe a gecko."

"That's random," he laughed.

"Well, you know, neither are overly cuddly," she said, studying his face. "Though, after today, maybe I can see you with a cat. A big fluffy beast who comes and sits on your lap while you're eating Cheerios in your pants. Maybe you give them the left-over milk."

"Have you been spying on me?" He grinned. "You've just described my Friday nights to a tee."

Darcy laughed but Devlin's smile soon faded as she pressed her lips to his. A subtle promise of what was to come.

CHAPTER 25

DARCY

Darcy didn't want to think about how Devlin spent his Friday nights, because she was sure it wasn't holed up in his penthouse with a cat. She couldn't think like that. It would drive her to distraction, especially after what had just happened between them. What was still happening between them. He had taken her to sweet oblivion and she wanted to make him feel the same.

In the soft light of the bunkroom, the snow-filled windows providing a screen from the setting sun, she could see his every single muscle was perfectly defined, the beat of his pulse just above his collar bone thumping hard and fast. And when she looked up from the wall of his chest, his eyes, all pupil, were focused on her lips.

She was helpless. This wasn't supposed to happen. Darcy hadn't expected to fall for Devlin, not like this. Not this easily or quickly. Not when she knew what he was like. Now, though, she couldn't help but think that *wasn't* what he was like.

Darcy ran her hand across his abdomen, her skin tingling as he groaned at her touch. She felt in control and powerful.

She was in charge now and her whole body was buzzing with the idea that he would let her take control.

Spreading her fingers under his waistband, she inched his trousers down until she found what she wanted. She gripped him and started stroking as Devlin moaned with satisfaction.

"Is this okay?" she whispered, lifting herself up and straddling him.

He took a moment to focus and then squeezed her fingers as a guttural noise came from deep inside him. Darcy watched as he studied her naked body, as though she was a work of art, her skin tingling at the intensity of his gaze. She had never felt more alive as Devlin lifted her hips and adjusted their position until they were perfectly aligned. He was reading her body like a favourite book he knew from cover to cover. And soon their bodies were moving together in perfect rhythm.

"You're perfect, Darcy Wainwright," he whispered in her ear.

Darcy wanted to reply, but her voice was lost, swallowed by the deep, aching pull of pleasure as she surrendered to him completely.

***

Darcy lay quietly smiling, the faint glow of the sun now gone, the bunkroom dark. She felt the weight of Devlin's arm on her stomach, the heat of his body next to hers. The outpost was still warm with the heating, but the lack of sunlight made Darcy shiver. The night had been perfect for her but what about Devlin? His girlfriends were all models and far more experienced than she was. What if she hadn't been good for him?

As if he could read her mind Devlin looked at her.

"I know what you're thinking. I know what people say about me. I know my reputation isn't exactly . . . decent."

Darcy raised an eyebrow. *Not exactly decent?* She thought about the stories she'd read in the papers and magazines, the exposés and scandals. According to the press, Devlin seemed to have a new girlfriend every week — and sometimes two or three. Those risqué stories didn't exactly match the man she was lying next to now, though, and the thought of hearing him talk about his past was surprisingly painful.

Her mind started spiralling back to reality. To the world outside the snow-covered outpost. A world where Devlin Storm was a figure larger than life, untouchable, reckless and adventurous. A man who never stayed in one place for very long. Or with one person. She didn't want to be a fleeting moment in his life. A story he could retell one day when they were home and safe. A soft sound escaped her, somewhere between a sigh and a laugh. Two days ago, the idea of being stuck with Devlin had been a nightmare, yet now she was afraid of losing him.

"What you have read about me, everyone's idea that I'm a heartbreaker, it's just not true." Devlin studied her with an intense gaze. "It is important to me that you believe that."

Darcy smiled softly, not wanting to say all her fears out loud in case it made them true.

"Let me tell you something," Devlin went on. "Something else you won't read anywhere. Something absolutely nobody knows about me, other than my mum."

A sudden gust of wind shook the cabin and Darcy leaned in towards him as if he might provide shelter, tugging the blanket up to their chins. Devlin wrapped his good arm around her, and despite the topic of conversation all she could think about was those lips, and how good they had tasted. She tore her gaze away, meeting his eyes instead.

"I've only had three girlfriends in my life."

Darcy frowned.

"What?" She wondered if he was lying to her, trying to put her at ease after what had just happened between them, but his face was open and honest.

"Three," he said again. "One when I was a teenager. Delia and I were together for years. Then I was with another woman, Anna, in my early twenties."

"Then there was Claudia, right?" Darcy asked, feeling a wave of jealousy pass over her. "Claudia Romano. The supermodel."

Devlin nodded, his face growing stony. Darcy had read a few stories about their tumultuous relationship, about the fights and the make-ups and the million-pound holidays. She was fairly sure it was reported they'd been engaged to be married at one point.

"She's beautiful," Darcy said, looking at the ceiling. "All long limbs and glossy hair and perfect features."

What had she been thinking, kissing this man, having sex with him? He was used to dating the most amazing women in the world. Why on earth did she think she was special enough to join their ranks?

"She was voted the most stunning woman in the world at one point, wasn't she?" Darcy went on, not able to stop the comparisons.

"Two years running," said Devlin, which didn't exactly help. He took a deep breath, his Adam's apple bobbing. Darcy watched his face twist as he thought through what he was going to say next.

"Claudia was the perfect model, yes," he said. "But she wasn't beautiful. Not really."

"Not if you're more into bog trolls and Jabba the Hut," she joked, looking away again.

"Hey," he said, tilting her chin towards him. "Eyes on me."

Devlin looked at her with a stare that stopped her in her tracks as he carried on talking.

"She really wasn't beautiful. I mean, I found her attractive in the beginning, but it soon wore off. Her beauty was superficial, all hard edges. She really wasn't very nice, you know."

He dropped a kiss on Darcy's lips.

"You were together for years, weren't you?" she asked. He nodded.

"Six, nearly," he said. "It was okay, if that makes sense? Grew into something I was comfortable with. Neither of us showed the other much affection, but that suited us, you know? But when I ended it she sold stories about us to the press. She knew I liked my privacy, to hide behind the image I had created, but she sold the stories anyway. She likes the front page and the celebrity status too much. I provided that."

"I'm so sorry, Devlin," Darcy said. "So . . . the press, all those articles about you, the supermodels and movie stars. They're made up?"

"They're just stories," he said. "I go on dates, sure, but they never lead to anything serious. It's not worth the risk. We have a few drinks, let the papers take their photos and concoct their lies. Then we part company."

"And the women go along with this?" Darcy asked.

He nodded again. "They have to. They have to sign a non-disclosure agreement before I will even see them."

"So they don't talk about you in your pants eating cereal?" Darcy asked, smiling sadly. "Why do it?"

"It all feeds into my reputation, and that's why my clothes sell and my business is so profitable."

"No," said Darcy, taking his good hand and holding it between both of hers. "No, that's not true. Your business works because you do. Your clothes sell because they're amazing, because you put so much of yourself into them. That story you told me, about making the dress for your mum. It was beautiful, and you put the same care and love into everything you design. It's there in every stitch, in every fold, in every seam. Trust me, I've tried on a few Devlin Storm dresses in my time — not that I've ever had nearly enough money to buy one — and they're amazing. They're life-changing. These hands are why your clothes are so wonderful."

She kissed his cheek and rested her forehead against his. "This mind is why you are so creative, and so successful. Forget about your reputation for a moment. People see your clothes and they see your soul in everything you make."

Devlin eyes grew heavy lidded, never leaving hers. His chest rose and fell steadily.

"I've never thought about it that way," he said quietly. "How do you know exactly what to say?"

"Because I feel like I know you," she said. "It's impossible, I get it. We have only been here a couple of days, but we've been through so much. I'm sorry, I know it must sound crazy."

"It doesn't," he said, his lips curving into a smile. "I think it's called trauma bonding."

Darcy hit his chest softly in jest.

"Oy," she said, smiling. "Don't belittle this. Sounds like we've both been through enough past trauma to have enough bonds with that to keep us going. This is—"

Darcy didn't have a chance to finish her sentence as Devlin covered her lips with his own.

"You're anything but trauma," he spoke onto her lips. "Now shut up and kiss me."

"Happily," Darcy whispered.

I would happily spend my life right here with you. Every last day of it.

And she was so certain it was the truth. She was so sure.

Until she woke up the next morning to find that Devlin had gone.

CHAPTER 26

DEVLIN

Of all the terrible things he'd done in his life, this felt like the worst.

Devlin stood for a moment, watching Darcy sleep. She was curled up on the single bed, burrowed into the blanket with a smile on her face. She was undoubtedly the most beautiful woman he had ever seen — her button nose was the cutest, her lips the sweetest. Memories of the previous night and the way she had looked made Devlin's body run hot with desire. But there was something else, too. Something that made what he was about to do, near on impossible. She had an inner strength, a core of goodness, that he hadn't seen in anyone for a long time. She wasn't afraid to stand up to him when he was wrong, and she wasn't afraid to fight for what was right. That integrity and honesty shone from her. It seemed to make her rise up above everyone else in his life.

"I'm so sorry," he whispered, kissing her gently on the head. "I hope that you'll be able to forgive me."

The thoughts of what this would do to her made him feel sick, but he had no other choice. What she'd said to him, the way she seemed to read him, shifted something deep inside him, as if the broken pieces of his heart were starting to move back together again. Could she really be right? Would people genuinely still admire him if he wasn't Devlin Storm 'the rebel'? If he wasn't the angry, alpha man who made the headlines for all the wrong reasons? If he was Devlin Storm 'the nice guy'? It was the very opposite of what he had believed for such a long time, he didn't know if he could trust that idea at all.

Back in the beginning, when he'd first started designing, that's all he'd wanted people to see: the clothes. He'd wanted people to look at those designs and see the happiness that had created them, the joy they could bring. Then somewhere down the line he'd forgotten himself, and he'd become somebody different. He wasn't sure how the change had happened or what had triggered it, but he knew that the persona he'd developed allowed him the space to sit back from people's views about him. It wasn't him they were talking about, was it? It was Devlin Storm the ego. But somehow the persona had taken over his whole life. And it had turned sour.

Darcy had shown him that it wasn't too late to change.

And he was repaying her by betraying her.

No, he thought, fumbling with the thermal trousers he'd found in one of the lockers. *Not betraying her, saving her.*

Because deep down he knew what it would be like for her if he didn't. All the press, all the interviews, all the gossip. It would hurt her, and he wasn't willing to do that. No. The real truth was that he had been Devlin Storm for so long that change would be impossible. Even if he tried, the world he lived in was so ruthless that anyone who got in the way would get hurt.

As quietly as he could, he slid on his T-shirt, a jumper, and a brand-new thermal jacket. He winced as his injured arm was squashed as he zipped up the thick, down jacket, and Darcy stirred. She mumbled something, reaching out and wrapping her arms around the pillow that Devlin had pressed against her in place of his warmth when he'd climbed out of bed. A moment of doubt passed through him and he wondered if he should just climb back beneath the blanket with her, pull her into his arms, and fall back asleep. He felt a powerful ache as he thought about the way her body fit so perfectly around his. Surely that couldn't be a bad thing?

But the truth was that it scared him. And wasn't that just the root of all his problems? No one would believe him, looking at the way he was from the outside. But Devlin Storm was scared. He was so afraid, it was paralysing.

When his mum had passed, he had been broken. If he opened up to Darcy and let her in, if he let himself be close to her, if something more developed between them and he grew to care about her as much as he feared he could, then there was a danger he could lose her too. That thought terrified him. *Better to be a mountain*, he said silently to himself. *Better to shut yourself off from the world so that nothing else can hurt you.*

He shook his head sadly, opening the door to the bunkroom and immediately catching sight of his small suitcase. That was the other reason he was sneaking away before dawn. He had a job to do, and he needed to do it alone.

He filled his pockets with protein bars and chocolate from the food cupboard, then grabbed a pen and paper and started to write.

Dear Darcy,
I'm sorry. You said I'm like a frozen lake, and you were right. But you deserve warmth and sunlight in your life, not the cold I bring. I don't know if I'll ever be able to thaw enough to give you what you truly deserve. I want you to be happy, to find joy and adventure, and live the life that's waiting for you. I'll wire you the money as soon as I'm back — use it to chase your dreams and create the life you deserve.
Devlin

He left the note on the table, beside their unfinished game of cards. He carefully rested the pen on the paper. Sadness gnawed at his heart, and once again he wondered if he was doing the right thing. No. This was the right thing, he was sure of it. For once, he wasn't acting out of selfishness. He was doing it for her, for Darcy. And he couldn't believe how much it hurt.

He hoped the letter would make her angry, because anger was easier to carry than sadness. It was better for her, a cleaner break. But the truth gnawed at him — he wasn't good enough for her. He, the man who could have anything, was unworthy of the one thing he realised he truly wanted. That irony cut deeper than he expected, a reminder that for the first time in his life, having it all wasn't enough.

A bright stream of sunshine burst through the windows of the outpost and through the bunkroom door, Devlin saw Darcy stir on the bed again, her hair fanning out around her face like a halo. He needed to go before she woke up. Taking one last look at the woman who had somehow broken through to his core, he then paused at the table, staring at the note, hoping he had done the right thing — for her.

It would be too difficult to carry the suitcase, he thought, so he opened it up and reached inside.

The tin seemed heavier now than it had two days ago. He was amazed it was still sealed shut, given what it had been through. He ran a hand over it gently, feeling his throat close at the thought of what it contained. Puffing out his cheeks, Devlin took a breath to compose himself. He could put up his wall again, protect himself from what he knew was coming. He slid the tin into his coat pocket and left the suitcase next to the leg of the table before tiptoeing his way out of the living quarters. The storm had blown through, and the mountain was utterly silent. The first few rays of sunlight were rising in the entrance hall, too, so bright that it seemed as if the peaks of the mountains were on fire. By the depth of the lights of the helipad he could see that a good few feet of snow had fallen overnight, but not enough to slow him down.

He checked his watch to see that it was 6.45. It was getting late. He should really have left by now, but he had the decency to wait until he heard the distant rumble of a rescue helicopter for Darcy before opening the door. Snow tumbled in and he kicked his way through it, shutting the outpost tightly closed behind him, doing one last thing to keep Darcy safe. The cold hit him like he'd fallen into a deep, dark lake, making his body shudder in protest. His arm felt like it was burning. Everything ached, and despite the sleep he'd had, he felt utterly exhausted. Devlin had no idea how he was going to be able to get to where he needed to get to, except that he was just going to have to put one foot in front of the other and push through. He knew that he should wait here, with Darcy, that he should climb on board the chopper with her and ride home to the warmth and some proper food and a doctor who could mend his broken arm.

Instead, he pulled up the hood of his jacket, clutched the tin to his chest, and trudged out into the snow.

CHAPTER 27

DARCY

The sound of thunder drew Darcy up from dreams of cold ice cream and warm cuddles. She rolled over, smiling, remembering the way she had felt last night. The happy, belly-aching warmth of how Devlin had made her feel. Thunder was good. It meant the storm was still raging. It meant that she would have more time here with the man who had made her feel like this outpost in the middle of the mountains was home. She gathered him close, pushing her face into the familiar smell of him, reaching for his arms, his hands, then his legs, and — he was softer than she remembered him being. Downy. Squashy. Smelled a little mouldy.

"What?" she said, sitting up. The thing she held in her arms wasn't Devlin at all — it was a pillow. For a moment she was grateful for that fact, because it was covered in her drool. Then she blinked the fuzziness from her vision to see that the bunkroom was completely empty.

"Devlin?" she called. The thunder outside was louder than ever, and with a jolt of her heart, she realised it wasn't thunder at all. It was a helicopter.

She clambered off the bed, threw the blanket around her body, and ran to the window. The snow had piled up on the other side of the glass, but past it she could see a huge, bright-orange helicopter spinning lazily as it dropped towards the landing pad. Its rotors kicked up another storm of snow, flecks drumming against the window.

"Devlin?" she cried, running through the bunkroom and out into the living quarters. "The helicopter is here!"

As disappointing as it was to know that her time alone with Devlin had come to an end, she was excited to be heading home. She couldn't wait to have a warm bath, a proper bed, a decent meal. Then maybe, just maybe, she and Devlin could carry on where they had left off last night.

She smiled to herself as she skipped back into the bunkroom and found herself the warmest snow-gear she could get her hands on. It had been one of the most wonderful nights of her life and her skin fizzed at the memory of his touch as she pulled on a jumper and a pair of oversized trousers.

"Devlin?" she called again, checking the bathroom.

It was empty so she washed her face and ran some water around her mouth as she called his name again, a feeling of dread starting to work itself up from her stomach.

He'll be outside, directing the helicopter where to land, she thought. *Or in the office, radioing for a new box of Frosted Flakes to be delivered to his hospital wing.* Tying her trousers tight and pulling on some socks, Darcy headed back out to the living quarters.

"Devlin, we're being rescued," Darcy shouted one last time, rushing past the table and almost tripping on the empty suitcase. The dread exploded into full-blown panic.

She ran to the hallway and the front door. The floor here was covered in snow, as if the door had just been opened. Darcy checked the garage to find it empty, then grabbed the front door and hauled it open. The cold gripped her like a fist and she squealed as the snow fell on her stockinged feet. Clutching her arms to her chest, she stumbled outside just as the helicopter was touching down.

"Devlin?" she cried out. "Where are you?"

He didn't answer, and he didn't need to. She could see the deep holes that his footprints had made in the snow, leading around the landing pad and disappearing up the slope.

"What are you doing?" she yelled into the sunlit snow, though she knew he wouldn't hear her.

There was no time to think, though, as two figures in orange thermal gear were already climbing out of the helicopter and running towards her. She retreated into the outpost so that they could get through the door.

"Darcy?" said one, pulling off a pair of reflective goggles and a hat to reveal a kind, wrinkled face. Darcy nodded at him, suddenly gripped by an intense round of shivers. The man put a gentle hand on her arm and steered her through the door, back into the living quarters. "Come on, let's get you warm. We don't want you catching hypothermia now you're about to be rescued."

The other ranger took off her hat and goggles and gave Darcy a smile that was full of compassion and relief.

"We're so glad to see you alive," she said. "Our choppers saw the wreckage of the bird you were flying in. You both did well getting out of that and making it here, especially in the middle of a storm like the one we just had. Are you ready to leave? We can have you down the mountain in fifteen minutes. How about that?"

"Leave?" Darcy said. "What about Devlin?"

The two rangers shared a look, then the man turned to Darcy with a sigh.

"Devlin radioed in this morning," he said. "He's asked us to take you back on your own. He said he had something he needed to do."

"What?" Darcy asked, retreating until her back hit the table. "What do you mean? I don't understand."

"We weren't given an explanation," said the woman, shrugging. "Now it's safe to fly, Devlin's chartering one of his own helicopters to bring him back this evening. But he didn't want you to be here longer than you needed to. It's a bit unorthodox, I'll give you that, but then he is Devlin Storm."

Darcy turned around, feeling like her bones had been replaced with ice. He'd abandoned her, just tossed her aside like she was rubbish. After everything they'd been through, everything she'd given to him last night, how could he do that?

"We really need to leave," urged the man.

He said something else, but Darcy ignored him. There was a piece of paper on the table next to Devlin's winning card hand, a pen resting on top of it. Snatching it up, she read the note that he had left her, growing colder with every word.

I'm sorry. You once said I'm like a frozen lake, and you were right. But you deserve warmth and sunlight in your life, not the cold I bring. I don't know if I'll ever be able to thaw enough to give you what you truly deserve.

"What?" she shouted, gripping the note so tightly it ripped at the edges. "It's best I leave. Never be able to thaw. You coward, Devlin."

She used the sleeve of her jumper to wipe away a tear. What had happened? Why was he doing this? She was boiling hot, a rash of anger creeping up her neck. Devlin had proved himself to be the ignorant, hard-faced man the press warned her about. And she'd fallen for his soft-boy act. The note fluttered onto the cards. Darcy moved them about with her hands, looking at the four Queens he'd laid out before he'd kissed her and made her whole world light up.

"You're an idiot, Darcy," she whispered, noticing the suitcase and half halting at the sight of it.

Devlin had left her, that she understood in so much as he had a reputation that had screamed from the rooftops that that's exactly what he would do. But to leave this suitcase? There was no way. Devlin had risked his life to get it from the helicopter. He'd shouted at Darcy when she'd gone near it.

He looked like a broken man when he thought it had fallen down the crevasse. Yet, there it was, sitting beside the table in the outpost, forgotten.

Something didn't add up.

"Darcy, we really need to get going in case another storm flies in," the man said. "We don't all want to be stranded here."

"Wait, just a moment, please," she pushed, pleading with the rangers. She opened Devlin's suitcase and peered inside. His passport was there, but the only other thing it had contained — that strange tin — was now gone.

"Miss Wainwright, please," said the female ranger, tapping her snow boots and sending a flurry of melted snow onto the floor. "We can't stay here and put ourselves at risk. You must understand that?"

"I'm sorry, I'm sorry," she said, closing the suitcase and forcing herself to think. "Please just give me a moment."

A metal tin that seemed to mean more to Devlin than anything. And a job he needed to do, right here on the mountain. Darcy paced around the room, moving back to the table and sifting through the cards strewn there.

Suddenly it made sense. A terrible, beautiful, heart-breaking kind of sense. Darcy lifted the Queen of Hearts and slid it into her pocket, looking back at the rangers.

"I'm sorry," she said. "I'm so sorry, but you have to wait."

"Why?" asked the man.

"Because Devlin needs me," she said. "He needs me, because he's saying goodbye to his mum."

CHAPTER 28

DEVLIN

It was harder going than he'd thought, especially with the pain that radiated from his broken arm. He felt like a car that was out of fuel, running on fumes and about to cut out completely. He stopped to take a breath, looking back down the slope he'd just climbed. The route he'd taken meant that he couldn't see the ranger's outpost anymore, but he'd watched the chopper drop. Any minute now he'd see it rise again, Darcy safely inside it.

The pain of that thought was somehow worse than the agony in his arm.

The tin had shuffled up as he'd been climbing, and it threatened to spill from his pocket. He pulled it out and clung to it with his good arm. The wind whipped around him, threatening to pull it free, but nothing would make him loosen his grip. It wasn't for much longer. The place he needed to get to was just on the other side of a mound of rocks, maybe a hundred metres further up the mountain. The whole journey had felt like a lifetime, and now he'd be there in a matter of minutes.

"Hang on, Mum," he said. "Not long now. We're nearly there."

He set off again, stumbling and just managing to keep his balance. The snow came up to the middle of his shins, so thick that it was like wading through wet sand. He'd eaten one of the protein bars, but it was barely enough to power him, and what little energy he had was fast being leeched away by the cold. He'd overestimated how little his body had recuperated overnight, and now he was paying the price. At least the sun was up now, hovering over the peaks of the distant mountains and doing its best to warm him up.

Except, it wasn't just the weather making him feel cold.

Shuddering, he clambered over a pile of loose shale and up the final stretch of slope. Seven gruelling minutes later and he'd reached the mound of rocks. He put a hand to them and rested again, panting hard. This wasn't exactly how he'd intended to get here, to this moment. The original plan had been to fly to the ranger station and trek up the slope — something he would have found easy, if he hadn't been so exhausted and broken. It didn't matter, though. He was here — he'd kept his promise.

Taking a deep, steadying breath, he walked around the mound of rocks, each step deliberate, as though something significant was about to happen. His heart thudded in his chest, the weight of what he was about to do pressing down on him like snow on a mountain. He paused for a moment, letting cold air fill his lungs.

As he rounded the last curve, the view before him opened up, and all at once the world seemed to shift. A gasp escaped him, unbidden, as his eyes took in the sweeping expanse of the mountains stretching to the horizon. The jagged peaks, crowned in snow and bathed in early morning light, seemed to glow with ethereal beauty. Their sharp edges softened by the gentle rays of the sun.

Ahead of him lay the whole world. At least, it looked that way. Fifty yards from where he stood, the mountain dropped away into a snow-covered valley, gentle slopes rising on both sides of it. It stretched for miles, pockets of forest gleaming like emeralds, and a frozen lake that glittered sapphire bright in the fiery light of the rising sun. It was the most glorious thing he had ever seen, even more so than the last time he'd been here.

For a long moment, Devlin stood frozen in place, overcome by a feeling that he couldn't quite name. Awe, yes, but something deeper than that too. The wind, which had howled so fiercely through the night, now whispered softly around him. Carrying with it the scent of pine trees and snow, crisp and pure.

Devlin allowed himself to breathe for what felt like the first time in weeks — the first proper breath since his mum had passed away. He inhaled until his lungs felt like they might explode, and when he breathed it out, he finally felt at peace. Like he was stepping into a new life he didn't yet fully understand but was somehow ready to embrace. For so long he'd been trying to outrun his demons, and more recently, trying to bury his grief under layers of success, adventure and distraction. But here, in this vast and quiet place, there was no more running. There was only stillness and the truth laid bare before him.

The last time he'd been here was three years ago, but it felt like yesterday. It had been another APEX Club Ball, and he'd flown his mum out for it too. This was before she'd become sick. She was still a picture of health, with a youthful exuberance that belied her years. He'd just had a huge row with Claudia, and his mum had been the one to keep him sane, keep him laughing. To say thank you, he'd flown her onto the mountain and led her here just as the sun was rising.

He remembered how she'd fallen silent, how she'd just taken it all in. She must have known, by then, that she was ill. She hadn't said anything to him, of course, but she would have had her diagnosis. She'd taken his hand in hers and smiled.

"When you've seen something like this," she had said to him, "it makes you realise how lucky you are to just be alive."

Devlin had nodded, and they'd hugged, watching the sun rise until the cold drove them back to the helicopter. Years later, when his mum couldn't get out of bed, she'd asked him for one last favour.

"Take me back there," she had asked. "To the mountain, to that view. I've never felt so at peace as I did there with you that day. That's where I want my for ever to be, Devlin."

And so here he was, that same magnificent view ahead of him, his mum's ashes cradled in his arms like a newborn baby. He wiped his eyes on his sleeve, his teeth chattering so much he could barely speak.

"Here we are, Mum," he said. "Just like you wanted. I mean, you could have picked an easier place to get to, like the beach or something." He laughed softly. "But I did it. I got you here. Well, not just me, Darcy too. You know that already, right?"

He could almost see her smile, the sparkle in her eyes. She would have taken his hand, patting it.

You're a fool, Devlin, he heard her say. *Coming up here with me, when you should be down there with her.*

He twisted the lid of the tin, knowing his mum would have been right, but the cold had sealed it shut and his arm wasn't strong enough to fight it.

"Come on," he shouted. "Come on, open."

He tried again, but the pain was too much — the agony in his heart worse than that in his arm. The tin stayed stubbornly closed, and with every passing second, Devlin felt his strength ebb away. After all this, after everything he'd been through, he couldn't even say goodbye properly. He collapsed to the snow.

"I'm sorry," he said. And he knew he wasn't just apologising for this, he was apologising for everything — for his arrogance, for his bluntness. His mum had always known it was an act, but she'd always wanted him to be kinder, nicer. She'd wanted him to show the world the real Devlin. "I'm so sorry."

"Devlin?"

The voice that called his name was gentle and soft, and unmistakable. He didn't need to turn around to see who spoke it, but he did anyway. Darcy stood by the mound of rocks, dressed in full mountain gear. She smiled at him, tucking a strand of windswept hair into her hat as she stepped forward. He didn't deserve that smile. He wanted to tell her to leave him alone, ashamed of the fact he'd abandoned her in the cabin, but he was too tired to get the words out. He just sat there in the snow, holding the tin.

"Let me help you," Darcy said, crunching her way to him. She sat down beside him and rested her hand on top of his. "Nobody should be alone at a moment like this. Nobody."

"But I need to be," he croaked. Darcy shook her head.

"You don't," she said. "There is no reason you need to be on your own to do this. Let me help you."

Her hand seemed to channel heat into his body, her smile warmer than the sun. He nodded, handing her the metal urn.

"I can't get it open with just one hand," he said.

She twisted and the lid came free.

"Here," she said, standing up and offering her free hand. He took it and she helped him to his feet. Together, hand in hand, they walked to the edge of the cliff. Darcy handed him the urn and he clutched it.

"She loved this place more than anything," he whispered.

"Have you ever thought that she loved this place because it reminded her of you," Darcy replied, and he smiled at her.

That was something he had never considered, but now Darcy had said it, he thought it was probably the truth. He nudged Darcy gently with his shoulder.

"Thank you," he said, then turned to the urn. "And thank you, Mum. Thank you for everything you did for me and all the ways you showed me love."

He tipped up the tin and the ashes drifted out. The wind caught them, gently lifting them away. Devlin watched them go until he could no longer see them, then he took another deep, wonderful breath. It was as if he had been carrying a mountain on his shoulders for weeks, and had only just slipped out from beneath it.

It was time to stop clinging to the past and start looking towards a future he had never allowed himself to believe was possible. A future where he didn't have to carry the weight of the world alone.

He turned to Darcy, who took his hands in hers and smiled at him in a way that made him feel perfectly warm, and perfectly happy.

"You always know how to make me feel better," he said.

"It's because . . ." Darcy paused, looking away for a moment. He saw her take a breath — the same deep, magical, mountain-aired breath he'd just taken himself — then she turned back to him. "It's because I think I love you, Devlin Storm. I don't know how it happened, but it did, and there's nothing I can do about it."

As if the mountains themselves had heard her, the sun caught the lake, making it shimmer. For a second, Devlin thought of his mum. She was here, he was sure of it, and proud of him for finally letting go.

"Let's go home," Darcy said, softly.

He nodded, and they walked away together, side by side. It was only when they had rounded the mound of rocks that Devlin stopped. Without a word, he turned to Darcy and pulled her close, kissing her warm lips with his cold ones.

When he pulled back, he grinned, his heart full. "You are the bravest person I have ever met. And I think I love you, too, Darcy Wainwright."

CHAPTER 29

DARCY

Darcy may as well have been carried down that last stretch of slope by the wind. She felt weightless, as if she was a flurry of snow. Only Devlin's hand in hers kept her grounded. He needed her as much as she needed him — more, maybe.

"Just think," she said, "if I hadn't been on reception that day you demanded your helicopter, you might be walking down this mountain hand in hand with Clive, the guy who does my off shifts."

Devlin laughed and doubled up, wincing.

"Please don't be funny," he said. "My body is broken and laughing hurts."

Darcy zipped her fingers across her mouth, but a few seconds later she had forgotten. Being with Devlin was a new high.

"Actually, you'd probably both be at the bottom of the hill in the helicopter wreckage. There's no way you'd have thrown your body over Clive to keep him safe. Butterfly wings and hurricanes and all."

"I was going for the controls," Devlin said, grinning. "Just the controls. Not at all distracted by the gorgeous woman who had talked my ear off the whole flight because she was so nervous."

"I tend to do that," said Darcy, treading carefully as they rounded the mound of rocks. "You'll have to get used to my noise."

"Good, because I tend to like it," Devlin replied. "It felt quiet when you were sleeping."

They walked in silence for a beat, neither of them saying it, but both of them thinking.

"So, elephant in the mountain," Darcy was the first to break. "Why didn't you wake me up?"

Devlin dropped his chin, blowing out air between his teeth.

"Mainly, because I'm an idiot," he said, squeezing Darcy's gloved hand in his. "But also because I thought I needed to do that alone. You know, the whole *Devlin is a mountain* thing."

"Well, do that again and I'll push you *off* the mountain," Darcy joked. The rangers came into view as they got halfway back to the outpost.

"Oh, no," Devlin said. "They're going to be so mad at me."

"Yeah," Darcy agreed. "But I explained what I thought you were doing, and they seemed less likely to leave when they heard. Besides, look at you. They'll be able to see by the exhaustion on your face just how much you have been through. Let's go and find out."

Darcy reluctantly let go of him so that the man could take Devlin's good arm. Together, both rangers helped Devlin down to the helicopter. Its rotors spun lazily, a third ranger sitting in the pilot's seat and giving them a thumbs up. The two rangers walked Devlin to the steps, but he shook his head and looked back at Darcy.

"Ladies first," he said, and she smiled. She hesitated for a moment, looking at the outpost and thinking once again about the amazing time they'd shared inside it. She wondered if they would ever be back. And if they were, if they could arrive in style as well as leaving in style.

"Thank you," she said, walking up the steps and sitting down on one of the seats. Devlin followed her, then one of the rangers strapped them both in before taking a seat opposite.

"We'll be back at base camp in twenty minutes," the woman said. "But I want to check you both over on the way, if that's okay?"

Darcy nodded, sitting back. She felt a sudden rush of nerves as the helicopter wobbled up from the landing pad, but soon they were high above the slopes and riding smoothly back down the mountain. It felt like a lifetime ago that she and Devlin had taken off from the resort and headed into the storm, and in many ways it was a lifetime, because so much had changed. She felt like a new person, and for the first time in a long time the future looked bright.

She turned to share a smile with Devlin, to reach out and hold his hand. But the day had already been too much for him. His eyes were closed, his chest gently rising and falling as he gave in to sleep.

Despite the terror of flying in a helicopter again, Darcy was almost asleep, too, by the time they dropped into the ranger station at the base of the mountain. When the helicopter rocked still, and the mind-numbing throb of the rotors began to fade, Darcy took a deep breath of relief.

Thank you, she thought.

"That was some adventure," said the male ranger, his eyes twinkling. "We'll have you back to normal in no time. How are you feeling?"

Darcy glanced at Devlin, who was still fast asleep.

"I'm good," she said. "Thanks to him. Is he okay?"

"The arm is broken," replied the female ranger, who was sitting beside him. "Badly, I think. He's also got some severe contusions, and he's suffering the effects of hypothermia. I gave him a sedative to help him relax and heal, but it'll take time."

"He had it worse than me," admitted Darcy, thinking about the crash, and the crevasse. "He gave me his coat."

"Devlin Storm gave up his coat?" the woman said. "Now that's a headline for you."

Darcy opened her mouth to argue, but she was too tired, and the rangers had risked a lot coming to rescue them. Anyway, if Darcy had heard the same thing four days ago, she would have been surprised too. Most people would have expected Devlin to put himself before anyone else. She really couldn't wait until he was awake and they got to share their story. The world would see how much he had changed, and actually what a good man he really was.

"I'll take you down to the infirmary while we wait for Mr Storm's stretcher," said the man.

"That's okay, I can wait," Darcy argued, looking again at Devlin. "We can go together."

"That's impossible," said the woman.

"What?" asked Darcy. "Why?"

"We've been given our orders," she explained. "Devlin's insurance policy states that he is to be taken to a private clinic for treatment."

"But . . ." Darcy started, shaking her head. "Orders from who? That's not right, we should stay together. I'll go with him. I can walk, so I don't need a stretcher."

"If you've got a spare 5,000 euro a night in the pocket of your coat, I'll gladly take you," said the woman. "It's not right, but it's the way it is. We have the papers, and somebody has already signed for his care."

"What do you mean? Who has signed for his care?" Darcy asked, but nobody was listening to her anymore, they were too busy fussing over Devlin.

She wondered if she should wake him. He would surely stick up for her, ask them to bring her as well. Wouldn't he? But she didn't have the heart to disturb him. He looked so peaceful, and so tranquil, and besides, she'd be fighting against the results of a sedative and didn't fancy her chances.

"Come on, miss," said the male ranger, offering her his hand. "Are you sure you don't need a stretcher?"

"No," Darcy said. "I can walk. What's the name of the clinic? Can you at least tell me that?"

The female ranger shook her head.

"Sorry," she muttered.

The male ranger was steering her towards the open door of the helicopter and she followed him, numb with uncertainty. After everything she'd been through in the last few days, this felt like the most painful experience to date.

"Watch your head," said the man, even though the spinning rotors were far above her. She ducked, walking swiftly off the landing pad. It wasn't exactly tropical down here, but it was so much warmer than the mountain face. The ranger led her towards a large, two-floor building that was surprisingly busy. A group of people who could only be journalists stood outside the main door, a security guard holding them back. Even from here Darcy could hear them clamouring at her, looking for a story. She ignored them, turning back to the helicopter.

"Will they tell Devlin where I am?" she said. "When he wakes up?"

The ranger shrugged.

"Do you really want them to?" he asked, brow raised.

Darcy glared at him.

"Of course I do," she said. "He might be worried about me."

"Sure," said the ranger. "Devlin Storm, the guy who only worries about himself."

He laughed, walking towards the building. Darcy waited for the helicopter to take off, but it stayed where it was, the rotors spinning.

Please let him wake up, she said. *Please let him run after me, pick me up, hold me tight.*

But there was no sign of Devlin. She turned, following the ranger to the base station. There might be somebody she could talk to inside, somebody who could give her more information.

"Miss Wainwright!" yelled one of the reporters as she passed them. "How are you doing? How did it feel to almost die?"

"Darcy!" called another. "How is Devlin? Is he seriously ill?"

"How was it being locked in a cabin with Mr. Storm?" shouted a third. "Most women would pay for that kind of experience!"

The reporters laughed, and Darcy felt her blood boil. She ignored them, walking through a door into the building. A medical team was waiting for her there, complete with a stretcher. A doctor stepped forward, smoothing back his slick, black hair.

"Miss Wainwright," he said in a strong accent. "We're here to take you to the hospital. After an experience like the one you have just had, you will most certainly need a check-up and medical care."

She didn't need medical care, she needed Devlin.

"Look, I . . ."

She stopped speaking when she heard a surge of excited shouts from outside. For a wonderful moment she thought it was Devlin, stepping out of the helicopter so that he could embrace her. But when she turned to the big glass door she saw that a sleek, black limousine had pulled up alongside the helicopter.

"Miss Wainwright, please," said the doctor, but Darcy ignored him.

Somebody was climbing out of the car, a stunning blonde wearing a fur coat and sunglasses. The helicopter door opened and she walked up the steps and climbed inside. Moments later, it lifted off the landing pad and soared into the perfect blue sky. The reporters were still calling out the woman's name, as if they expected her to answer from up in the air. Darcy didn't need them to tell her who it was, though. She didn't need anyone to tell her who had climbed into the helicopter beside Devlin. She had recognised the woman instantly.

It was Claudia Romano.

CHAPTER 30

DEVLIN

For a moment, when Devlin opened his eyes, he thought he was back in the snow. It was freezing, and his teeth were still chattering. The room around him was dark, the soft glow of early morning creeping in through the windows, but his mind was foggy, disorientated. He rubbed his eyes, trying to piece together the events of the last few days.

Slowly, the memories came rushing back. He remembered the crash — the chaos, the biting cold, and the sheer panic that had followed. He remembered finding the research cabin, the desperate trek through the mountains, the ravine that had nearly swallowed him whole. But more than anything, he remembered the outpost, the quiet sanctuary where he'd found shelter from more than just the storm.

He remembered Darcy.

The night he'd spent with her was still vivid in his mind. The warmth of her body, the way she made him feel. They way she'd ignored his stupid note and helped him to spread his mum's ashes. He'd only had the strength to do it because of Darcy. She'd been there for him, as steadfast as the mountain they stood on. If it hadn't been for her, the experience would have broken him.

Then what, though? He dug into his cloudy memories, seeing the walk back down the slope, then the chopper ride, the relief of being rescued, and the joy of flying home with Darcy. He must have fallen asleep, or maybe even passed out.

He sat up, squinting into the sleepy darkness of a small room. The blinds were drawn, although beads of warm light squeezed through and pooled on the floor. There were machines everywhere, bleeping softly, and through a half-open door he could hear the unmistakable sounds of a hospital.

"Finally," said a voice from the far corner of the room. Devlin peered into the shadows to see a woman there, nothing more than a silhouette. He broke into a smile without even realising it.

"Darcy," he said. "You're okay, thank goodness."

"Darcy?" the woman said, and as he recognised the Italian accent, his temperature dropped back to dangerous levels.

The woman sashayed to the bed, the light falling on her face. Claudia was as superficially perfect as ever. Devlin shook his head.

"What are you doing here?" he asked.

Claudia pouted as she perched on the side of the bed. She laid her manicured fingers on his hand and he pulled it away, gasping as the pain burned out from his broken arm. He looked down and saw it was plastered from his wrist to his shoulder.

"Careful, dear," she said, reaching for him again, more insistently this time. "You don't want to make it worse."

"Claudia," Devlin hissed, his voice as cold and hard as steel. "I asked you a question. What are you doing here?"

"Is that any way to talk to your beloved?" she asked, planting a kiss on his cheek, her lips leaving an icy imprint.

"My *what*?" Devlin snorted. "You have to be kidding, right?"

He looked past her to the door, wishing that a doctor would come in. He opened his mouth to call for security, but

Claudia leaned in and placed a finger on his lips. He shook her away.

"You're being unfair," she said, fluttering her lashes, her eyes huge. "I saw the news, and I was worried about you. As soon as I heard you were missing in the Alps, I flew here to join the search. That's a lot for me to do, Devlin. I was working on a luxury shoot, which I had to drop to look for you."

Devlin found that hard to believe. Claudia had never had to look for anything in her life. Born to a wealthy Italian banking family, if she'd ever lost something she'd just bought another one. It's what she had done to Devlin, too. The moment they had broken up, she'd found herself another billionaire. So why was she here, sitting on his hospital bed as though she belonged there?

"Claudia, we're not together," he said, but she batted away his suggestion.

"Let's not argue about little details," she purred, stroking his cheek. "My *petite amour*. I hated the thought of you being out there alone."

"I wasn't alone," Devlin growled. Claudia's expression hardened.

"So I heard," she said. "You were out there with some secretary. Some poor, frumpy nobody. I can't imagine what that must have been like, stuck in a cabin with her. No wonder they had to sedate you."

Devlin's anger roared like an engine.

"She's not a nobody. Her name is Darcy, and she saved my life."

Claudia smiled. Her fingers tightly gripping his as Devlin struggled up in bed, still shivering.

"I have no idea what you want with me. Another story to sell?" he growled. "Well whatever it is, you can't have it. I told you I never wanted to see you again. Now leave."

"Poor Devlin," she said, putting a hand to his forehead. "The doctors tell me you have a fever. You aren't thinking straight." She leaned in, that cold smile still on her face.

"The truth is, I'm bored. Hunter and I didn't work out. And because I left that shoot, I'm out of work, too, which is your fault may I add. I need us to be back together. And what better chance for you to declare your love for me again than now, when you're front-page news."

"What are you talking about?" demanded Devlin. "That will never, ever happen, Claudia."

"Oh, come now," Claudia kidded. "We had fun, didn't we?"

There was a gentle knock at the door and it swung open to reveal an older man in a doctor's coat, his grey-blond hair tied back in a long ponytail.

"Good morning," he said, flicking on the light. "Nice to see you're awake, Mr Storm. How are you feeling?"

Claudia stood up, flashing another smile at Devlin.

"The poor man is burning up," she said. "I really should let him rest. *Ciao*, my beloved. I will see you soon."

She nodded to the doctor and left the room. It was only when she'd gone that Devlin remembered to breathe. The brief exchange with Claudia had left him even more shaken than the last three days in the wilderness. He felt his heart thrashing in his chest. What was she playing at? He'd always known she was an opportunist, and a predator, too, but this was low even for her.

"Let's check that fever," said the doctor, prodding a thermometer into Devlin's ear and waiting for it to beep before removing it. "Good, good. Your temperature is within the normal range — looks like you're on the mend. How's the arm?"

Devlin looked at the cast covering his arm. It still ached, but there must have been some heavy-duty painkillers in his system because everything felt a little fuzzy.

"It was broken in two places," the doctor said. "It's a good job you had the sense to splint it and then strap it up, otherwise it never would have healed. You could have lost it, Mr Storm. You're a lucky man."

"It wasn't my idea to splint it," he said. "It was Darcy's. Do you know where she is? Darcy Wainwright?"

"The young woman you were stranded with?" the doctor asked. "I'm afraid I don't know. She was never brought here. I think she was taken to the local hospital for treatment."

"What? No, that's not right," Devlin said. "I would have paid her fees. She should have been brought here with me."

"We had no way of running that by you, Mr Storm," the doctor said. "I'm sorry, but we have to follow protocol and the paperwork wasn't signed."

Devlin cursed himself for passing out in the helicopter. How could he have been so stupid? Now Darcy was in a different hospital, in a different town. What on earth would she think of him? He glanced at his watch, which sat on the bedside table. It was almost noon — he'd been out for hours. He lifted his sheet and sat up, ready to climb out of bed, but the doctor held up his hand.

"Please, Mr Storm," he said. "Just give yourself some time. Your body has been through a gruelling experience, and you need to rest."

"I need to find Darcy," he argued, feeling his head lighten at the shift in movement. "Where is she? Which hospital?"

"Please sit back, Mr Storm," said the doctor. "I'll find out where Miss Wainwright is and let you know. You should have asked your fiancé before she left."

"My *fiancé*?" Devlin asked, bursting into a humourless laugh. "Not even close. She's my ex-girlfriend. *Very* ex. Why would she know?"

"Because she's the one who refused to sign the paperwork allowing Miss Wainwright to accompany you for medical treatment," the doctor said. "She said that you wouldn't have wanted her here."

Devlin's fury was volcanic. He wanted to rage from the rooftops, but his spinning head was stopping him. Besides, the poor doctor didn't deserve it, though he must have seen it in Devlin's eyes because he took a step back.

"Please don't worry, all Swiss hospitals are world class. She will be in good hands." The doctor looked stoic.

"Just find out where she is," Devlin said, his voice low and powerful. "And get me a phone. Please."

"Mr Storm, you need to rest," the doctor urged again.

"I don't need to rest," he said. "I need to know that she's okay. I need her to know I'm okay. It's been over five hours — she'll be worried sick."

The doctor sighed, looking at the floor.

"What?" asked Devlin.

"It hasn't been five hours," he said. "You were badly injured, you had hypothermia, you were suffering from extreme exhaustion and a fever. I'm not sure you realise just how ill you are."

"How long?" Devlin asked, leaning forward in the bed. "How long has it been?"

"I'm sorry," the doctor replied, looking up at Devlin. "You've been out for two whole days."

CHAPTER 31

DARCY

"Anything?"

Darcy looked over at Penny, whose nose was practically pushed up against her computer monitor. The lobby of the Royal Alpine was eerily quiet, its usual energy sapped after the ball. Most of the guests had flown out, their luxurious stays cut short after the excitement had died down.

According to Penny, half a dozen of them had stayed on to join the search for Devlin and Darcy — including Blake Fielding and Jackson Brodie — but even they had now departed since they had been found safe and well. The lobby, usually bustling with guests in chic winter gear, felt like a hollow shell, echoing with a silence that was pressing on Darcy from all angles, not least her phone which she was checking every few minutes for a message from Devlin. He might not have taken her number, but he was Devlin Storm and if he wanted it, he could have found it.

The whole resort was oddly quiet, so quiet that manager Abigail Lamb had told Darcy not to come back for a day or two. But the truth was that the silence at home was even worse, so she'd dragged herself to work that morning, hoping for a semblance of normalcy.

"Nothing," Penny said, flatly. "Just the same official message from Claudia Romano."

"I don't believe it," said Darcy, feeling her heart freeze over again. "I don't understand."

The last forty-eight hours had been nothing short of a nightmare — worse than crashing in the mountains. Way worse. After being flown to the base camp, Darcy had been transported by ambulance to the nearest hospital. It had all been a blur — the white lights overhead, the cool, efficiency of the doctors and nurses as they had poked and prodded her. Their conclusion had been a relief, pronouncing her surprisingly healthy if a little dehydrated. They'd kept her in for that first night anyway, just to be sure. Sleep had been elusive, and the sterile smell of the ward had done nothing to soothe her nerves. All she wanted to know was where Devlin was and how he was doing. But when she'd asked the hospital staff to contact the clinic where he was being treated, they had refused. She'd pleaded with them, begged them, but to no avail. Celebrity privacy was taken very seriously here, it would seem.

No matter how much she told them Devlin wouldn't mind, they still refused. And the longer the silence went on, the more Darcy wondered if Devlin would, in fact, mind.

The drive back to her apartment had felt endless as she clung to the hope that there would be something waiting for her when she got there. A message, a phone call, something to let her know if he was alive or not. But there was nothing. It felt worse than anything she'd ever endured, worse than the days when she'd nearly died in the helicopter crash and then endured in the freezing cold snow.

At least, that's what she had thought until she'd flicked on the TV.

The image on the screen had hit her like a sledgehammer to the chest. The leading story on every channel had been that billionaire Devlin Storm was alive and well. There was footage of the helicopter landing at the private clinic, Devlin being wheeled out on a stretcher looking pale but very much alive. There had been a brief, dismissive mention of Darcy — the 'unnamed woman' who had been with Devlin was also 'believed to be well'. No name, no recognition of what they'd been through together. Just a footnote to the story of Devlin Storm, billionaire survivor.

But the real devastation had come moments later when Claudia Romano appeared on the screen. Darcy had sat on the floor, cross-legged like a child, in front of the little television and watched with growing horror as the beautiful, icy, blonde woman spoke to the reporters with such grace and poise. Her words like daggers to Darcy's heart.

"Thank you for being here," Claudia had said, her voice smooth and practised as if she'd delivered these lines a thousand times. "Thank you for caring. Devlin has been through a truly terrifying experience, and the doctors say he hasn't fully regained consciousness. Being out there, alone, I just can't imagine what it must have been like. I've flown in especially from a shoot in Tuscany, and I plan to be here by Devlin's side until he fully recovers."

Darcy had felt the blood drain from her face as the woman had paused, flicking back her hair and looking right at the camera.

"In fact," she had added. "I plan on never leaving his side again. Devlin is the love of my life. I just had to almost lose him for ever before I truly realised it."

The reporters had swarmed Claudia with questions, but she hadn't faltered. With the ease of a runway model, she had turned on her heels and strode away, disappearing into the clinic, and leaving Darcy shattered in front of the television. The tears had come then, hot and heavy as she tried to reconcile the man she had been in the snow with to the man Claudia had spoken about.

"Are you sure you don't want to get out of here," said Penny, bringing Darcy back to the moment. "I've got this under control. Why don't you go and relax? Maybe Abigail will let you use the spa."

Darcy shook her head. "I don't want to be on my own." The words came out in just a whisper, a confession she hadn't meant to make, but it had just slipped out.

"Maybe she'll let us both use it," Penny replied with a laugh. Darcy's face fell even further and Penny reached over, putting a gentle hand on her arm. "Look, I don't know what happened out there. I can't even begin to imagine how hard it's been — it must have been terrible — and I don't know what Devlin was like, what he was *really* like, but you've got to remember who he is. He's Devlin Storm, Darcy. He's famous. And he's with *her*." She nodded to a picture of Claudia on her monitor. "I hate to say it, but three days freezing your behinds off together in the snow isn't going to put you in the same league. I'm sorry, that's horrible, but it's true."

And the worst thing was, Darcy knew it was true. It wasn't a fairy tale. It wasn't some grand romance where the billionaire fell for the ordinary girl. Yet, she couldn't shake the memory of their time together. She couldn't erase Devlin's words from out of her head.

I think I love you, too, Darcy.

He'd been so sincere when he'd said it, she just couldn't accept that he didn't mean it. There had been a vulnerability in his eyes, a rare softness that she was still clinging to. But the doubts were creeping in. What if it had been a lie? What if it had all been a lie, an empty promise, a fleeting sentiment to get him through scattering his mum's ashes after the trauma they'd already suffered together?

And then there was Claudia — stunningly beautiful, sophisticated Claudia Romano. Everything Devlin had told Darcy about her, how cold and detached she was, how their relationship turned into a facade the moment she sold their story — were those lies too? Could he have been playing her? Was she a diversion, a distraction from the reality of life? Or was Devlin just attracted to that kind of woman? Maybe everything he'd said to her, everything he'd done, was an act. Maybe the arrogant, devilish Devlin, the ones the tabloids adored, who charmed and discarded women like toys, was the real one after all.

No. She wouldn't believe it. She just wouldn't.

"Just go stretch your legs," Penny said. "Get some air. No point sitting here pining over him. You'll drive yourself crazy."

Darcy nodded, pushing herself to her feet. This whole thing was torture. She left the reception desk and crossed the lobby, seeing the reporters clustered outside. Abigail had strictly forbidden her from speaking with the press, saying that it would be a direct violation of the resort's privacy policy. But what would she say anyway? She didn't have answers to her own questions, let alone theirs.

She turned around and headed for the staff door instead.

"Darcy!" Penny called her name.

"What?" Darcy asked, turning back.

"It's just been announced," Penny said, cautiously. "He's awake."

Darcy felt her world tilt, her pulse thudding in her ears as she ran and stood behind Penny, looking at the screen. It was true, Devlin had woken up a short while ago and was doing fine. Darcy let out a breath in a hard stutter, bracing herself on the back of Penny's chair so that she didn't fall over. So that was the reason he hadn't been in touch — he simply hadn't been able to. The relief was like stepping into a warm bath after a cold day. Any moment now Devlin would call her. He'd tell her how he felt, and everything would be fine.

"Thank goodness," she said.

Penny was scrolling down the article, but Darcy didn't care what it said. At least, she *thought* she didn't, but then something caught her eye at the bottom of the page that made her stomach lurch.

"Wait, what did that say?" she asked, her voice tight.

Penny scrolled back to the section, her face paling.

"Devlin has announced that he will be holding a press conference shortly after one," Penny read. "Alongside his girlfriend, Claudia."

"No," said Darcy, her voice just a breath.

But how could she deny it? Beneath the text was a photograph, snapped through the hospital window that very morning, of Devlin and Claudia, their hands tightly clenched.

CHAPTER 32

DEVLIN

"Don't do that again," Devlin growled, his voice a dangerous, low rumble.

Claudia merely laughed, the sound of it cold and brittle like cracking ice. She reached for his hand again, a gesture meant for the camera, but he yanked it back, fury rising in him like a wave. They were standing in the corridor outside his room, next to a bank of huge windows that let in the morning light and the nosy lens of a reporter.

The clinic was ridiculously expensive, and one reason for that was it was supposed to be completely private and completely secure. But Devlin had already spotted at least three people — including a staff member — taking photographs of him through the windows. One of those photos had been snapped just as Claudia had grabbed his hand, and he knew it wouldn't be long before it hit the news outlets and the rumours would explode.

"Oh, Devlin, do stop being such a child," said Claudia, barely sparing him a glace as she examined her nails. "Did you leave your spine out there in the mountains?"

The hatred he felt for her was immense, like a dark storm brewing out on the horizon. It wasn't just a flash of anger, it was something that had been building in him for a while now. Fuelled by her cruelty and manipulation, by her relentless need for fame and to control his narrative. But she refused to leave, and the clinic was reluctant to throw her out — too intimidated by her status. Claudia Romano was a big name and no one wanted the bad press that came with crossing her, especially when she was still listed as next of kin on his paperwork.

All Devlin wanted to do was get out of here and find Darcy, but there were hurdles at every turn. His release papers weren't signed and his clothes were nowhere to be seen. If they didn't hurry, then he was going to walk out of the door in his hospital pyjamas. Let the press take photos of *that*.

At least his fever had broken, the haze of illness lifting now that he was awake. His body still ached all over — his arm especially — but there was a newfound energy thrumming through him. A sharp clarity that hadn't been there before. He felt as good as new. He felt better than new, because he felt like a different person entirely. Something fundamental had shifted in him during his time on the mountains. He could feel it in his bones and he was pretty sure it wasn't just the morphine.

He walked back into his room, pacing like a tiger locked in a cage. Claudia followed him.

"I'm not going to tell you again," he said. "I want you to leave."

But Claudia just smiled a smile that didn't reach her eyes. It was the smile of someone who knew they held all the cards and it made his skin crawl.

"And I've told you, that's not going to happen," she said. "I've scheduled a press conference for an hour from now — your suit is on its way from the resort. You're going to sit in front of the world's media and tell them that we are back together."

"Why on earth would I do that?" he said, shaking his head at the absurdity of her demand. "You're out of your mind if you think I'd ever want to be back with you."

"You have to do it," she said, walking up to him and running a hand through his hair. "Or I'll tell the world who the real Devlin Storm is."

Devlin shook his head. Her words gave him pause.

"What do you mean?" he said.

"I mean, I'll tell them exactly what you're like," she went on, smiling. "All the ways you manipulated me. How you controlled me. And, of course, they'll believe me. I was young, vulnerable, hopelessly in love with you. And you're . . . well, you." She let out a soft laugh, tilting her head. "By the time your lawyers scramble to deny it, the damage will have been done. You won't just lose your reputation, you'll lose everything."

"That's a lie," Devlin roared, his hands clenched into fists at his sides. "Even for you, that's just pathetic."

"Of course it's a lie." Claudia shot back. "I'm asking for one tiny favour. That's all. Pretend we're together. That way I get back in front of the camera. But you won't do it because of this secretary you kept mumbling about when you were drugged. I won't lose my lifestyle because you've lowered your standards. One word from me and your reputation is in tatters. Everyone will see just how much of a fake you really are, and Devlin, no one buys a fake."

Devlin felt as if he'd been drenched in ice-cold water. She was right. If the world believed Claudia's lies, then it was over. Everything. Everyone loved the image of the famous arrogant designer who had his life together. But if he didn't do this for her, then it wasn't just his reputation on the line, it was his entire life. His business employed thousands of people who depended on him. Could he risk all that just to save his reputation?

He knew the answer, and though he hated himself for it, he nodded at Claudia. His image, his brand, it was too big, too important for too many people.

Devlin shut off his emotions the way he'd always done, regarding Claudia with a hard, blank stare.

"There he is," Claudia said, smiling. "My Devlin. Welcome home. Now wait here while I check on your suit."

CHAPTER 33

DARCY

The fresh air wasn't helping. If anything it was making her chest tighter.

Darcy paced back and forth in the open stretch of ground between the main building and the hangar. She barely noticed the frozen landscape around her, the mountains looming in the distance like silent sentinels. The thick snow crunched beneath her boots, and her angry breaths came out as little clouds that floated up, escaping towards the blue sky. But Darcy wasn't so lucky. She was trapped here. Trapped with her thoughts, her heart tangled into knots she couldn't untie.

She wished she could follow her breath into the mountains, far away from this place and what was happening in front of her eyes. She wished she could be back up there with Devlin, in that strange, isolated world they had shared for a few brief moments. She could feel it now. Cuddling in front of a log fire, or on the sofa, his arm around her. The memory of his touch, his lips against hers, his hands on her skin sent a wave of heat through her, even now. Even when she knew it was all gone.

Because the truth was, Darcy would never be that close to Devlin again. She would never snuggle up with him on a sofa, or play cards, pretending the rest of the world didn't exist. She would never again get the chance to feel his lips on hers, to drown in the heat of his embrace. The grief of it, the finality of it, was a weight she couldn't bear. It was so intense, so all-consuming, that it made her physically ill. Her stomach churned with the pain of losing him, and her heart felt like it was breaking into pieces.

Maybe Abigail had been right — maybe she shouldn't be back at work yet. It was impossible to keep her mind on anything other than Devlin. She sighed heavily with the weight of the decision. Maybe it was time to go home and admit she wasn't ready to be back yet. Darcy made her way around the side of the building, deciding she would tell Abigail she needed the rest of the day off.

As she was rounding the building, she saw another member of staff walking swiftly along the path that led to the exclusive villas. The young woman was holding an armful of bags, and she was obviously struggling. Darcy ran over, trying not to slip on the icy ground.

"Hey, do you need a hand?" she called out, her breath puffing.

The woman turned, her face a mixture of relief and exhaustion. She nodded gratefully, shifting the bags in her arms.

"That would be amazing, thank you," she said, lifting a heavy-looking bag from the pile.

As Darcy caught up to her she handed over the travel bag and a suit in a carry case. The smell that came from them was divine, and Darcy felt her heart do a loop-the-loop as she breathed it in.

She knew that scent. It was him. For a moment she almost convinced herself he was nearby. It was a ridiculous thought, but it sent a surge of emotion through her all the same.

"These are Devlin Storm's," said Darcy, trying not to be too obvious when she leaned her head forward and breathed in the scent.

The young woman looked at her surprised.

"How do you know?" the girl asked, eyebrows raised.

"Oh, uh, I recognised the suit bag," she lied. "Where are you taking them?"

The girl glanced around nervously, as if she wasn't supposed to be talking to anyone.

"I'm not supposed to tell anyone about it," she whispered, looking around nervously.

Darcy's heart sank a little. These bags were heading to Devlin and she wanted to go too.

"It's okay," said Darcy. "I work here. I'm just off to see Abigail now."

"I know," said the girl. "I recognise you. How was it, being up there with *him*? Is he as awful as everyone says?"

"He was..." Darcy hesitated. She wasn't sure how much to say, but she wanted to defend him and tell the truth about the man on the mountain. But it wasn't her story to tell. "He was fine. Are you taking these to the clinic?"

"Yeah," the girl said quietly as they reached the front of the building. Parked at the entrance was a sleek Royal Alpine Resort sedan, its engine idling. The girl glanced at the car. "He requested his things. I think he's got some kind of press conference happening soon. Abigail asked me to take these up to him myself, to make sure they arrived safely. There's a driver waiting."

Darcy stopped walking, her mind racing. This was her chance. She could go to him, explain everything, talk to him away from the media circus that was surely already surrounding him. She couldn't let this opportunity slip away. Her heart pounded in her chest as she turned to the girl, a plan forming in her mind.

"Listen," Darcy stopped, taking the woman's arm until she stopped walking. "What's your name?"

"Sophia," said the girl. Darcy leaned into her.

"Listen, Sophia, can I ask you a huge favour?"

The girl shook her head, her eyes wide and uncertain.

"What kind of favour?"

"Let me take Devlin's things," said Darcy. "Let me go instead of you."

"No way," she argued. "I'd get in so much trouble."

"One hundred thousand," Darcy said, the words out of her mouth before she even had time to think about them. "I'll give you one hundred thousand pounds if you let me go instead."

Sophia's mouth fell open.

"Seriously?"

"Yes," Darcy said. "I promise. We can shake on it."

Sophia looked around, clearly torn. She hesitated, biting her lip as she considered Darcy's offer. Finally, after what felt like an eternity, she nodded.

"All right," she said. "But you'd better not get me in trouble for this."

Darcy breathed a sigh of relief. "I won't. I promise. Thank you. Thank you. Here, I'll help you to the car."

They walked to the road together, the driver clambering out and opening the boot for them. Carefully, they laid Devlin's clothes inside and the driver closed the boot, opening the back door. Sophia held out her hand and Darcy shook it.

"Thank you," said Darcy, climbing inside. "I won't forget this."

"You'd better not," replied Sophia. "And good luck. If he's worth this much money, then he must mean the world to you."

"He does," said Darcy as the car pulled away. "He means everything."

CHAPTER 34

DEVLIN

What am I going to do?

Devlin rested his head against the wall, his forehead pressed against the cool surface as he tried to calm the swirling blizzard of thoughts that whirled around his mind. The press conference was in twenty minutes. Twenty minutes until he would be expected to sit in front of the world's media, smile for the cameras, and pretend like everything was fine. But it wasn't. Everything was falling apart, and he had no idea what he was going to say when the cameras started rolling. Claudia would stay true to her word, he had no doubt about that. If he didn't play along with her twisted plan, then she would hijack the entire conference and make it all about her. She would lie to the world and in doing so, she would ruin everything.

Devlin could already picture it: Claudia, with her flawless smile and icy demeanour, standing at the podium, weaving a tale of betrayal and lies, exposing him for the man he had always feared people would see — a fraud. His reputation would be destroyed, his business would crumble, and everything he had built over the years would be reduced to ashes.

The weight of it was suffocating.

Devlin had nobody to talk to. His mum was gone, he had no brothers and sisters. That was the trouble with retreating from life, he knew. That was the trouble with being a loner. Sure, there was nobody who could hurt you, but there was nobody who could help you either. And as much as Devlin hated being helped, he could really use some now.

But the only person who could help him was miles away, with no idea where he was.

Darcy.

With a grunt of frustration, he pushed himself off the wall and left the room. Claudia was nowhere to be seen, thankfully, and he made his way down the corridor towards the clinic's large, open lobby. His doctor was there, speaking with a nurse, and he smiled at Devlin as he saw him approach.

"Mr Storm," he said. "You're recovering faster than I expected. It's remarkable."

"Please, I need a phone," Devlin said, ignoring him. He didn't have time for small talk.

The doctor blinked, taken aback for a split second with the sudden request.

"Of course, if you'll follow me." He nodded.

The doctor led Devlin to the reception desk, and the receptionist politely vacated her chair. Devlin sat down and picked up the receiver, using the computer to Google the number of the Royal Alpine. After a couple of rings, a young woman answered.

"Hello, the Royal Alpine. How may I help you?"

"I need to speak to Darcy Wainwright," Devlin said.

"I'm sorry," said the girl. "She's not here. She left a little while ago. Can I take a message?"

She left? His chest tightened, a wave of panic crashing over him.

"No."

Devlin hung up the phone. He thought about trying to find out Darcy's mobile number, but there was no time.

Anyway, the chances were she wouldn't answer his call. He knew that photos of him and Claudia were splashed all over the news, and Claudia had told him they were trending on social media again. Darcy would have seen it all by now. She would have assumed he'd betrayed her, that he was back with his ex, and in twenty minutes or so it would be confirmed at the press conference. How else could she take it?

The thought of it was unbearable. It tore at his heart in a way he hadn't expected. He had been prepared to live with regret, to carry the burden of the decisions he had made to protect his business, but he hadn't been prepared for this. He hadn't been prepared for the idea of losing Darcy. The truth was, he needed her more than he had ever needed anyone. She had been his lifeline in the mountains, not just physically but emotionally. She had seen him at his most vulnerable, and she hadn't turned away.

But now she was gone, and it was his fault.

"Thank you," he said to the doctor, walking out from behind the desk, barely noticing his polite nod.

Through the window he could see the clinic's beautiful formal gardens. They were packed full of people, most of whom were holding video cameras or cell phones and waiting eagerly. There were two empty chairs at the head of the crowd, and Devlin knew that he would soon be sitting in one, Claudia in the other.

The sight of those chairs filled him with dread. They should have filled him with excitement. Under any other circumstances, this could have been a moment of triumph — surviving the Alps, returning from the brink of death, sharing his story with the world. It should have been a celebration of life, of victory. Of love. He should have been sitting in that chair next to Darcy, telling the world about the adventure they had shared, the connection they had found in the harshest of conditions.

But instead, it felt more like a trial. A punishment.

Devlin clenched his fists, trying to calm the fury simmering inside him. It wasn't fair. None of this was fair.

"Mr Storm," the doctor called from behind him. "We've just had word that your belongings have arrived. Would you like to come with me?"

No, Devlin replied, but only inside his head.

He didn't care about his belongings. He didn't care about the suit Claudia had arranged for him to wear at the press conference he didn't want to take part in. All he wanted was to find a way out of this mess, to find Darcy and tell her the truth before it was too late. But that was impossible now. The wheels were already in motion, and he was trapped, caught in a web of lies he didn't know how to escape.

With a weary sigh, Devlin nodded, his body heavy with the weight of his decisions. He followed the doctor out of the lobby and down a short corridor, his mind racing. He didn't know what the future held, but one thing was certain — the hurt wasn't over. Not by a long shot.

CHAPTER 35

DARCY

The journey was shorter than she'd expected. Darcy had sat silently in the backseat, watching the landscape change as they descended from the Royal Alpine. The driver had steered them cautiously down the weaving mountain roads, keeping his speed low until they hit the highway. The snow-covered mountains loomed on either side, their jagged peaks piercing the blue sky. Darcy pressed her face close to the window, her breath fogging up the glass as she gazed at the scenery passing by. She didn't say a word, not wanting to draw attention to herself. If the driver knew who she was or why she was really there, he might try to stop her from going any further. And she couldn't risk that — not now. Not when she was so close to seeing Devlin again.

Just twelve minutes later, the car turned off the highway onto a private service road, the tyres humming as they glided up towards a secluded plateau nestled between two mountains. The scenery was breathtaking — vast expanses of white snow stretching out in every direction, with the rugged mountains rising in the distance like guardians of a hidden world.

And there, perched on the edge of the plateau, was the clinic. The building itself was low and sleek. A luxurious building of modern architecture that seemed to blend into the landscape. It looked almost like something a James Bond villain might live in.

The parking lot was packed, and there had to be dozens of people waiting outside the main doors. Most of them were holding cameras, their lenses trained on the doors, waiting for their moment to capture a glimpse of Devlin or Claudia.

"I'll take you around the side, ma'am," said the driver, and he steered the car through the crowd before pulling into a narrow alleyway between two buildings.

He cut the engine and got out, running to Darcy's door and opening it for her. She stepped out, her heart pounding as she felt the cold air hit her face. The driver popped the boot, and together they carefully unloaded Devlin's belongings — the travel bag, the suit, the personal items that had been requested.

A young woman, one of the clinic staff, appeared at the fire door and gestured for them to follow her. They carried Devlin's things through the narrow hallway, the sterile smell of the clinic mixing with the faint scent of pine from the snowy air outside. The hallway led them to a small room, and as Darcy walked through the door, her breath caught in her throat.

Claudia Romano.

The supermodel stood there, typing something into her phone with her immaculate nails. Actually, there wasn't a single piece of her that wasn't immaculate. Darcy didn't know whether it was because of the press conference, or if she looked like this every day, but it had an intimidating effect. She almost backed out of the room, afraid of what Claudia would say when she recognised her.

But when the model finally looked up from her phone, her gaze landed on Darcy with complete disinterest. There was no recognition in her eyes — just cold dismissal.

"Put them on the table," she ordered. "That will be all."

The driver carefully placed Devlin's bags on the only table in the room.

"I'll wait for you," he said to Darcy, and walked out of the room.

Darcy placed her own bags on the table, but made no move to leave. If Claudia was here, then Devlin had to be close. Claudia looked at her again, an expression of distaste wafting over her features.

"I said that will be all. Are you deaf?" Claudia snapped.

She obviously hadn't seen any photos of Darcy, but that wasn't really surprising considering all of the news footage had been about Devlin. Darcy had been nothing more than an afterthought, a footnote in the story.

"I'm sorry," said Darcy, "but I was told to deliver these things to Devlin himself. I'll get fired if I don't. Where is he?"

Claudia's eyes narrowed, her grip tightening around her phone as if she were about to throw it.

"None of your business," Claudia spat. She clutched her phone and walked to the table, picking up a suit and inspecting it for a moment before turning her attention back to Darcy, surprised to find her still there. "Leave. Now. Or I can guarantee you that you will lose your job. I don't care for staff outstaying their welcome."

Darcy's stomach churned with anger, but she stood her ground. She'd try to find Devlin by herself, before the press conference started. She was almost out in the corridor before she had a sudden thought.

"Sorry, Miss Romano. Can I ask you a question?"

Claudia looked at her, her face twisted with impatience. "What?"

"You and Devlin, is it true? Are you back together? I'm . . ." She had to swallow her pride before speaking the next part. "I'm a fan."

Claudia's expression softened, just a little, and she gave a small, self-satisfied smile.

"We never really stopped loving one another," she said. "He told me he spent the entire time on the mountain thinking about me and praying that he would have the chance to tell me how he felt. I've never seen him so regretful. We're the power couple that everyone wants a piece of, that's what he told me."

With that, she turned back to the table. Darcy had expected to find herself bursting into tears when she heard what Claudia had to say, but to her surprise she felt a smile spread over her face. It took her a moment to work out why.

Claudia may have been a portrait of beauty, a professional supermodel, and an actress, too, but she wasn't convincing in the slightest.

She was lying.

CHAPTER 36

DEVLIN

It was almost as if he was walking to his own execution.

Devlin did his best to keep his back straight, his chin high, his expression neutral. He had to keep reminding himself who he was. He was Devlin Storm, a man known across the globe, a name that carried weight and power wherever it was spoken. He had more money than he could ever spend, more influence than most could dream of. But right now, none of that seemed to matter. None of it could stop the creeping dread that gnawed at him from the inside out.

Just four days ago he would have walked into this press conference with nothing but confidence. He would have regaled the press with tales of his heroics, then left them wanting more. He would have been icy, and arrogant, and selfish.

He would have been miserable, too, although he never would have let them see that.

Now, all of that was gone. Stripped away, leaving him exposed and vulnerable. Now, he just felt scared.

His life, once so meticulously controlled, was unravelling before his very eyes. It felt like being in a helicopter caught in a blizzard, the wind whipping all around him, blinding him, making it impossible to pilot. No matter how hard he tried to hold on, he knew it was only a matter of time before it all came crashing down.

"Just in here, Mr Storm," the doctor said, interrupting Devlin's spiralling thoughts.

Devlin nodded a weary thanks to the doctor, walking into the small room. He stood there for a moment, rubbing his eyes and making a wish.

Please let her find me.

But Darcy was nowhere to be seen. Instead, Claudia was there, waiting for him with a look of fury.

"Where have you been?" she demanded. "You're a mess, Devlin."

Devlin stared at her for a long moment, too tired to argue. She was right — he was a mess, physically and emotionally. But he didn't care what Claudia thought of him anymore. All he wanted was to get this over with, to survive the next hour without losing his last shred of his dignity.

"Let's just get this over with," he replied wearily, walking to the table. His arm throbbed from the effort, the pain a constant reminder of everything he had been through.

Claudia, unfazed by his tone, picked up a suit and tossed it at him.

"This one," she said. "Five minutes to make yourself look decent."

The suit hit his injured arm, sending a jolt of pain shooting through his body. Devlin yelped in agony, clutching the suit to his chest as his eyes watered. He blinked rapidly, trying to regain his composure as Claudia turned on her heel and walked towards the door, her stiletto heels clacking loudly against the floor. She smiled at the doctor as she made her way into the corridor.

"He may need some help," she said. "He's weak."

Devlin heard the clack of her heels fading as she walked down the corridor, her words echoing in his mind. He wasn't weak, not really — but he felt weak. He felt like a shell of the man he had once been, hollowed out by everything that had happened and the weight of losing Darcy.

"I'll be fine," he said to the doctor.

The doctor nodded and quietly closed the door, leaving Devlin alone. The silence felt too loud, amplifying his thoughts. All he wanted to do was escape, just leave through the back door and make his way into the mountains again. But if he did that then Claudia would destroy him. With the world's eyes watching, she could say anything she wanted to. Whether she told the truth or lies, he would be finished.

And if he did that, Darcy would never know where to find him.

Wincing, he struggled out of his pyjamas. It took quite a few attempts and over fifteen minutes before he managed to dress himself, and the effort exhausted him. Leaning on the table, he took a few deep breaths to get his strength back. He needed Darcy. In the mountains she had done nothing but give him strength, and he needed her now more than ever.

But Darcy was nowhere to be seen.

Devlin gritted his teeth, forcing himself to focus on the task at hand, and after what felt like an eternity, he managed to get the suit on. It was a sleek, expensive suit — exactly the kind Claudia would have chosen for him. The kind that screamed power and control. But Devlin felt none of that. He felt exhausted, drained, like all the fight had been sucked out of him.

Sighing, Devlin straightened up and opened the door. Claudia was there waiting for him, her foot tapping. She looked at her watch — the £60,000 BVLGARI she had made him buy her — and shook her head. She took hold of his hand in an iron grip, making him wince with pain.

"Don't mess this up," she said, a cold smile on her face. "I need this. I need people to think we're back together. One wrong move, and the myth that is Devlin Storm dies."

Devlin met her gaze, his eyes hard. He always knew her celebrity status mattered to her, but to do this, ruin his image and his company just to get back onto the front page. It was pathetic. But she would enjoy every second of it.

As they walked down the corridor, following the doctor towards the private entrance that led to the press room, Devlin thought of Darcy. Her smile. Her bravery. She believed she was afraid of adventure, but she was the strongest person he knew. She would fight for what was right, not what was easy. Looking at Claudia, Devlin knew it wouldn't be easy but perhaps it was time to tell the truth. Time for the lie that was Devlin Storm to die.

CHAPTER 37

DARCY

She was running out of time.

Darcy had walked up and down the corridors of the clinic, her heart pounding in her chest as she desperately searched for Devlin. But no matter where she looked, there was no sign of him. Worse still, people were starting to notice her. The clinic was highly secure — everywhere she turned the doors were locked tight, accessed only by a keycard, and the staff seemed to be on high alert. Twice now, a staff member had stopped her, asking who she was and what she was doing there. She'd managed to bluff her way out of both situations, but it wouldn't be long before somebody kicked her out.

The only reason she'd lasted this long, she thought, is because she blended in. The press had descended on the building in droves, eager to cover the story of Devlin's miraculous survival. The air outside had been electric with anticipation, and Darcy knew that once the press conference began, the attention of the staff would shift entirely to managing the media frenzy.

But she didn't have that kind of time. If she didn't find Devlin before the press conference started, it would be too late.

Grunting with frustration after reaching yet another dead end, Darcy spun on her heels and retraced her steps towards the lobby, her head down as she navigated the maze of corridors. As she neared her destination, the distant sound of voices grew louder, a low hum of activity that made her stomach tighten with nerves. She needed to stay invisible, to blend in with the crowd until she could find Devlin.

Pushing open the door to the lobby, Darcy was immediately met by a wall of sound. The place was packed with people — journalists, photographers, camera crews — all buzzing with excitement. Through the glass doors that led to the formal gardens, Darcy could see even more people outside, a veritable sea of bodies filling the space in front of the clinic.

She kept her head down as she made her way to the formal gardens. Two seats sat empty at the front of the crowd, like thrones. The sight of those chairs sent a fresh wave of fear washing over her. Soon, Devlin and Claudia would be sitting there, side by side, presenting a united front to the world. The thought made Darcy's heart twist painfully in her chest. What was she doing here? What had she hoped to accomplish by coming?

Even if Claudia had been lying, and she and Devlin weren't getting back together, what chance did Darcy really stand with Devlin? She was naive, and poor, just a foolish girl from Wisconsin who'd made a terrible decision and got herself stranded in Europe. She wasn't glamourous like Claudia. She was plain and dull. Her life was the very definition of boring. Most of all, she was scared. She was scared of commitment, scared of adventure, scared of change.

She was scared of life.

The truth hit her like a punch to the gut, and for a moment, Darcy felt like the wind had been knocked out of her. What was she thinking? She didn't belong here. She didn't belong in Devlin's world. He was a billionaire, a global icon, a man whose life was filled with luxury and excitement. She was just an ordinary girl who had stumbled into something far bigger than she could handle. It would be better for everyone if she just left, if she turned around and walked away right now. Devlin could go back to his life, and she could go back to hers. Nothing would change. Life would go on.

The definition of insanity is doing the same thing again and again and expecting different results.

The words echoed in her mind, and Darcy stopped in her tracks, her pulse racing. She couldn't go back to her old life. She didn't want things to go back to the way they were. She had been so unhappy, drifting through life without purpose, without passion. And Devlin — he had been unhappy too. She had seen it in his eyes, heard it in his voice. They were both trapped, both searching for something more.

"No," Darcy said.

This was her chance to change everything. It was time for her not to be afraid anymore.

She turned around, searching for something. There had to be a way to reach him, a way to get a message to Devlin before it was too late. She dug into her pockets for a scrap of paper and her fingers closed around the playing card from their unfinished game. Queen of Hearts. It didn't take long to spot a journalist scribbling notes in a small pad. An idea sparked in her mind, and without hesitating, she weaved her way through the bustling crowd towards him.

"Excuse me," she said. "Can I borrow your pen? Just for a second."

The man eyed her suspiciously, but didn't seem to recognise her and he reluctantly handed over his pen. Darcy had only just started to write on the front of the card when she heard a surge of noise. Glancing up, she squinted through the sun-drenched window and there, she saw a familiar face walking to the door.

Devlin.

Darcy's heart did a leap of joy, but she didn't have time to savour the moment. She quickly handed the pen back to the journalist.

"Thanks," she said, flashing him a grateful smile before turning her attention to the chairs at the front of the crowd.

The noise level was growing by the second as the journalists scrambled to get into position, their cameras trained on the door. Darcy resisted the urge to join them, to see Devlin for herself. There wasn't time. She had to act now.

Pushing her way through the throng of people, Darcy made her way to the front of the assembly, her heart pounding with adrenaline. She didn't stop to think about what she was doing. There was no time to question it. She reached the empty chairs, the ones meant for Devlin and Claudia, and with a quick glance over her shoulder to make sure she wasn't being watched, she swapped out Devlin's name card with the Queen of Hearts onto his seat. She couldn't risk being seen. If Claudia worked out who she was, then she'd have her thrown out of the clinic.

Please let him find it, she thought, her pulse racing.

It was only when she got to the back of the gardens that she stopped and turned around. Past the assembly of bobbing heads she made out Devlin and Claudia walking across the garden. They were side by side, but from here Darcy couldn't tell how close they were, or whether they were holding hands.

Please be strong, she thought, trying to broadcast the message into Devlin's head. *Please, just be you.*

"Excuse me," said a voice behind her. Darcy wheeled around to see a security guard there. "May I see your press ID?"

"Oh, sorry," she said. "I'm just leaving."

She kept her head down as she walked away, heading for the alleyway where the car was still waiting for her. Climbing inside, she leaned over to the driver.

"Can you tune in to the local radio?" she asked. "Can we listen to the press conference on the way?"

"Sure," the driver said. He pressed the buttons until he reached the right station, and Darcy's tummy flipped as she recognised Devlin's voice.

She hoped the note would be enough, that Devlin would understand it.

Because if he didn't, then everything was lost.

CHAPTER 38

DEVLIN

The cold hit Devlin like an icy hammer as he walked out of the clinic. He struggled to breathe, his entire body breaking into shivers. Back on that frozen peak, he'd been exposed to the elements, surrounded by snow and ice, but it hadn't felt this bitter. It wasn't just the temperature that made the difference — it was Darcy, her presence a warmth. And it was Claudia — her presence brought nothing but bitterness.

It was a ridiculous idea to hold a press conference outside — the gardens were the only space in the clinic big enough for the sheer number of people who had turned up — but at least he had an excuse to make it quick.

Claudia walked out beside him, sliding her arm through his, and as soon as they left the building the cluster of reporters went wild. Questions flew through the air like arrows and Devlin put his head down, making his way to the empty chairs. There was a scrap of colourful card on one, fluttering in the breeze. It almost flew away, but he snatched it up and held it on his lap as he sat down, no time to look at it, as the doctor had walked to his side and was waving at the crowd to be seated.

"Thank you, thank you," said the man. "Mr Storm has kindly agreed to a brief press conference focusing on his time in the mountains, and his recovery. He is a strong, determined patient, but I would like to remind you that he *is* a patient. He was incredibly poorly, and is still convalescing, so I ask you to be respectful."

The pack of reporters settled down, but there was still an electricity in the air that Devlin could feel on his skin. He shuddered, but it was more to do with the fact that Claudia had taken his hand in hers. He glanced at her and saw her smiling at him, but there wasn't a shred of warmth or compassion there.

"Be good, Devlin," she said.

"Don't worry," he whispered, holding on to the scrap of paper without really thinking about it. "I told you. You win."

"Mr Storm," came a voice from the crowd, a young, female reporter bundled up in fake furs. Devlin recognised the dress she was wearing beneath her coat as one of his. "I'm glad to see you alive and well, we all are. Welcome back."

The crowd applauded, and despite everything, Devlin managed a smile. Maybe Darcy had been right. Maybe people did love him, despite his awful behaviour.

"May I start by asking a question?" the reporter went on.

"Mr Storm has prepared a brief statement," said the doctor, but Devlin held up a hand.

"I'm happy to take questions," he said. "Go ahead."

"I think what we'd all like to know first and foremost is what happened in the mountains to make you realise you wanted to be back with Claudia Romano."

Devlin opened his mouth to reply, but he had no idea what to say. The urge to stand up and walk away was overwhelming, but he resisted it. The old Devlin would have upped and gone without a single care in the world about who he might have hurt. But Darcy had taught him a great deal in the mountains. She had shown such integrity, and honour. He stood his ground, gritting his teeth.

"I . . . uh . . ." He swallowed hard. If he denied Claudia's rumour, then she would take him down. If he agreed to it, then he would lose Darcy for ever. Claudia squeezed his hand, more of a warning than an attempt at reassurance. "It did get a bit hairy out there on the mountain. So can I just start by saying that I'm glad to be back. Thank you all for being here."

He cleared his throat, still trying to work out what to say. What would the old Devlin do now?

"I knew it would be okay," he said. "And I had a reason to come back."

Devlin glanced at Claudia, her smug smile making him feel sick. All he had to do was agree with her story, tell the reporters that he still loved her. Then he could get out of here and get on with his life.

His sad, lonely, emotionless life.

"I had a reason to come back," he said again, faltering.

He looked down to collect his thoughts, and that's when he noticed the card in his hand. The edges were slightly crumpled from where he had been gripping it without realising. His eyes fell on the red hearts and the queen's crown and around the edge were small, neat letters — just six simple words.

I'm not afraid of adventures anymore.

A jolt of electricity flowed through him as he understood who had left it. He scanned the crowd, searching for Darcy, but there was no sign of her. She had already disappeared into the sea of faces.

He glanced down at the note again, reading those six words, knowing instantly what she was telling him. And if Darcy wasn't afraid any more, then why should he be? He folded the paper up, sliding it into the pocket of his suit jacket. He felt lighter, freer. As if he had crawled back beneath the blanket in the cabin where they had spent their first night together, the fire roaring. The chill he'd felt since waking began to melt from his bones, his body thawing.

He sat up straighter, his heart steady, and the bitterness of the cold faded. He was ready.

"Let me tell you all a story," he said, his voice louder than before, full of the strength that Darcy had given him. "Let me tell you a story about a man called Devlin Storm."

The reporter nodded, everyone in the crowd pointing their cameras and cell phones at him. Claudia clutched his hand even harder, her nails digging into his skin.

"This man, he isn't the man you think he is. He has a reputation for arrogance, for selfishness, for causing trouble. And he deserves that reputation, sure."

"Devlin," said Claudia with a beaming smile. "They were asking about me and you."

"I'm getting to that," Devlin said. "But I need to say this first. That man . . . He's a lie."

Small gasps rose from the crowd.

"What are you doing?" Claudia hissed.

"I'm not this arrogant, impulsive man I've made myself out to be," he went on, ignoring her. "I became him because it was easier being alone where no one could sell my stories to the highest bidder." Devlin glanced at Claudia before continuing. "But in doing that, I forgot how to trust people, I forgot how to let people in. And I forgot how to love."

"But now you've remembered," said Claudia, her voice full of desperation. "You've remembered that you love me. Coming so close to death in the mountains, it was inevitable really."

"Claudia is right," Devlin said, and he felt her hand relax a little. "Coming so close to death in the mountains did make me remember something. It made me remember the man I used to be, made me remember the things that I used to find important. I . . ."

He had to pause, feeling overwhelmed. He searched the crowd again for Darcy, but there were just too many people.

"I went into the mountains to scatter my mum's ashes," he said, taking a breath. "Many of you will know she died a few weeks ago, and she wanted to be laid to rest there. I kept that part quiet because it's private, but also, to the world, I was this unfeeling giant of fashion and it didn't fit the picture you all had of me."

The formal garden was perfectly quiet, everybody waiting to see what he was going to say next.

"And Claudia was right about something else," he said. "Being out there, nearly dying, I did fall in love again."

He pulled his hand away quickly, before Claudia could react.

"Just not with her."

CHAPTER 39

DARCY

The crowd broke into such a cacophony of chatter that Darcy couldn't be sure she'd heard Devlin right. The voices from the radio meshed with the thrum of the car's tyres on the road, and for a moment, everything felt distant, surreal. Her heart was racing, her fingers gripping the edge of her seat as if bracing herself for whatever came next.

"Can you turn it up?" she asked, and the driver obliged.

With a quick twist of the dial Devlin's voice blasted from the speakers, clear and strong, pulling her back. She closed her eyes, picturing him there in front of that army of reporters, letting his words wash over her.

Be strong, she thought.

"I didn't fall back in love with Claudia Romano," Devlin's voice echoed through the speakers. "I fell in love with somebody else."

Darcy felt a perfect bubbling fountain of happiness rise up inside her, but before she could fully process the moment, she heard Claudia's voice cut through the airwaves, shrill and panicked. She could almost picture the other woman's face

— twisted with rage, her carefully crafted persona crumbling in front of everyone.

"Oh, Devlin, you poor thing. Doctor, we should get him back inside," Claudia said, her words crackling over the radio. "You're not well. He's, uh, obviously not in his right mind. Perhaps we should reschedule this for another—"

"No, I think today is absolutely fine," Devlin said. "I am in my right mind. I don't think I've ever been so sure about anything in my life. I woke up today to find Claudia here, uninvited. We haven't spoken in almost a year. But she's trying to blackmail me by threatening to lie about who I really am to ruin my business and my life. She's sold private stories about me before, but this time she was going to make up awful lies. She used me for leverage once before, and I'm not going to let her do it again. Certainly not by holding my company hostage."

Darcy could hear the sound of cameras clicking, of shocked gasps. Devlin had been right about Claudia — she was wicked.

"I won't allow it." Devlin continued. "I let you get away with selling stories about me once before but not again. Not when you are risking my employees for your own gain."

He paused, a small smile tugging at his lips, as if recalling a moment. "Like Claudia, I used to think image was everything. But then I met someone. Someone who, when she managed to stop talking for more than thirty seconds, showed me that being strong isn't about shutting everyone out. It's about caring for others, letting people in. And when I found myself in a situation where survival was the only option, she showed me that I could survive — and thrive — by being myself."

Darcy's heart swelled. It was as if Devlin was speaking to her alone. She could hear the truth in his voice, the raw vulnerability that he had kept hidden for so long.

"It's about letting yourself love somebody," Devlin continued. "And letting them love you back."

Darcy's smile was almost too big to fit on her face. All she wanted to do was ask the driver to turn around so she could run into Devlin's arms, but she could hear the chaos as the reporters all tried to get answers. There was no way she'd be able to get close to him now.

Through the radio, she heard Claudia's voice again, but this time it was distant, almost drowned out by the noise. From the sound of it, Claudia was storming off, pushing reporters out of her way as she walked back into the clinic.

Then there was silence. A relative calm settled over the scene.

"I'm exhausted, and injured," Devlin said. "But I have never felt more alive. And I just want to say sorry. Sorry to everyone I have hurt. It wasn't me, not really. I was afraid of what would happen if I let the world see the real Devlin Storm. And it took somebody amazing to show me that isn't a bad thing. And that someone was Darcy."

Darcy blushed, her heart skipping a beat as she realised what he was saying was absolutely, 100 percent about her.

"Sometimes you have to walk through the darkest of moments before you see the light," Devlin said, steady and thoughtful. "But Darcy walked with me, she never left my side, she pulled me out of that darkness — quite literally. She showed me that happiness can only come from being myself."

The reporters went wild at that. She could hear the sound of camera shutters like hail pounding on a tin roof, raised voices clamouring for more. Luckily for them, Devlin wasn't done yet.

"I will be taking a leave of absence from my company," Devlin said. "I feel happy. I feel good. To quote a friend of mine: find love, and everything else makes sense."

The next words were almost a whisper, and once again Darcy felt as if he was speaking to nobody but her.

"Everything makes perfect, wonderful sense."

"Mr Storm," somebody called out. "Where are you going to go?"

If he replied, Darcy didn't hear it. Chaos had broken out again, and she could almost picture the surge of reporters pushing forward towards Devlin. She thought she heard his voice again, but it was drowned out.

"Please," she said to the driver. "Please turn it up a little more."

He did so. The thunder of the crowd was almost deafening, but just for a second, Devlin's voice rose up above it, perfectly clear.

"You know where to find me! You know where we belong!"

And then it was over. The press conference faded into static, the radio cutting to the familiar voice of a newsreader summarising what had just taken place. But Darcy wasn't listening anymore. She had heard everything she needed to hear.

You know where to find me! You know where I belong!

She did. She understood exactly what Devlin meant.

"Take me home," she said to the driver, tingling with excitement. "I've got a bag to pack."

CHAPTER 40

DEVLIN

Devlin tried to fight the current of bodies pressing in from all sides, but it was like swimming against a relentless tide. Reporters were rushing towards him, their voices a chaotic chorus of shouts and questions. Microphones and cameras were thrust in his face and the clinic's security staff were struggling to hold them back, all of their shouting lost in the madness. Despite their best efforts, the sheer number of people made it impossible to maintain control. The noise was deafening, and for a moment, Devlin felt his heart race in response to the overwhelming pressure.

But then he let go and allowed himself to be carried along with the tide, knowing the doctor would steer him where he needed to go. The older man guided him through the confusion, his hand on Devlin's shoulder as they made their way through a side door. It clicked shut behind them, sealing off the noise, and suddenly the clinic felt like an oasis of calm compared to the madness outside.

"Are you okay?" the doctor asked, his brow lined with worry. "I'm so sorry. I thought we had them under control."

"I'm fine," said Devlin, feeling his heart rate start to slow. He smiled. "I really am. I don't think I've ever been better."

The doctor still looked uneasy, clearly unconvinced by Devlin's calm demeanour.

"Let me take you back to your room," the doctor said. "You need your rest. We'll clear the press from the grounds immediately."

But Devlin shook his head, already feeling the familiar pull of action. He didn't want to rest. Not now. Not when everything had finally fallen into place.

"No," he stated, firmly. "I'm checking out."

"Checking out?" the doctor repeated, a note of alarm creeping into his voice. "But you're still recovering—"

"I'm fine," Devlin said. "Please pack my clothes for me, and can I request a few new items? Oh, and I need to borrow a helicopter."

The doctor blinked in astonishment.

"We can't just let you borrow—"

"Then I'll buy it," said Devlin. "Whatever you have, I'll buy it."

Not waiting for a reply, he turned on his heel and walked down the corridor towards his room, his mind already spinning ahead to the next steps. He wasn't going to linger here, not when there was something much more important waiting for him.

He wasn't surprised to see Claudia in his room, her fury pulsing from her in dark, angry waves. She had her phone in her hand, holding it so tightly her knuckles were white, and her face was twisted in a mask of rage.

"Do you know what you've done?" she said. "I'm a laughing stock on Twitter, on Heartbook, *everywhere*!"

Devlin looked at her calmly.

"I didn't ask you to be here," he said. "You did this to yourself."

"That's not fair," she snapped, stepping towards him. "After everything I did for you."

Devlin tried not to laugh, shaking his head slightly.

"Everything you did for me?" he repeated, incredulously. "You threatened to destroy me, Claudia."

Claudia scoffed. "Just you wait, when your empire crumbles, you'll come back to me," she spat. "You need the front page as much as I do."

She pushed past him, and he listened to the sound of her heels clacking down the corridor. He knew it would be the last time he heard them, the last time he heard her voice, and the thought of it made him grin.

But it was nothing compared to the thought of seeing Darcy again.

He wasn't sure if she was still here, or if she'd left, but he hoped she had been listening and had heard his words at the end of the press conference. She would know what he meant, he was sure of it. She always did. He didn't need to explain himself to Darcy. She saw him — truly saw him — in a way no one else ever had. And that's what mattered.

With a newfound sense of purpose, Devlin grabbed the few personal items he had in his room, packing them quickly. He didn't need much. Just the essentials to keep him going for the next few days. What mattered was that Darcy would come.

He zipped up his small bag, slung it carefully over his good shoulder, and walked out of the room without looking back.

CHAPTER 41

DARCY

"Darcy! Oh my god!"

Penny greeted Darcy with a squeal as she walked back into the lobby of the Royal Alpine. She shot up from her chair and ducked out from behind the desk, running over to her.

"You're all over the news," she said. "Heartbook is going wild! Is it true? You and Devlin Storm?"

Darcy couldn't help but smile, even though she felt terribly embarrassed at the fact her face was being broadcast to the world. She nodded, and Penny squealed again, drawing the attention of a few staff members nearby. They quickly returned to their tasks, but Darcy could feel the curious glances being thrown her way.

"I'm so jealous!" her friend said. "But I'm so, so happy for you. I mean, Devlin Storm. What are you even doing here? Shouldn't you be off on some glamourous adventure with him?"

Darcy hefted her travel bag higher on her shoulder, feeling the weight of it pull her back into reality. The driver had taken her back to her apartment and kindly waited for her there while she gathered a few essential items — warm clothes, scarf, gloves, thermals, thick pyjamas. She had packed quickly, almost on autopilot, her mind too full of the events of the day to process what she was doing. Yet, somehow, everything had fallen into place. And now, here she was, back at the Royal Alpine, with a flutter of nerves in her stomach that had nothing to do with the helicopter waiting outside.

The truth was, she wasn't entirely sure what she was doing back here. But she understood exactly what Devlin had said to her during the press conference — and those words had been for her, and her alone. She knew, without a shadow of a doubt, where she was supposed to go.

"I came to say goodbye," she said. "For now, anyway."

"You're leaving?" Penny asked. "With Devlin?"

Darcy nodded, a shy smile tugging at her lips.

"Yes, with Devlin. He's . . . waiting for me."

"You look radiant," Penny told her. "Honestly, you look so happy. It's like you're a completely different person."

"I am, I think," Darcy said. "I don't feel afraid anymore. I think I'm ready for an adventure."

It was the first time Darcy had ever said those words out loud, and the realisation filled her with a quiet strength. She had spent so much of her life afraid — afraid of failure, afraid of the unknown, afraid of opening herself up to love — but something had changed. Devlin had changed her, or rather, had shown her the person she had been all along, buried beneath the layers of fear and self-doubt. She was no longer the timid girl from Wisconsin, scared of stepping out of her comfort zone. She was someone new — someone stronger, braver, and ready for whatever came next.

The staff door at the far side of the lobby opened and Abigail Lamb walked out, a bundle of winter gear in her hands. She smiled at Darcy as she walked over.

"You're here," she said, handing Darcy a thick thermal jacket and a pair of climbing boots. "There's a helicopter waiting for you, as Devlin instructed, but the pilot doesn't know where he's supposed to go."

"It's okay," Darcy said, taking the jacket and boots with a grateful nod. "I can show him."

"Then put these on," she urged. "And come with me."

Darcy slid the coat on, zipping it up to her chin, then kicked off her heels and slid her feet into the boots. The heavy-duty nylon felt stiff on her ankles, but the warmth was immediate.

"Good luck," said Penny.

Darcy flashed her a grateful smile and hugged her tightly, before following Abigail out of the lobby and down the staff corridor that led towards the hangar. It was a familiar path, yet everything felt different now. It was still freezing outside, but the sky was blue. She'd listened to the weather report while she was packing and there were no more storm warnings. Everything was perfectly clear. It was as if the universe itself had conspired to give her a smooth journey, a clean slate.

There was a helicopter on the landing pad, its rotors spinning.

"There's a job here for you if you need it," Abigail said with a grin. "But something tells me you probably won't. Maybe we'll see you again one day, as a guest."

"Thank you," Darcy said. "For everything."

With a wave of gratitude, she clutched her bag and ran up to the landing pad. The pilot, a tall man in a flight suit, held the door open for her and she clambered in, fastening her belt and putting the headphones on. She'd thought that being on yet another helicopter would scare her, but it didn't. She did feel like a new person, stronger and braver, and she knew that Devlin had enabled her to change. Adventure was waiting for her, and for the very first time in her life she was excited about it.

"Where to, miss?" the pilot asked, settling into his seat and glancing at her expectantly.

"East," she said. "Head into the mountains. I'll tell you when to stop."

The pilot nodded, and with a gentle jolt, the chopper lifted off the landing pad, rising steadily into the air. Darcy looked down at the resort, waving a goodbye to Abigail and the life she had known there. Then they banked to the side and the mountains filled the windscreen, bathed in golden light. The peaks all looked the same, and for a moment she wondered if she would even be able to find her way, but she didn't have to worry, the location was locked inside her. A place she would never forget.

"There," she said after fifteen minutes of flying. "Can you see the lights?"

It was hard, because they were almost covered by the snow falling around them, but the pilot nodded, steering the chopper towards the slope. They touched down lightly.

"Are you sure you're going to be okay out here?" the man asked, his voice fed into her ears through the headphones. Darcy nodded as she took them off.

"I'll be great," she said, giving him the thumbs up.

She pulled the door open and climbed out, ducking beneath the still-spinning blades as the helicopter lifted off again, its powerful roar echoing in the stillness. Darcy stood there for a moment, watching as the helicopter disappeared into the sky, leaving her alone on the snowy slope.

Then she turned around to face the little wooden cabin.

Her heart fluttered as she took in the sight of it. The place where everything had changed. It looked just as it had before — small, unassuming, nestled against the mountainside. Yet somehow, it felt different. It felt like home. Darcy should be worried, she knew. What if she'd misunderstood? What if she'd got it wrong? What if Devlin hadn't been able to get here?

But there wasn't a single trace of anxiety or doubt in her. She knew he was here. She just *knew*.

She trudged to the cabin, the snow crunching beneath her boots, her footprints covered almost immediately by the new snowfall pattering around her. There was no sign of life inside, the windows dark, and she stopped by the door. It felt like a million years ago that she had left this little place — another life, another her.

Taking a deep breath, she reached out and knocked on the door.

There was no reply. The cabin remained silent, the snow-covered world around her still and quiet.

Darcy knocked again, and this time she heard footsteps from inside. The door swung open and Devlin was there. He was dressed in winter gear, his arm strapped in a huge cast and a sling, and he gave her the most amazing smile she had ever seen.

"Sorry," he said. "I was just lighting the fire."

Darcy's heart fluttered at the thought of the two of them, curled up by the fire together, just like they had been the first time they stayed in the cabin. The memory of that night, the warmth of the flames and the way they'd fallen asleep next to each other, but still so oblivious to what would happen between them, washed over her, making her knees feel weak.

She couldn't explain the change in her. Somehow, in just a few days, everything had turned upside down. It was surreal to think how she'd gone from not liking Devlin to something far, far better. Somewhere between survival and surrender she'd found a confidence she didn't know she had, and with that had come a turning point.

"And so we meet again," he said. "You knew?"

Darcy nodded and smile. "I knew."

Without another word, Devlin reached out with his good hand, and Darcy took it, their fingers intertwining as if they had always belonged together. His hand was strong but gentle, and in that touch, Darcy felt everything — his love, his devotion, his trust. It was all there, unspoken but understood. She felt high on the victory of it all.

"I would carry you over the threshold," he said, gesturing at his arm. "But, you know . . ."

Darcy laughed.

"Then how about a kiss instead?" she said, reaching up on her tiptoes.

He granted her wish, his lips impossibly warm. Darcy melted into him, feeling the world fade away. When he stood back, his green eyes twinkled intensely, and Darcy thought she saw flashes of colour there, like the fish moving beneath the ice.

"It's great to see you, my little adventurer," he said, pulling her gently into the cabin.

"Right back at you, my work-in-progress," Darcy laughed, taking off her jacket and boots at the door. "In fact, you absolutely rocked that press conference, maybe you're a work-no-longer-in-progress."

The cabin was exactly as she remembered it — the smell of woodsmoke, the cosy warmth of the fire crackling in the hearth, the rustic simplicity that made it feel like a world apart from everything else.

Devlin closed the door behind them, shutting out the cold and the outside world, and Darcy felt a deep sense of peace settle over her. This was where she was meant to be. With him. In this cabin, in this moment. Nothing else mattered.

"Come on," Devlin said, leading her over to the fire. "Let's get warm."

They sat together on the floor in front of the flames, the heat from the fire wrapping around them like a blanket. Devlin draped his good arm over her shoulders, pulling her close to him. She leaned into him, resting her head on his chest, listening to the steady beat of his heart.

For a long time, they didn't speak. They didn't need to. The silence between them was comfortable, filled with the unspoken understanding that they had finally found what they had been searching for.

After a while, Darcy lifted her head to look at him, her heart swelling with love. He was so handsome, stupidly handsome really. And he was hers.

"This is equal parts exciting and terrifying," she said, grinning.

He smiled, a slow, contented smile, and kissed her. "It wouldn't be a Devlin Storm adventure if it wasn't a bit of both."

EPILOGUE

DARCY
One Year Later

"I see him!" Darcy pointed excitedly through the helicopter window, her heart racing at the scene below.

Devlin nodded, steering them to the side. The helicopter banked so hard that Darcy felt her stomach do a loop-the-loop, the mountain slope looming up through the window. Two tiny figures came into view, both dressed in bright-red climbing gear, their silhouettes stark against the white backdrop. One of the climbers was lying motionless, while the other waved frantically, trying to get their attention.

"I can't see a place to land," Devlin said, his voice steady despite the tension in the air. He skilfully guided the helicopter lower, trying to get as close as he could to the stranded climbers. The slope below was steep, with jagged rocks and thick snow making it impossible for a safe landing. "You'll have to drop."

Darcy nodded. There was no room for hesitation. She unbuckled her seatbelt and climbed out of her seat, moving into the back of the helicopter where the equipment was stored. Her hands moved swiftly as she rigged up the winch line to her safety harness, the metal clinking against her karabiner as she checked everything twice, making sure it was secure. She couldn't afford any mistakes.

With a deep breath, she reached for the sliding door and pulled it open. Cold air rushed in, snatching Darcy's breath away. She was used to it, though, bracing herself as Devlin levelled out the Bell 525 ten metres above the slope. For an instant she thought back to the woman she had been just a few months ago — scared of adventure, scared of anything new, scared of herself. If somebody had told her that one day she'd be jumping out of a helicopter in order to rescue stranded climbers from some of the highest peaks in Europe, she'd have burst out laughing.

But here she was, about to do exactly that. She'd been doing it for five months now, ever since she'd completed her training. Devlin had bought three new helicopters for the ranger team and had devoted himself to piloting rescue missions. It was as if he had found a new purpose — a way to give back, to live a life of meaning beyond the world of fashion.

He still designed, of course, and his business was doing just fine. In fact, his business had never been better. Devlin's speech during the press conference had gone viral around the world, and everybody had praised his honesty and his transformation. Once upon a time, Devlin Storm's name had been synonymous with arrogance and selfishness, a man who cared only about his own success. But now, he was a symbol of something else — a man who had found redemption, who had become a bastion of decency and integrity.

Devlin's public apology had been genuine, raw and vulnerable, and people responded to it. Instead of damaging his reputation, it had strengthened it. He had become someone people respected, someone they admired. The shift had been profound, not just in how the world saw him, but in how he saw himself, and Darcy had been at his side ever since. She had never felt prouder.

He'd even made good on his payment of £100,000, although it had gone to a delighted Sophia, not Darcy. Darcy didn't need his money. She had the man himself.

She looked over at him, grinning. He grinned back, his smile still powerful enough to make her feel giddy. He looked like the same man, but he was also so different from the Devlin she had first met. Goodness seemed to flow out of him, his expression was open and welcoming and kind. He was the man in the ice, the man who had always been there, and she had helped him escape.

That's why she loved him. That's why he loved her.

"Be safe," he mouthed as he flashed her the OK sign with his hand.

Darcy nodded, a grin spreading across her face as she secured the final piece of her gear. She felt the exhilaration rise in her chest, the thrill of the jump buzzing through her veins. Taking a deep breath, she leaned forward into the cold, biting wind, feeling the rush of adrenaline as her body prepared for the descent. Then, with a gasp of excitement and exhilaration, she dropped out of the helicopter, her harness catching as she dangled in mid-air, the snowy slope rising up to meet her. This was her life now — her adventure. And she loved every second of it.

* * *

DEVLIN

"We're late!" Devlin said as the helicopter bumped down on the landing pad forty-five minutes later. He checked his watch, his brow furrowing. "Really late!"

"They'll wait," said Darcy with a playful grin from the seat next to him. "It's not like they have a choice. We're the only ones who can fly them off the mountain."

Devlin laughed, leaning across the cockpit to steal a kiss. Darcy met him halfway, her hand on his cheek. They were late because they'd had to fly the stranded climbers down to base camp. One man had broken his leg in a fall, but thanks to their quick rescue, they were both healthy, and hypothermia hadn't had a chance to set in. They had been delighted to be rescued, but it was Devlin who was happiest. He sat back in his seat, feeling the thrill of the rescue give way to a wonderful, unbeatable sense of relief and satisfaction.

It had been Darcy who had suggested they offer help to people lost or hurt in the mountains. Of course it had. She was the kindest, most selfless person he knew. She was the bravest, too. The girl he'd first met had been terrified of everything, but that core of bravery had been in her even then.

"You've changed me," he said, as he had so many times before. "I'm so glad you climbed into that helicopter with me."

"Like I always say," she replied, eyes sparkling with mischief, "I'm not sure I really had a choice. But I am glad I did, too."

Without her, he never would have survived that first trip. She had changed his life. She had changed *him*. He had gone to the mountains to say goodbye to his mother, but in doing so he had found his soulmate, and he gave thanks for that every single day.

Devlin checked his watch again.

"Ready?" he asked.

"I've been ready for this for eight wonderful months," she said.

He opened his door, ducking beneath the lazily spinning rotors, and offering his hand to Darcy as she stepped down. They walked away from the landing pad and past the outpost station, heading up the familiar slope. It was the middle of summer, and even though there were still scraps of snow here, most of the slope was lush with grass, alpine flowers blooming and filling the air with their scent. It was so warm that Devlin had to take off his coat. Beneath was a tuxedo, complete with a bow tie.

"We may as well change here," Darcy said. "Do you still need help getting out of your clothes?"

Devlin laughed, flexing his arm. The break had healed, and even though it still ached in the cold, he barely noticed it anymore.

"I'll be fine," he said. "This time. Can't say for sure I won't need a little help later on though, so park that thought and we'll come back to it."

He kicked off his boots and his snowsuit trousers, and before long he was standing there in his wedding suit. Darcy did the same, struggling out of her rescue kit to reveal the beautifully tailored white dress beneath.

"It's unlucky for me to see it before the wedding," Devlin said, and she smiled.

"I don't think that counts when the groom actually designed the dress," she said, brushing her hands over the silk. "It's a little wrinkled."

"It's perfect," he said, taking her hand and starting to walk again. "You're perfect."

They began walking together up the slope, heading towards the group of guests gathered near the top. As they neared, Darcy's smile grew wider when she spotted their ring bearers — Nibbles and Norman, their beloved rabbits — sitting primly at the top of the slope, each with a little ribbon tied around their necks, holding the rings in a tiny pouch. Nibbles, her fluffy white fur contrasting beautifully with the green grass, twitched her nose as if she knew she had an important job to do. Norman, slightly larger and more regal-looking, sat beside her, his ears perked up, looking every bit the dignified rabbit.

"Devlin!" Darcy cried, her hand flying to her mouth. "You brought the kids. You know they're going to steal the show, right?"

"I wouldn't be surprised," Devlin chuckled, watching the two rabbits with amusement. "Norman looks like he's taking this whole ring-bearer role very seriously."

The slope levelled out as they reached the top, where their friends and family stood waiting, champagne glasses in hand. They broke into a round of cheers and applause when they saw Devlin and Darcy coming. Blake Fielding was there, and he jogged towards them with a beaming smile on his face.

"Everyone safe?" Blake asked, and Devlin nodded.

"Well done. I always thought Devlin Storm was a great name for a super hero."

"Darcy's the hero," he said. "I'm just her sidekick."

Blake grinned. "Well, either way, you're a lucky man."

Devlin glanced at Darcy, his heart swelling with love. "I know I am."

Blake gestured towards the guests gathered near the rocks.

"Everyone's here," he said. "This place is amazing. You picked the perfect spot."

Devlin nodded, taking in the view. He'd once risked his life to get here, and it turned out to be the best decision he'd ever made. And the last reckless one.

"It's pretty special, all right," he said.

"I'll go get in place," Darcy whispered, leaning up to kiss him on the cheek. "See you in a moment."

As she moved towards the rocky outcrop, Devlin turned to Blake, a hand on his shoulder as they made their way upwards.

"Thank you," he said.

"For what?" Blake asked, frowning.

"For what you said to me months ago, back at the Royal Alpine. You were right. I found love, and everything makes sense. *Everything.*"

Blake face lit up with a knowing smile.

"I'm happy for you," he said. "Now come on, let's get you married."

They walked up the slope together, rounding the rocks. Even though he'd been here countless times since the day he'd scattered his mum's ashes, the view still took his breath away. Now, in the middle of summer, it was better than ever. The lush, green, burgeoning valley stretched for miles, cradled by the sun-drenched mountain slopes. It felt even more beautiful, knowing that this was where he would marry the woman who had changed his life for ever.

Hey, Mum, he thought, closing his eyes for a moment and seeing her there, smiling. *Look at me now. I hope this makes you proud of me. You'd have loved Darcy and she would have loved you.*

His mum would have been so happy to know how much he had changed. She would have been so happy that he had found love.

Two dozen seats had been arranged next to the rocks, facing the stunning view and a small archway adorned with thousands of tiny wildflowers. Beneath the arch, a priest stood waiting. Nearby, Nibbles and Norman, sat patiently, keeping the rings safe as the guests took their seats. Devlin and Darcy had wanted a small, intimate wedding, but nothing was going to stop their friends celebrating the nuptials, and at least half the seats were taken up by the people they'd rescued from the mountains.

Devlin made his way to the front, a little nervous now that everybody was watching him. Blake straightened Devlin's bow tie, then brushed something from his shoulder.

"Good luck," he said.

Devlin met his friend's gaze, his heart full. "Thank you," he replied quietly.

"Congratulations, my friend," he said. "You've earned this."

Blake sat down on his seat, and the priest began the ceremony. Devlin wasn't listening. Every ounce of his being was taken up by the sight of Darcy walking around the rocks, her face lit up by mountain sunshine, her cheeks perfectly pink, those beautiful eyes sparkling. She walked to his side and he took her hand.

"I love you, Devlin Storm," she whispered.

"And I love you, Darcy Wainwright Storm," he replied.

Together, they turned to face the priest and Nibbles and Norman. Behind them, the world seemed to glow, the future stretching infinitely out for them, bright and full of possibilities. And Darcy and Devlin knew that this was just the beginning of their adventure together.

THE END

ACKNOWLEDGEMENTS

Writing this book has been an incredible journey, and I am deeply grateful to the amazing people who helped make it possible.

First and foremost, my heartfelt thanks go to my wonderful agent, Tanera Simons, for believing in me and guiding me through every step of my author journey. The support and insight from both you and Laura have been, and continue to be, invaluable.

To my brilliant editor, Becky Slorach, your keen eye and unwavering dedication helped shape this book into what it is today. Thank you for your patience, wisdom, and for pushing me to do my best work. You've made this book shine.

To my family, whose love and encouragement have been my foundation throughout this entire process — thank you for always being there. And to my daughter, your joy and boundless creativity inspire me every day. I am so lucky to have you by my side.

Finally, thank you to all the readers who choose to spend their time in the worlds I create. I hope this story brings you as much joy as it brought me in writing it.

Katie x

THE CHOC LIT STORY

Established in 2009, Choc Lit is an independent, award-winning publisher dedicated to creating a delicious selection of quality women's fiction.

We have won 18 awards, including Publisher of the Year and the Romantic Novel of the Year, and have been shortlisted for countless others. In 2023, we were shortlisted for Publisher of the Year by the Romantic Novelists' Association.

All our novels are selected by genuine readers. We are proud to publish talented first-time authors, as well as established writers whose books we love introducing to a new generation of readers.

In 2023, we became a Joffe Books company. Best known for publishing a wide range of commercial fiction, Joffe Books has its roots in women's fiction. Today it is one of the largest independent publishers in the UK.

We love to hear from you, so please email us about absolutely anything bookish at choc-lit@joffebooks.com.

If you want to receive free books every Friday and hear about all our new releases, join our mailing list here: www.joffebooks.com/freebooks.